PRETTY PERFECT TOY

A TEMPTATION COURT NOVEL

ANGEL PAYNE

T0105126

This book is an original publication of Waterhouse Press.

This is a work of fiction. Names, characters, places, and incidents either are the product of the author's imagination or are used fictitiously, and any resemblance to actual persons, living or dead, business establishments, events, or locales is entirely coincidental. The publisher does not assume any responsibility for third-party websites or their content.

Copyright © 2018 Waterhouse Press, LLC
Cover Design by Waterhouse Press, LLC
Cover Photographs: Shutterstock

All Rights Reserved.
No part of this book may be reproduced, scanned, or distributed in any printed or electronic format without permission. Please do not participate in or encourage piracy of copyrighted materials in violation of the author's rights. Purchase only authorized editions.

Paperback ISBN: 978-1-64263-072-5

PRETTY PERFECT TOY

A TEMPTATION COURT NOVEL

ANGEL PAYNE

WATERHOUSE PRESS

"Love takes off masks that we fear we cannot live without, and know we cannot live within."

— James Baldwin

CHAPTER ONE

MISHELLA

I am going to hell.

A choir sings in Latin. People speak in reverent tones. Sun streams through angels and saints on stained-glass windows, dappling rainbows across pious stone effigies...

And all I can think about is undressing the golden perfection of a man next to me.

And that would only be the start.

I want to touch him. Caress every muscled, chiseled inch of him. Wrap my naked body around his. Guide his erect, straining body deep inside mine...

Not. Now.

But why not now?

Cassian. I ache...

Nearly six weeks have passed since the moment that changed our lives. Forty-one days, to be exact—since the night he confronted a group of hoodlums attacking me in a dark corner of Bryant Park, not knowing one of them was carrying a gun—that the thug then fired three times.

Even here, in the streaming sun of mid-July, I relive that horrific midnight as if it has just happened. The minutes, seeming like hours, of gripping his pale hand, locking my terrified gaze into his glassy one, screaming across the park for help until I was hoarse...and then screaming some more...

"Please! Come quickly! His name is Cassian Court. Yes, that Cassian Court. You must help him! You must—"

"Ella."

My head snaps up. He is not pale any longer, thank the Creator—a little patch on his elegant nose actually peels from the sunburn he incurred during our sailing trip on New York Harbor over the weekend—and his eyes are glittering instead of glassy, as deep a forest green as the T-shirt hugging his flawless torso. Regrettably, *that* is mostly hidden now, layered beneath a tan sport coat paired with matching slacks atop his muscled legs...

With a backside to match.

Get your mind off *his backside.*

Stop thinking of how those perfect mounds would feel, clenched and naked against your palms, as his thighs slide between yours...

Ohhhhh...*my.*

"Hmmm?" I hope he does not expect more. Likely, he does not. These moments come upon me often. It is a bizarre mix of the awe I felt when we first met and reverent thanks for his simple aliveness—meaning I am now an idiot barely capable of logic or speech.

The sensation is...

wonderful.

And troubling.

I am rarely described by anyone, myself included, as the fanciful one in the room. And while Cassian Court is often labeled as New York's crown prince, I spent much of my adult life just steps away from real royalty. True, the halls of Palais Arcadia, on the Mediterranean island I called home until two months ago, would not qualify as a *wing* of some New York buildings—but they were perfect training wheels for the world I am now a part of. Many times, even in the center of, as Cassian's...

What?

As I gaze at his chiseled face, the query burns deeper than ever. *What* am *I to him?* Girlfriend? Companion? The ideal decoration for his arm...for now? Or...something else? Something he does not want to see nor even has to, thanks to the giant whale still flopping in the middle of the room between us. A whale possessed by a ghost named Lily Rianna Court.

His wife.

Until four years ago.

It is the sole detail I can get out of anyone about her—including the man's own mother. Yes, I have tried. And *tried.* Struggled to give him time and room to come to me—the considerations I did not give him the night I first learned about Lily. Instead I stormed off, making him chase me across a park—

The park he left on a stretcher. With three bullets in his body.

"Knock knock." Cassian's playful tone wrestles me from the flashback. He taps a finger to my forehead. "Anyone home?"

I gaze at his retreating hand. Despite my dark reminiscence, fresh need curls low in my belly. Finger porn, Cassian Court style, is not a temptation for which I have girded this afternoon. "*Désonnum*," I mutter, jerking my stare to meet his instead...

As if that helps.

His eyes have turned smoky—and an alluring kind of reproving. When I use native Arcadian, it hits him like an aphrodisiac. I have not simply "guessed" at this fact. He made sure I knew it shortly after the shooting, when he was still horizontal in a hospital bed and unable to do anything about it. Since then, we have certainly been able to do a few things about it—just not all the "things" we did before that terrible night.

Things he always had such perfect names for.

I want to fuck the color from your eyes, Mishella.

Take me deeper, favori.

Of course you can come a fourth time for me, little girl.

We have dealt with the dearth. We have had to. Compensated in ways our relationship definitely needed. We have been on real, honest-to-Creator *dates.* Have seen some movies (he likes Tim Burton and Peter Jackson), flown out on some day trips (I have decorated his refrigerator with tacky tourist magnets from Niagara Falls, the Hudson Valley, and the White House), and even gone bowling and sailing (a thousand gutter balls and a sunburn of my own later, I am in love with both). I have learned about his love for omelets and bacon and good Scotch. He has learned I prefer milk chocolate over dark—and now, thanks to him, cannot get enough of New York street tacos and red velvet cupcakes from Billy's Bakery.

By all the rules of a "good" relationship, we have done very well.

Good.

It is a category. A definition.

For a relationship that has none.

Moments like this are simply the silent, screaming proof of it. Where even désonnum does not belong. As our stares weave tighter and tighter, a tapestry unfurls, brighter and brighter—and I suddenly see every thread of his thoughts and every color of his soul as if they are my own.

We smile.

He lowers his hand. Scoops mine into it.

"The director was just saying that much of the stained glass in the museum wasn't acquired until the nineteen seventies," Cassian explains. "But that now, it's a crucial part of the Cloisters' collections."

"Oh." I blink, focusing on the large glass pieces. "Hmm. Very interesting." Lying on top of lusting now—in the glow from large glass panels where every figure has wings, a halo, or both.

Yes. Hell-bound.

The man to whom Cassian is referring, a handsome fellow with the beginnings of gray around his angular face, warms and then preens. The "Cassian Court Effect" has claimed another victim. I have yet to meet anyone in this city, from car valets to waitresses to heads of huge corporations, who is immune to it—the largest casualty, of course, being the girl in the mirror. It is a sentence I fully accept—though at first, it was like turning my skin inside out. After twenty-three years of learning to see only the scheming side of humanity, it has been strange—and amazing—to shift my lens, seeing things through Cassian's focus. He stuns me, this man with the shadows in his eyes and the ghosts from his past, who can still rouse so much of the light in others. Or perhaps that is the drive behind his laser focus on it—that seeing the Eden in others helps banish the hell in him.

In that case, maybe I am glad that is my destination too.

"What an honor and privilege it has been to escort you through the museum this afternoon, Mr. Court." The director still glows as we make our way out of the little stone room, into a pair of galleries lined with elaborate medieval tapestries.

"Rarely do we get a chance to see our benefactors outside of the fundraising special events, which are usually such clusterf—"

As the man colors, Cassian smirks. "It's all right, Blythe. You're among friends." He wraps an arm around my waist. "Fly that clusterfuck flag with pride."

The man chuckles—and clearly enrolls himself as a new member of the Cassian Court Fan Club. As its president, I join him in worshiping the man with my upturned smile—though the next moment, it is impossible to even remember Blythe's presence. As soon as Cassian dips his head to return my gaze, electricity arcs and zaps and binds us, even stronger than before...heat rocketing into desire, and then desire coiling into lust, as the world spins far away and we breathe hard together, barely recalling we are in public and cannot simply shred each other's clothes away...

"Shall we continue out to the garden?"

Cassian blinks. His jaw compresses before his head jerks up, a forced smile on his strong, sensual lips. Hell overtakes me prematurely, simply having to stare at those lips instead of pulling them to mine...and then to other places...

"Of course," he tells Blythe, shooting me an apologetic glance while slipping his grip from my waist to my hand. It is certain and commanding, his thumb caressing my knuckles as we follow the director out to the little square courtyard, with its lush plants, manicured lawns, and stone fountain surrounded on all four sides by arched walkways. The echo of our steps on the stones seems a perfect—and agonizing—echo of the desire pinging through our bodies.

By all the powers.

When we make it through the garden and finally enter another soaring chapel, I press back into Cassian's side.

Perhaps letting his arm rub my chest will relieve at least the ache in my breasts...

And the pillars will magically turn into soaring red velvet cupcakes.

"The Romanesque Hall and the Langon Chapel," Blythe rambles on.

I smile and nod in all the right places, attempting to focus on his litany.

Constructed in stone sourced from Moutiers-Saint-Jean...

Burgundy, France...

in the grand gothic architectural style...

"Gothic." Cassian is more engaging than I can hope to be, even adding one of the most classic versions of his subtle smile. "Well, obviously."

"Oh, *oui!*" The director laughs loudly, earning himself high-holy glares from a cluster of women nearby. Cassian fields it like the verbal version of a fist bump, encouragement and camaraderie in a pleasant mix. I am as grateful for it as Blythe, because I now start to wonder if the man is actually making a play for Cassian. That should make me amused, but...does not. The sensation getting in its way is a complete flummox. What is this twisting in my belly, this irksome stab in my chest?

The feeling intensifies as the director claps a hand to Cassian's shoulder and starts regaling us with details of the chapel's ceiling. I am not as easily "called" as Cassian, barely listening to the narration, even as Blythe guides us to a small side doorway, through a portal accessed by a swipe of his museum key card, and then up a flight of private stone steps into private offices and event preparation rooms. As the men continue to talk, I am only interested in the man's rapt stare at Cassian—even as he swings another door wide and shows us onto a balcony with a jaw-dropping view of the sunset over the Hudson.

That is only where the magic begins.

The alcove is aglow, though not by artificial means. A hundred white candles burn in ornate medieval candelabra, their stone bases carved with a menagerie of animals and—of course—angels. More candles are arranged in the center of a table set for two, with a plate of fresh meats, cheeses, and vegetables accompanied by a tall bottle of Italian red wine. Another plate holds an assortment of fancy desserts. The air is a rich mix of sinful and spiritual, the savory food blending deliciously with the tapers' warm wax.

"*Oh.*" I gasp it before I can help it. While the museum tour has been wonderful despite Blythe's bizarre behavior, this is the last—but absolutely best—thing I have fathomed as a grand finale. A medieval-style dream come to life, with my own gorgeous knight.

I *hope* that is what the *two* chairs mean...

Especially when Blythe lifts both brows expectantly at Cassian and then prompts, "Wellll?"

Cassian squares his shoulders. Sweeps an appraising look across the balcony. As a result, *I* do not stop gazing at *him*. Is he adopting "CEO Face" just for me? He knows what it does to me; I have *told* him in words of his own language—words borrowed from my best friend Vylet, a self-proclaimed "Americano junkie," to make sure he understands the point, loud and clear.

Turn-on. Panty dissolver. Invitation to lick.

Without looking at me—another purposeful move?—he pivots his attention back toward Blythe. Waits through one more pause before speaking.

"It's perfect." He grins big, hauling the other man in for a one-shouldered bump. "Thank you, Blythe. Can't express my gratitude enough."

"Oh, you already *do*, Mr. Court." Before I can decipher *that* bit of gushing, the man is back in professional mode, bowing to both of us with formality rivaling any Sancti Palais page from back home. "With that, I bid a fond *bon soir.* Simply pick up the red courtesy phone when you're ready to depart. Security will phone your car to the front and let you out."

"Outstanding."

Blythe bows low over my hand before leaving completely, ensuring I stand in a pool of my own confusion as soon as he shuts the door and is gone. Though I direct my frown out toward the glistening waves and watercolor-bright sky, my unease has not escaped Cassian's observance. Not that I expected it to. The man has been my personal mind reader since the moment we met.

"All right." He demands it in a murmur against my hair, tucking me close to his body. "Out with it."

"With what?"

"You *really* giving me that, *armeau*?"

"And are you really using *that* word...now?"

Armeau. It is not a term he throws around lightly— because he knows that I do not. The Arcadian word for "gift" carries a double meaning, used to denote a person who is special above others in a person's life. When used, it...*elevates* a conversation.

"Sure as hell am." Though his reply comes without a skipped beat, he lets one pass while drawing up and relocking our stares. "You're troubled. Why?"

I wrestle my gaze away. Turn it back to the horizon, banking that the sunset will hold it still for more than a few

15

seconds. The gamble was worth it. The sky is a palette of pink and orange, the river a collection of purple and gold. I walk to the balcony's edge. For a moment, I can truly imagine we are a knight errant and his lady, enjoying a respite as day transforms into night. "There is no room for troubled here." I hope my peaceful breath proves how much I mean it.

"You accuse me of pulling the armeau card, then use a line like that?"

Dismissive shrug. "Worth a try."

Cassian chuckles hard enough to make me join in. Soothes my frayed nerves a little more by stepping behind me, caging me against the stone ledge, hands flattened just next to my elbows. "You weren't comfortable during the tour."

I shift a little. Enough to assure myself his warmth is real...

Including the stiff ridge between his thighs.

"Not true." I curl one of his arms forward, around my waist. *More...* I want so much more. Though keeping our hands from each other would be a feat close to achieving world peace, his recovery from the shooting has stopped us short from being fully passionate for the last six weeks—meaning everything about his nearness coats my senses like a wizard's spell. His scent, cedar and soap and musk. His muscles, now leaner but more defined because of the changes in his workouts. His masculine force, potent and stringent, as if trying to gash its way out of his body and into mine. "The tour, I was very comfortable with."

"But...?"

His voice vibrates along my ear. I swallow, struggling not to let that fire course through the rest of me...but as my toes burn with it, I embrace the defeat. "But Blythe..."

"Blythe?" He jerks back. Just a little. "You're in a twist about *him*?"

"He…" My lips purse. Borrowing serenity from the sky, despite how the man swirls heat through my belly with tiny circles of his fingers, I push on. "He…wants you, Cassian. In *that* way."

He resettles behind me. Expands the caresses, playing at the top of my panties through my light cotton dress, while teasing my neck with a soft chuckle. "Is that all?"

I take my turn for a little jerk. "Is that *all*?"

"I've known the man for years, Ella. And he isn't subtle."

"Isn't—? Wait. You mean he's…tried to…"

"*Tried.*" He has the nerve to chuckle about it. "Long ago."

"*How* long?"

"Long enough."

"And…and did you…errrm…*return* his…his…"

Another chuckle, huskier and sexier, before he dips in to nip at the space beneath my ear. "What do *you* think?"

I squirm. Battle through the steam he has thickened through my senses with his oh-so-talented fingers and lips. "I think you are a man of many passions—"

"*Specific* passions." He trails that incredible mouth down, lining my shoulder with tingles of perfect heat. "Most particularly, for strawberry blondes with the sky in their eyes and heaven in their kiss." One of his hands sprawls across the front of my throat, compelling me tighter against him. "Oh yeah…and accents. Ones that remind me of Mediterranean islands with trellises full of possibilities…"

Even in my confusion, I smile. His reference to the night of our first kiss, when he scaled a trellis to get onto my balcony and then into my bedroom, can bring nothing else. "But only one of us in that room was still a virgin, Cassian. And I can accept that, even if I do not understand all of it—"

"And I don't want you to." His voice, deepening with new solemnity, sends vibrations of emotion through me. And confusion.

"But—"

"Ssshhh."

"*Cassian.* We have been open with each other since the start..." When we had to negotiate the terms of the contract that brought me here. Forty million of his dollars. Six months of my life. And the possibility of having exactly this. A connection my spirit has never felt with anyone...

"And I'm being open with you now." He turns me back to face him, stroking tendrils of hair from my face as the wind kicks up—and pointedly clearing his throat as our lower bodies fit against each other again. "As a matter of fact"—his brows jump and his nostrils flare—"if I'm any *more* open about things..."

Against my better instinct, my lips tip up. Against the same intuition, let him see the shudder claiming me as we mesh, soft to hard, woman to man...*perfection.* "I...I do not want you to think I am prying. It is not my place. In just four months—"

He does not allow me to finish. Correction: commands me not to, in the form of a kiss bordering on punishing. His mouth is so incessant, half the air punches from my lungs. The other half funnels strength into my arms, seizing him by both biceps as our lips crush and meld and ravish each other.

A cacophony of heat and heartbeats later, he draws back, gaze thick with sage smoke. "I've imposed few rules about this whole thing, favori," he utters. "But right now, I'm invoking a new one." His hand moves in, spreading across the back of my head. "No more countdowns." His fingertips curl in, pulling at my hair. "I need to have this." Tightens even harder. "Just this.

Just...you. Okay?"

He yanks a third time. I let my head tilt, succumbing to the bite of pain. Slide my eyes closed for an instant. "Okay."

His grip eases a little. "So we're good?"

"Good." I manage to volume into it. "Yes. Of—of course. We are good." *Just do not stop holding me like this.* "We are completely...squalid."

He chuffs. "You mean *solid*?"

"Oh. Hmm. That makes sense."

He brushes his lips down over mine again. Raises back up enough to murmur, "You sure about that?"

"About what?"

"Me. Making sense." He dips both hands back down—pulling me harder against him, making my legs widen for him. "Maybe I need to *show* you solid, instead of just telling you."

"*Ahhh.*" It spurts out on a gasp as my limbs shudder, my skin tingles, and my sex pulses. My head falls back again, whirling in a new vortex of color and feeling, letting Cassian completely take over again. I am lost in his ruthless strength as he lifts me to the balcony's thick brick ledge. Engulfed in blood red, in the sunset that bathes his taut, sharp face. A delighted quarry of joy, without sorrow or penance. If we *are* in hell, I gladly relinquish my rights to heaven.

Obscenities blur, steaming from Cassian as he clamps lips to my neck and suckles his way down, down, down... "God*damn*," he echoes, twisting free the buttons at the front of my dress and then nosing aside my bra...to find my erect tip awaiting his attention.

As his mouth closes in, a strangled choke bursts up my throat. We are not officially "in church" but might as well be, with hundreds of spirits, saints, and martyrs immortalized in art below us. My cries of arousal cannot be any more welcome here than in a real house of worship—though that is exactly how I feel right now, as Cassian licks me, laves me, and adores me, his attention not skipping a single inch of my breasts, now jutted up at him in twin spikes of need.

"Cassian." It is a whisper of desperate, burning need. I shove a hand beneath his shirt, seeking his nipples too... repeating his name as I pinch them both. He hisses and then grimaces, letting the pain jolt through him, before crashing his lips atop mine again.

Inside my mouth, his tongue is a vengeful animal. He tackles, twirls, punishes, penetrates. Scrapes my lips...and sucks out my breaths. By the time he is done, my hands have circled to his back, scratching down his shoulders and spine...

And his hands are under my dress...toying with my panties.

"Tell me they're white."

I smile against his mouth. How this man can enchant *and* empower me, in the space of but four words, takes my breath away again. Is it something all men feel about the woman they've deflowered—and their panties? And does the answer really matter...as long as I only care about what *this* man feels?

And how I continue to make him feel...

And *oh*, all the things he continues to make *me* feel...

Especially as I whisper in reply, "Yes, Cassian. They are white." I jot in one of my mental journals, which by now have begun to outnumber my physical ones: *buy more white panties.*

He growls in approval. Drops a stare of the same intent down over me while working his hands around my hips...and then beneath the very garment responsible for pumping both our lusts higher...

and higher...

"*Fuck.*" The stunned flare in his voice is mirrored in his

gaze. "Ella...your sweet parts..."

Before I can help it, a giggle overflows. "My *sweet parts*?" It is interesting to be the one *not* fumbling for words. Is Cassian Court, the man with a thousand dirty synonyms, suddenly out of golden prose? And why is stunned and awkward just as stunning on him as commanding and knowing?

"They're—" His breath hitches again as he explores my mound more thoroughly. "They're so—"

"Trimmed?" I barely get it out at full volume. As he slips fingers past the neat patch of hair and then farther, between my intimate lips, my most sensitive button shivers. Heat races through my sex. My hands tighten, gripping the ropes of his muscles. My body arches, lifting toward him...blooming for him as if it is the first time he has stoked this sparkling fire in me. In many ways, it is. We are not the same two people who burst into our first kiss, in the shadows of my bedroom on Arcadia, two months ago. Now, he is much more than the riveting billionaire come to strike a deal with my father—and I am not the virgin girl melting in his arms. I am a woman. The woman who knows what the zenith of his passion looks like. Tastes like. Feels like. Who has been without it for so long...*too* long. Who needs it so badly, I am dizzy from the need.

"When did you do it?" His question, just as much a demand for *why* I did it, is rough along my cheek.

"You mean tame the forest?" I quip. "Yesterday. You had the big meeting about the Singapore power grid integration, so Kate and I took a long lunch. She might have mentioned something about how you like...things...this way."

His brow knits. "How the hell does *Kate* know about—"

"Because she has been your trusted friend since college?" I am glad for the chance to tease a little more—and wrestle my libido to a semblance of control. "And...she might have mentioned that you chattered about it during a night of excessive drinking. And...I might have coerced her into taking me to the spa, once I knew. It was *my* idea, *not* hers, so place the blame properly. I just wanted to please you."

"Mishella." A subtle growl advances up his throat. He resettles me with harsher jerks, fitting our crotches back together again. "You please me just by being here with me. You please me with the brilliance of your mind, the challenge of your spirit, and the music of your laugh." His stare slides to my mouth. "And you *definitely* please me with your passion..."

"And now, my waxed sweet parts."

After joining his chuckle to my giggle, he dances his reply across my lips. "Ah. Yes. Certainly those." Another nip in but not the full kiss I expected. "But the forest was amazing too."

"Bullshit," I return—before the breath leaves me as if he did deliver the kiss. By the powers. I am still a mess of shivering need, craving that kiss. Craving *him*...

Even more now...

He trails his mouth along the line of my jaw, into the dip behind my ear, down the tight strain of my neck. Knowing every spot that makes me tremble harder, gasp louder, wrap myself to him tighter... *Ohhhh, don't stop*...

"Amazing." He issues it in a snarl, making it all too clear he is not to be debated this time. "All of you, Ella Santelle." With one hand still spreading my most sensitive tissues, he raises the other to my nape, securing my head so I am angled back, compelled to gaze at the brutal determination on his face. "*You* are amazing. The most incredible person I've ever known." The force of his hold intensifies, responding to what must be the doubt on my face, before he grates, "Including her."

He does not elaborate. He does not have to. The words vibrate on the air between us as if he already has.

Including Lily.

His face gains a dozen new lines of harshness. Clearly, his belief in the words is absolute—and it frightens me.

I bring a hand in, spread fingers along his jaw. "Cassian—"

"Hush."

"But I do not expect—"

"Hush."

This time, he backs it with a smash of his mouth—an assault injecting him into my blood, fusing him into my skin, and branding him into my senses until I possess no breath, sensation, or *thought* without him there. He is against me. Around me. Inside me.

And still I need more.

A message my body does not have to repeat. As always, the man simply knows—and delivers.

Sweeps his tongue deeper in—as his fingers spread wider into me below.

As his hips roll and his erection throbs harder between our bodies.

He groans.

I gasp.

He growls.

I mewl.

And the last six weeks fall away...replacing the agony of our abstinence with a flare as bright, perfect, and electric as the first time we ever drove our gazes into each other like this—

And knew our bodies were soon to follow.

I no longer yearn to soothe away the tension from his face. I scoop my fingers in, savoring all its magnificence. The forceful lines at the corners of his glittering eyes. The tension framing his nose, flared with the breaths of his arousal. Even the defined hills of his lips, parted to show me his locked, white teeth.

The look intensifies as he pulls his hand from my sex—and redirects it between his own legs. In one twist, he unbuttons himself. In another, takes care of his zipper.

Only then does my voice find its way past the brushfire of my arousal. "We—we cannot. Doctor Rudd said you needed six weeks after the shooting to—"

"Fuck Doctor Rudd."

A heated breath staggers out as I watch him shove down his black briefs—and take his beautiful shaft in hand. "I would rather fuck you, Mr. Court."

"That can be arranged, Miss Santelle." One side of his mouth kicks up in a grim smirk. Disappears beneath a sensual grimace as he works the milky drops at his tip along his heavily veined length. "With one important change."

"Ch-Change?" I struggle to remain focused. By the Creator...so much of this man is flawless, but his penis has to be the most perfect part of him. I have certainly not seen thousands in my lifetime—but growing up with a boy-crazy kinkster for a best friend has certainly yielded some special fringe benefits. After helping Vy ogle *many* online crotches, I can attest with certainty: Cassian Court's cock is flawless in every single way.

"Yes." He wraps his fist around that long, stiff length and strokes, making himself harder, redder. "Don't you remember?"

I blink and attempt to shake my head—though at the moment, I barely remember I *have* a head, let alone coherent thoughts inside it. The cause turns hopeless as he slides back in, slotting his hard, commanding body into the welcoming V of mine.

"*You* don't fuck *me*, Miss Santelle." He pushes back the cotton between my legs, exposing me—before widening me. "*I* fuck *you*."

And then...he is the force that fills me. A rod of heat. A ram of pressure. An invasion of lust. Impossible to hide from. Impenetrable...incredible.

He is mine.

And I am completely, hopelessly, his.

My body, not used to him after so many weeks, fights the penetration—but my soul welcomes the sting...craves the new wounds he opens from the inside out. The emotional blood I spill...

The tears it is now all right to shed.

They cleanse me. Heal me. Open the faucet for all the other tears, too. All the things I have kept so carefully stoppered since the night I knelt beside his bleeding body in a dark corner of Bryant Park...

The terror.

The guilt.

The nightmare of thinking he might die...without ever knowing how deeply I had fallen in love with him.

"Armeau. What is it?" The flinty edges of his voice slice into the side of my neck in all the best ways, making long-forgotten parts of my body tremble...reminding me why our surface satisfactions of the last six weeks have not come close to this. "Getting to know him" like a girlfriend has been enjoyable, even fun, but it is not the completion of having him like this...possessing him in the deepest regions of my body...

letting him into the sweet, wordless places of my soul...where even I cannot venture without the strength and boldness of him...

"Mishella?" he persists. In answer, I can only shake my head once more before tucking my face against his neck. I breathe in, cherishing the scents of our soaps and the musk of our arousals. I lick his skin, savoring the salty, masculine taste of him.

"Just...go deeper," I finally beg. "Fill me up, Cassian."

He groans, cupping my backside with his masterful hands and opening my body wider for his. "I won't stop until I have."

We rock in a steady, primal rhythm, my hips rolling to meet his plunges, his cock impaling me a little deeper with each new thrust. As the sun dips lower and twilight merges into night, shadows play over the focus of his face, the power of his body. I am entranced, scarcely believing a creature so perfect derives such pleasure from joining with me...but I accept the gratitude of knowing it as truth. Of feeling it with every perfect sink of his rigid, taut flesh.

"Almost there, favori." As he mutters it, his hands spread me wider. "Open up, Ella. Just a little more." His head falls back. His grimace is a flash of white. "Yes. Fuck...*yes*."

I cannot echo the words. Nothing but a cry spews as he penetrates me with his full length. I shiver as his sack slams my ass, but then he withdraws, preparing to stab in again. When he does, it hurts worse—and tingles better—than ever before.

"By the powers!" I tremble again, from head to toe. He is so big—and growing by the moment.

Before he lunges again, just for a moment, he pauses. I look up, confronting his gaze. Its deep-green patina reminds me of the art deco demons adorning the ledges of his Upper

West Side mansion, shining down on me with equally carnal intent...

Which explains why he has stopped.

Because he is readying the words.

The words he knows I will hate him for. Worship him for.

"There's only one power you need to concern yourself with right now." An arch of one whisky-colored brow. An enticing roll of his hips...teasing my most sensitive tissues. "You know what that is, don't you?"

Yes. I hate him.

Have never wanted him more.

"Yes, Cassian." I hope he does not make me say it. Pray he makes me say it.

"Then say it."

"The...the only power here is...is yours."

"Good girl." He reverses the roll. Adds a smooth slide so his erection brushes my clit as he pushes back in. "And what am I going to do with that power?"

My breath shakes. My tunnel convulses. Oh, the terrible, incredible things he does to me. My body...but more vividly, my mind...and my spirit.

Taking me. Breaking me. *Wide open...*

"You will pleasure me."

"What else?"

"You will fuck me."

"And...?"

"You will—" The words turn into a tight swallow.

He dips his head. Sinks teeth into my neck. "I will do *what*?"

"You will make me come."

He licks the abrasions along my carotid. "How many

times?"

I swallow hard. By the Creator, he does not hold back a single, dirty syllable of what turns me on the most...soaks my channel, dominates my mind...consumes me with longing for nothing else, *nobody* else, but him.

"How many times, Mishella?"

"As—as many times as you say."

A sound of rough satisfaction rumbles through him. "As I *shall* say." Candlelight plays across his face, flickers in his eyes, turns his mouth into sensual cruelty. As the night deepens, my golden demon thrives. "As I shall dictate before watching you crumble for me, piece by perfect...fucking...piece." He emphasizes with defined lunges, ensuring the head of his cock delivers the meaning deep inside my sex.

"Yes...Cassian." I do not wait for his prompt now. I simply know it is what he wishes...just as he sees completely inside me and knows every detail of every passion I have—perhaps I ever *will* have. A distinct possibility, since I cannot think of wanting anything else but this—or anyone but him.

He pulls back, swirls his wet crown along my most tender folds, and plunges once more inside. Then back out, repeating his torturous teases...

"Powers that *be*..."

"*Not them*." His snarl burns the front of my neck, the curve of my chin, my slightly parted lips. "*Who* do you beg for this, Mishella?"

"You." I make the amendment on a gasp. "I beg *you*, Cassian."

"Then do it." He is back inside, taking me with swift passion, hurling us both into our special, spectral space— where the universe peels back and we are exposed, as naked as if we were doing this skin-to-skin...soul-to-soul.

"Please." The command in his stare turns it into a shaking rasp. "*Please*, Cassian."

"Please...what?" He growls it out but punctuates with a hitched breath. Half-second gloat. He might be covering it in black-dagger attitude, but this is just as mind-blowing for him as it is me. Six weeks and two days after receiving my birth control injection, we are now able to fully enjoy its benefits—which should be *Benefits*, capital *B*.

"Please, Cassian. Let me come!"

He shifts his hands to my hips—controlling their motions as well as his. Setting our pace. "You need it bad, armeau?"

"Dammit! *Yes*; you know I do." I cannot quell my frustration. How is he able to hold back from this? From giving us both what we want...and need? The answer is nonessential—as soon as he releases my right hip long enough to reach beneath and swat that butt cheek. "Ahhh! What—"

"That wasn't begging."

"Dammit." I am not so nice about the repeat. He answers with a new pound of his lips over mine. Our tongues battle. Our mouths wrestle. By the time we break apart, we are breathing hard—and fucking harder. His desire ropes around me. His heat soaks into me. His cock controls me—completely.

My world narrows, becoming only the light of our union...the lightning of his body, striking over and over again, promising a cataclysmic cloud break...

"Oh..." I choke it out, fingernails making tracks down his spine, emulating the electricity building along mine. "All right; all *right*! I am begging. I am *begging*."

"For what?" He kisses me again. His lips are gentler, but his breaths are sharper. "You know what I want, Mishella."

I gulp again. Dammit, I *do* know. He wants the words. Not just any syllables. He wants all the filthy, naughty phrases from my dark, dirty fantasies...the fantasies only he knows how to fulfill...

"I am begging..."

He growls when I hesitate. Does not surrender a beat of his body's rhythm. "And I am waiting."

"I—I am begging to come. For you to fuck me until I do. Until my pussy soaks every inch of your cock and then vibrates around it until—until—*oh!*"

He grunts hard. I shudder harder. Something in the way he angles down and in, merging us in a tighter grind, converges every nerve in my clit and inch of my sex. I fall deeper into the cave, bouncing against the walls, stumbling toward the abyss at its core, where nothing but sensation and consummation await. I pant hard as I hurtle toward it, letting the bittersweet pressure mount inside. My buttocks quiver. My thighs clench. My vision turns into stars, forming a dizzying frame around his beautiful, unmerciful face.

"Now." The brace of his hand, thumb against my chin and fingers along my jaw, hauls me deeper into the darkness. "Your cunt will come for me *now*, Mishella."

And I am falling. Throbbing. Vibrating.

Bursting.

Screaming...

Though muffled at once by his mouth, sucking in my ecstasy like a parched man at an oasis—while his body continues to pump, brutalizing me like a sheikh with his concubine. Creator help me, just the thought enflames me again, especially as he peels back more of my dress, baring my breasts for his new licks and suckles. The moment he draws my nipple between his teeth, my second climax hits, twice as violent as the first—and then a third as he boldly presses my clit with the pad of his thumb. By the time he is finished, I am a shuddering, sobbing mess, coming apart beneath him like melted sugar.

Only he is not finished.

I *am* melted sugar, but he is still a stalk of hard cane—and ruthlessly uses that fact to his advantage. He looms over, capturing my gaze with his brilliant emerald focus, working my body with his knowing strokes. At the end of each plunge, he hitches his hips up and in, knowing exactly what place, so deep inside, he is determined to stimulate. My body reacts beyond the realm of my mind, coming for him yet again, answering instincts older than the cathedrals these stones used to be a part of. My head falls back, my gaze flying into the indigo sky, shooting my senses to the realm of the stars. While I have never felt more connected physically—maybe because of that—I have never flown further spiritually. Every inch of me vibrates at a new frequency, echoing harmonies as perfect and beautiful as my love for the creature who has brought me here...

The man now surging deeper into me.

Stretching me.

Throbbing deeper than he ever has before.

Then groaning, harsh and low, his breath filling my ear... his essence erupting into my sex.

"Fuck," he grates. "*Fuck.*"

One of his hands wraps around my head. The other is still flat between our bodies, finding the tender pearl at my center... coaxing it with harsher tugs, unstopping and unforgiving, bringing fresh flutters to the channel in which he is still embedded so tightly.

"Cassian!" I grab him, though am unsure whether to welcome him or punch him. It is so much. *Too* much. "I—I *cannot*—"

"You can." His snarl shakes the chest upon which I am now pressed. "You will."

Tears stab my eyes. The sensations he elicits... They begin to demand more than orgasms. A *more* I am not sure how to give—or if I *can* give. Not holding the knowledge that I do now.

Not while I still look the whale in the eye.

Not while I think of a faceless ghost named Lily—and the fact that she once wore Cassian's wedding ring.

And the fact that I did not know about it until the night he was shot.

How can I give him everything I am...when he has not done the same? Or even considered doing the same—until he was forced to? Outed by a sloshed ex-girlfriend who finagled her way into the gala we were attending and blurted the truth about Lily in front of a crowd of New York's social elite...

The *ugly* truth.

"*No*, Cassian. I *cannot*."

The violence in my voice punches the air—

And him.

He pushes back. Erupts with a fierce sound from deep in his chest. Slides out of me as if yanking a knife from his ribs instead.

Our breaths are still fast and fevered—as synched in our frustration as they were in our passion. Wordlessly, with my juices still coating him, he stuffs his cock away. Just as silently sweeps a napkin from the table and dabs at me, attempting to help my own cleanup. After a few seconds, I take over the task—but do not stop watching him from beneath my lashes.

Reading him like a neon sign.

On the surface, his face is stoic and gritted—but in the shimmer of his eyes and the grit of his jaw, I see the true torment biting at him.

The anguish of recognizing the whale too.

And the acceptance that we can no longer let the damn animal suffer like this.

CASSIAN

Remorse is the old sweater in the closet of my life.

It fits entirely too well to throw away—no matter how many times I've attempted to throw it out, give it away, or burn it.

Now, the thing falls over my shoulders again. All too familiar. All too disgusting. No ignoring it anymore. No giving it a glossy shine or turning the dirty threads into silk with another glamorous date—because Mishella Santelle doesn't care about the silk. She sees right through the shit because her life has already been draped in too damn much of it.

She actually wants the filthy sweater.

She wants my honesty.

Even after everything.

After knowing I wrote a check to be with her—and that her parents didn't blink about telling her to jump at the chance. Knowing that initially, my dick drove the decision as much as my brain did—and then after arriving here, knowing that the "sweet deal" of her billionaire benefactor came with a past full of fucked-up and a lover full of lies.

All right...not lies, exactly.

Then what is *it called when you take a woman thousands of miles from her home, claim her virginity a day later, and then profess you're falling in love with her a few days after* that— *without bothering to tell her about the woman you were once* married *to?*

So maybe I withheld a few things for too long.

So maybe I lied.

But now it's time to suck it up, swallow my pride—and my fear—and put on the goddamn sweater.

Starting this very second.

Only that's impossible.

Not without dragging her on one final journey.

I should feel better about the decision. Aren't difficult choices supposed to be easier once made?

Fucking fairy tale.

As I angle back toward her, my bones are like lead, my tendons turned to steel cables. I move with matching heaviness, lifting an awkward hand. At least I'm grateful she accepts it. Gently, I help her down from the balcony's ledge. Greedily steal a moment to hold her tight to me again, pushing the gold curls back from her face, marveling at how the candlelight dances across her features...though she'd light up the night without the extra illumination.

So. Fucking. Beautiful.

Her lips, pursed in curiosity, are still stung by my kisses. Her gaze, wide and searching, is as pure as the heart of a flame. Even the tiny stains of mascara on her upper cheeks are breathtaking—because I know exactly how they got there. Can still practically feel each of her orgasms, fluttering around my cock...

Thoughts for another time.

A much *different* time.

It's time to take care of things even more important than that.

"Cassian—"

"Ssshh." I take her lips in a small but insistent kiss. Tug her toward the door leading back into the museum offices.

"But the food and wine—"

"Will be appreciated by someone around here, I'm sure."

She stops. Pulls me back. A glorious flush suffuses her cheeks. "I—I did not mean to ruin the whole night."

"*Ella.*" My second kiss isn't so benign. *Ruin.* I'm not sure the woman even grasps the meaning of the word as a verb. "The night has hardly started—so that's null and void as well."

She doesn't move. Tightens her lips. "'Null and void,' Mr. Court?"

"Rolling our eyes, Miss Santelle?"

"And now with the royal 'we'?"

"And now with the sass that's begging for another spanking?"

No eye roll—but a deliberate pout full of just as much cheek. Little minx. She can rout my bullshit as easily as I catch the drift on hers.

I'm so fucking tempted to cap it with another swat to her delectable ass, but remembering what happened after the last spank makes me overcome the lure. The next time I'm inside her, we'll be more than simply skin-to-skin. We'll be twined again, spirit inside spirit. Thoughts so meshed, they'll feel like one. Hearts so bonded, they'll hammer in the same perfect time. No more secrets—and dammit, *no* more ghosts.

Tonight, it all ends.

The only ending I *ever* want with her.

And I am a man used to getting what he wants.

Because I am a man willing to pay for it. No matter what the price.

No truth has been less of a shock, while clanging through me exactly like one. It makes everything more real. More... permanent. A future I now envision having with her, despite the "strictly business" deal I struck to get her here. The contract that officially frees her to return home in just four months.

Home. To an island nearly five thousand miles away.

Unacceptable.

But *that's* an action item for another day.

Another price I'll have to pay.

Worth it.

No matter what...she's fucking worth it.

Is there some mental baggage in that one? *Bet your ass.* If I learned anything from the years with Lily—the knowledge I bring to every step I make now—it is that love doesn't pay lip service to every goddamn cliché ever conceived for it but a lot more that haven't been.

Flowers and honey. Victor Hugo. Got it. Check.

Smoke and sighs. Shakespeare's always good for this kind of shit.

Wonder of the wise. Amazement of the gods. Plato lends credibility.

But now for the Cassian Court entries in that journal.

Love...

is a gift.

This woman's love...the most priceless of them all.

Which throws the onus on the asshole peering back at me from reflections in the museum's glass cases as I guide her through the now-empty museum.

Great gifts require great gratitude. And the great commitment toward caring for them. And the actions proving exactly that.

And the recognition that many times, fate doesn't offer tomorrow for that proof.

There is only today.

And by this point, only the four hours we have left of it.

As if I need any further justification for rushing our steps out the front of the museum.

We emerge into the sticky summer night and make our way toward the Jag XJL limo, my driver Scott waiting with an open door and a lopsided smile. I climb inside after Ella—to find her already pivoted in the seat, waiting for me with an expectant frown. I settle in, letting her curve a hand into mine, but answer the questions in her eyes with steady silence.

For a few minutes, as we speed along the Henry Hudson, she seems content with that. But I know better.

The river begins to glow blue and silver instead of gold and red. The GW Bridge rises into view, its sweeping suspension cables lined in aqua lights.

Sure enough, as the bridge and the park disappear behind the bend in the road, Ella blurts, "Where are we going?"

I'm ready for it. I'm actually ready for a lot worse—not that she'll receive a different answer from me either way. From now on, I hide nothing from this woman.

Famous last words?

I pray they won't be.

With every goddamn bone in my body, I *swear* they won't be.

I made it through private school and college by shining shoes and slinging newspapers. Began a global empire with my own sweat and smarts. I can sure as fuck figure out how to do an open, honest, healthy relationship with a woman willing to bring the same thing to the table.

Starting with this.

"We're going where we can punch the restart button, armeau." I squeeze her hand. Kiss her forehead. "With the truth."

"All right." Her answer is like music, filled with her sweet trust and soft affection. "Where is that?"

"Home."

CHAPTER TWO

MISHELLA

"You're back early."

Mallory Court leans over the kitchen's granite counter as she murmurs it like juicy tabloid gossip instead of a statement of the obvious. Her green eyes sparkle. They are a shade lighter than her son's, like leaves in the sun compared to leaves in the shade, though her shoulder-length hair is the same shade and texture. Her bone structure is so similar to his, looking at her is like beholding Cassian with colored contacts. And...well...as a woman.

Unbelievably, that fact is secondary to another—for as much as Mallory Court resembles her son on the surface, she is a startling replica of Vylet Hester on the inside.

Vy.

A twinge of melancholy hits. Yes, my best friend and Mallory would be quite a pair. While night and day on the outside, both women are full of dry wit and raunchy imagination, balanced by huge hearts capable of delivering just the right encouragement at just the right time. That has made me love Mallory—and miss Vy—in increasing chunks each day.

"It would appear so." I scoot onto one of the dark wooden stools on my side of the counter. Follow that by tugging a knee beneath my chin: a simple feat since changing out of my "date dress" and into comfier attire of a T-shirts and cotton shorts, per Cassian's instructions as soon as we got back. It appears he is still off doing the same, though I would not put it past the man to sneak in a call to the office, his assistant, or both.

Ugh.

I tack on a heavy sigh. As if that will change anything.

And once again, doubt the decision to become the man's "girl next door," Temptation Manor style.

The guest bedroom certainly does not lack for comfort— with the exception of moments like these, when Mr. Court and his capital *A* personality determine it is acceptable to override medical orders and—

The same medical directives you let him violate an hour ago, between your thighs?

Maybe it is best that the sleeping arrangements remain as-is.

I originally conceived the move for emotional separation, following the whole Lily bombshell—but three gunshots and a week in New York Presbyterian later, my decision returned in the name of practicality. And desperation. That much was obvious just hours after Cassian's release. Despite doctor's orders, healing sutures, and enough pain medication to topple a horse, the man was clear he didn't believe "bed" and "rest" belonged between the sheets with us. Shamefully, I was beyond tempted to agree. Just days apart from him, and every cell of my skin reignited like dry brush...

Just like now.

Just as it did an hour ago, back at the Cloisters. *By the Creator.* Such soaring, tingling, amazing moments...now, just the memories refilling me with such abject need...

Before the memories become haunted.

Just like our passion was.

An invasion we both allowed—perhaps inevitable now, in light of how we successfully kept Lily beneath the rug for six weeks. Why it comes as a shock that we did not expect her wraith to rear up tonight, when the two of us dropped clothes, defenses, and all self-control, should be a stunner all on its own. But I do not feel that either. I am only mad at her—and madder at myself for letting her ruin one of the most perfect hours of connection Cassian and I have ever shared...

And wonder when we will be able to recreate again.

I miss him so.

My longing steals over my face before I can help it—or prevent Mallory from seeing it too.

"Uh-oh." She pushes up. Leaves behind the cat-with-the-canary grin. "So in this case...'back early' doesn't mean 'early for *other* things'?"

"Errrmm..." I hurl my gaze at a bowl of fresh fruit across the counter, though my cheeks must be the shade of the shiny apples perched on top.

"Oh, goodness. I've embarrassed you."

"Of—of course not!"

"Please, Mishella. Don't take away my special moment."

I jerk my head back up. Have forgotten what fruit to compare myself to now, especially as Mallory leans back over, grabbing one of my hands. "Your—"

"Moment." Her grasp tightens a little. "Yep. Just let me savor it a second longer."

"Uhhh." I eke out a smile. "All right. Savor away?"

To my deeper confusion—but infinite relief—a laugh bubbles on her lips. The kind only a *maimanne* can get away with, filled with teasing but loving warmth. The sound is so odd, it takes a moment to recognize it—and then understand it.

Then swallow back the heat behind my eyes because of it.

Mallory angles her chin up. Gives me the benefit of an assessing breath. "In case you can't tell, cutie, I'm not exactly a prude. One can't be when bringing up a boy who knew all the parts of his jolly roger, by their English *and* Latin names, before he finished third grade."

A giggle eclipses the tears. "And how long did you get away with calling it his 'jolly roger'?"

"Longer than I likely should have." She swipes a cluster of grapes out of the bowl. Pops one in and cants a smirk. "Still doesn't mean I don't want to think of him choosing a female of quality to share his world with."

"Oh." It is all I can blurt for a moment. "And that was why..."

"The moment?" Another grape goes in. Her grin tilts the opposite direction, deepening the dimples Cassian has inherited. "Yes. That's why I needed the moment."

"Well." I curve a little smile too—a tricky thing, since I must conceal as much as I reveal with it. Mallory is a woman who speaks all her truths, and since she has not talked about how I truly came to be here with Cassian, I am certain he has not told her. I am also certain *I* will not be that messenger either. "I enjoy...sharing his world."

At least for another four months...

She reaches over and pats my hand. "Not a subject we have to beat in right now. Besides, I believe we're due for another Monopoly match soon."

I laugh fully now. Relief is so much simpler to shield that way. "As long as we try to talk Cassian into joining us this time."

A beat goes by. Just one.

Before she tosses the remaining grapes on the counter—in favor of rushing around it to crush me into a hug.

"Errr? Mall—"

"Ssshh. I'm having another moment." She pulls me tighter. "Hang on. Adding a prayer this time."

"A prayer?" Alarm stabs my chest. "For what?"

"Just thanking the Almighty that Cas took that trip to Arcadia." She steps back far enough to give me her full smile again. "And came home with such a great treasure."

I laugh again—and can mean it this time. "It is my pleasure to be so, Mallory." Hopefully, she does not discern just how *much* pleasure. If she does, then it is her own son's fault. Between Cassian's seduction and the romantic spell of the Cloisters, is it any wonder I am a satisfied woman right now?

"Uh-oh."

As if summoned by the sensual force of my thoughts, the syllables are delivered with a gorgeous growl—replacing the alarm in my chest with butterflies.

Cliché? Yes.

But accurate? Absolutely.

I try breathing away the critters, but as I join Mallory in looking to the doorway where Cassian has ascended from the floor below, they refuse to heed me. Why should they? He is worth scrambling in a million directions for—especially now, with the museum slacks and coat off but the form-fitting T-shirt still on, paired with black workout pants accentuating his long legs even more.

Creator's mercy. Only fifteen minutes have passed since we arrived home, but I feel jittery, as if treated to his golden beauty for the first time. Is it like this for every woman in love? And for the men too? If so, how has anything on this earth gotten accomplished beyond the Stone Age? Despite every confusion and frustration I wrestled with during our episode at the Cloisters, all I want to do is get him alone again. *Now.* Do all the things that scenario implies. *Right* now.

"'Uh-oh' *what*?" Mallory's cheeky comeback eases the edge of my lust a little. A *little.* I would dare any woman to keep pious thoughts when exposed to the tender smile Cassian reserves only for his mother. "You implying something, sweet little one?"

Cassian grimaces. I smile, despite my tangled heart. No amount of repetition will make me forget the first time I heard the woman use the endearment. After Cassian survived his post-shooting surgery, his friend Doyle finally contacted Mallory. She rushed to the city from her home in Connecticut, sweeping into the room at the hospital without care for how things "appeared"—and leaned over him with love so fierce, it eclipsed every sterile inch of the room. Cassian had been sleeping and did not hear her fervent whisper, but I had—and was shattered to instant tears. He had landed in that damn bed because of me. My stupid actions...

To my shock, Mallory Court had held me through those tears. And as soon as she heard the whole story behind them, embraced me even harder...

Before giving me words that became my guideposts for the next six weeks.

He clearly thought you were worth those bullets, Mishella. So prove him right.

By the Creator, I hope I have fulfilled her expectation.

"I imply nothing that my instincts won't confirm, Mom."

He leans and kisses her cheek. "But my instincts are pretty good."

They both arch one brow. His left, her right. "Is this supposed to be fresh news, darling?" Mallory cracks.

Cassian puckers his lips in a funny way—a look that would approach stodgy on most other men. On him, it is simply... determined, with a twist of hot.

"What are you up to with my woman, Mother?"

My woman.

I do not miss the glimmer in Mallory's eyes—as one sparks in my heart. The glow expands as he loops an elbow around my neck, drawing me close. I have to remind myself— forcefully this time—that this may not be forever. But for now, I will allow it to feel...

utterly

wonderful.

"Up to?" Astonishment again, as Mallory's glare mirrors her son's. Or is it *his* that has copied *hers*? "We were just making plans for a new Monopoly match..."

"Just?" Cassian zips a look between she and me. "*Just?* After the way you two edged me out during the last game?"

"Stop pouting," Mallory chides. "Mishella can't help where the dice tell her to land."

He snorts. "Maybe if we played a *real* version of the game."

"What's wrong with *Scooby Doo* Monopoly?"

"Other than the fact that Boardwalk has been replaced by The Creeper Bell Tower?"

"You love *Scooby Doo* Monopoly."

"*Loved*, Mom. When I was ten."

"*Scooby Doo* is eternal."

In tandem, they swing gazes at me. My bottom lip gets

gnashed again. Truly, I should be used to the role of tie breaker, thanks to Brooke and Vy—but two generations of Courts elevate the stress to a new level. "Errrm...the dog is cute. Is that one Scooby?"

Mallory preens. "See? Eternal."

A sigh leaves Cassian—though does so through his smiling lips, officially stirring mud into the conversation's waters. Two months away from Arcadia, I have learned only one clear thing about the world beyond my borders: that nothing is clear. One day, people are fighting about the size of sugared drink cups. The next, they are using children as custody battle pawns. The next, they are pitching tents on sidewalks to buy new cell phones. The merit of "Scooby Doo" in all this is still not clear to me.

"Maybe it's best that we back burner this one."

Mallory's glower tightens. "Now trying the back-burner tack, Cassian Cameron Jonathan?" She slants a brow toward me. "You hearing this, missy? You're my witness. He *back burnered* Scooby."

Cassian breaks leans away from me long enough to buss her forehead. "Not far back, I promise." A new solemnity sets into his elegant features. "But right now, I need to borrow back Mishella." In the barest of mutters, he finishes, "Before I lose the nerve."

In the space of those five words, Mallory is transformed too. Like me, she hears every slight tremble beneath his soft sarcasm—and in seconds becomes a different person for it. With eyes glowing and lips tender, she cups his set jaw. "Since when do you lose?"

Cassian rolls his eyes and tosses back his head, though chuckles the whole time. Something tells me it is not the first time Mallory has challenged him this way, nor for his reaction to it—though the laugh was probably not always part of the mix. For a few perfect moments, it is like years peel away from both of them. Suddenly, I am looking at a teenage Cassian being encouraged by his young, single mother—and loving her for it, no matter how hard he tries to cover the reaction with adolescent attitude.

I am...fascinated.

Is *this* what it is like, when a parent believes in their child?

I can only rely on instinct to answer the question—but in the affirmation, I recognize another piece of Cassian that makes new sense.

But more that do not.

With the love and belief of a mother like this, why does the man still look at the world with so many shadows in his eyes? *Ghosts.* That is what Kathryn Robbe called them, when I first met his friend after arriving in New York. The word fits. For all of Cassian's confidence, arrogance, business savvy, and sanity-stealing sexual prowess, this man's spirit is stalked by darker things...monsters that drag him into places where the only way out is by fighting for himself.

Fighting desperately...

Against creatures he refuses to let me see...

Except for rare moments like this.

As he turns from Mallory, sliding his hand down my arm—and his gaze back into mine. Fits our palms firmly together before murmuring, "Don't worry, Mom. I *don't* intend to lose this one."

"Good." The riposte does not spark a single mother-son chortle. Before I can fathom if that is a good or bad thing, she nudges his free shoulder. "You got this, tiger."

"Tiger?" Even my attempt at a mood lightener gets swallowed by the depths of their new solemnity—a flow defining all of Cassian's steps as he leads me away from the kitchen. We walk through the dining room and living room, both drenched in shadows—appropriate symbolism of what lies ahead?—before he stops at the landing bracketed by two arched doors.

Two significant doors.

I already know where they lead—because I have already been through both of them. Temptation Manor's turrets are among its most fascinating architectural features, identical when beheld from the outside. Inside, they cannot hold more divergent contents. In the upstairs room of Turret One, Cassian and I commemorated my first night in New York with hours of lust and passion I shall never forget. Surrounded by the lights and energy of the city, I gave him the key piece of my innocence—and the beginning of my heart.

And Turret Two?

Well...I can say I have entered it. And climbed six of its steps—before being stopped and nearly hauled out by the roots of my hair by the woman who, for all intents and purposes, has appointed herself Cassian's ninja patrol. Since that day, Prim Smith—Temptation's seemingly self-appointed mistress of household—has made some small efforts to warm to me, despite the vigilance for Cassian that once had me fearing her as one of his preferred ex-lovers. It is not a stretch, considering how I had barely met the man before Vy showed me internet hits that brought up as many links to his "romantic adventures" as his international business deals.

Now, that still makes Prim a glaring—and even more confusing—exception.

And fully justifies why, as Cassian crosses the landing toward that door, I wrench my hand away from his. Back away, Pavlovian instinct kicking in, as he looks back and frowns.

"Armeau." He reclaims my hand. "It's all right."

"Is that so?" I twist again, but he is on to me, clutching hard. "And you have come to such a conclusion...how?"

A long breath leaves him. *The thief caught with the bag.* He does not fight the not-so-veiled allegation. One look into my eyes, and he must see it all there. How the memories assault me, as bitter as the incident that spawned them, of the night *after* Prim ordered me out of the turret...

"This isn't something I want to talk about anymore, Mishella."

"Is that why the only sound louder than your fist against that desk is the grind of your teeth? Why you look as if you yearn to collapse where you stand but run as fast as you can at the same time?"

"This conversation isn't going to happen. Period."

"I think this conversation is long overdue."

"Then you think really wrong."

The confrontation did not end any better—but like the stars that rebelled from the cosmos to first bring us together, we pushed back the mess and found each other once more. *Reconnected.*

Dear Creator, if I only know we always will...

And then the comprehension strikes.

Is *this* the meaning of having faith?

No wonder all those saints at the Cloisters looked so terrified.

No wonder I commiserate so thoroughly with them now.

But if the fear were gripping me tenfold, I would still

endure every moment. For Cassian. To know everything about him—no matter how ugly or hard or terrible it is—I will walk through Hades itself.

So maybe this *is* faith.

And maybe that is simply a huge part of falling in love.

"*Mishella.*" He reaches over, grabbing my other hand. Brings my knuckles up to his lips. "I love you. And I don't want to silo the explosives anymore. Not with you." Before my perplexed frown has a chance to fully form, he rushes on, "If this blows up on me, then I want *your* finger on the launch button."

Oh, Creator.

Oh...this man.

I lift our joined hands. Extend just my fingertips from their clasp, spreading them over both sides of his jaw. The warmth of his skin mixed with the stab of his stubble inspires a similar contrast of sensations. Excitement, energy, awakening, even arousal...but also deeper versions of nervousness...fear.

This is faith.

And I *do* believe it.

Believe in him.

In us.

The surety reaches like roots of a tree, twining through the ground of our connection, reaching for him. I feel his stretching for me too...coiling deeper into me. We are strong, ready for the storm of whatever may come.

"I only want to love you too, Cassian. As best I can, in whatever way you need. That is all."

For a long while, his stillness is my only reply. Nothing moves through him, not even a breath. I shiver harder. Terrified but turned-on. Unsure but utterly heated.

He steps back. Exhales roughly. "Christ, armeau. That's all I still pray for...after this."

CASSIAN

As we climb the spiral of stairs, I start to tremble.

Me.

Fuck.

This isn't the surface shit, like jitters funneled into productivity. This is the shakes from the inside out. The vibrations claiming the ends of my nerves, the pith of my bones, even the molecules of my breaths. The last time I felt something close to this, I held a shovel in my hands, breaking ground on Court Towers.

This is even more unfamiliar ground. And the route is riddled with quicksand.

But I'm determined. Right now, just this once, it's time for the silos to go. For the first time, one person alone will have access to every single bomb that can destroy me.

One person...who, as it stands right now, will not even be here in four months.

Is that why I've even thought about doing this?

No. Plenty of women—people I've even dared to called "relationships" before—have come along before this.

This is different.

She is different.

Reassuring...right? Somebody needs to relay that to my bile-filled gut.

One mire at a time, man. One foot in front of the other. And watch the fucking quicksand.

I sure heed *that* little tidbit—by hitting the top of the stairs

51

with a step made of lead. One more. *Great. You're doing soooo great.*

New acid boils up, scorching my throat as I lift my head, already knowing the dark vista that awaits my gaze.

The room is sealed in perpetual gloom but kept meticulously clean, thanks to Prim. It's still centered by the ornate daybed, covered in that pristine gold brocade, a dozen pillows, and the stuffed animals in shades of cream and white. Nearby, the little chaise with the throw blanket is still positioned next to the reading table with its small stack of books, purchased by me but never read by their recipient. Long ago, during those numb days when I couldn't move from the floor next to the couch, I committed every one of those spines into bitter memory.

Stop The Insanity: Pills No More

Beating Back the Beast

Serenity in Stillness: An Addict's Prayers

Quitting and Sticking

Why Can't I Say No?

Addiction Understood

But nothing in the room diverts from its main attraction.

The wide curve of the turret almost appears to fall away from the building, due to the ripped wallpaper at its edges. The walls were kept like this on my dictate, along with the dried blood smears on the exposed surface beneath.

Lily, stop it. Stop it. *You're bleeding, dammit!*

But she didn't stop.

The center window of the turret, its original pane still broken out except for a few chunks of glass, bears the harrowing proof of that. Forming a seal over the outside of the panel is the Plexiglass cover Hodge mounted from the outside, since I ordered that the original window also remain as-is. The cover is now clouded by dust and spotted with rain. I wish to hell my memories would grow as dull...have surrendered hope they ever will.

Ella sees that too. More vitally, she understands. I see it in every inch of her bearing as she turns from the window back to me. While new questions flow from her eyes, her lips are firm and her bearing straight. Simply from our shared stares, she knows answers are finally going to come.

I just beg God to get me to the end.

"Cassian."

Her voice breaks on it. My whole jaw clenches, crushing down on my hatred of the sound. *I am the subject of nobody's pity.* But as she uses our joined hands to pull me across the room, I let her. When she stops before the chaise and then hesitates to sit, I make the decision for us both—by falling to my knees next to it.

"Cassian."

She utters nothing but a rasp now. I hate *and* cherish the sound, drawn to it like an orphan to shelter. As soon as she plummets to the chaise, her hands are in my hair and my head is in her lap. I reach up, compelled by forces I cannot control. Grip her by the ribcage, confirming she is real and warm and *here.* Dark sarcasm sneaks in. *Fuck*...I'm going to have to tell Kathryn she's been right all these years. I've been living with ghosts too damn long.

But what the fuck to do with them now? I grapple for the answer past the swamp in my head and the boulders in my throat. The only path to clarity seems to lie in holding this woman harder...in breathing in her strength and warmth, wrapped tighter around me in return. The new pressure brings a strange sensation. Amazement. That she can sit here, overflowing with humanity and tenderness even after two insane months in a city that should be *named* Insanity, shatters my mind. That she can surround me with devotion, even sitting in a room where Lily whispers from every shadow, smashes apart my soul.

Or maybe she's just become as insane as the city already...

As if that matters now.

I burrow deeper against her. Battle for more eloquence than what *does* come out. "I don't know...what to do with them now."

Them.

How an attempt at confessing about Lily turned into a catch-all for Damon too is too tangled a mystery right now. *Eye on the goal. You're best at that above all, remember?* In this moment, I just need to get this shit spilled—before survival instinct blasts in and shuts me down.

Because this feels a little like dying.

Maybe a lot like it.

"Cassian."

"*What?*"

Yeah...my voice is now the husk and hers the command. I ignore the recognition. And the new hammer in my blood. And the dread coiling into my grip, seeking more of her warmth.

"Just start at the beginning."

A scrape of a laugh. "Sure, favori. I'll get right on that." This shit has been a part of me for so long, I have no damn idea where "the start" is.

She folds herself tighter around me. Yeah, she knows that too.

"Tell me how you and Lily met."

Remarkably, I exhale. Unbelievably, layers of tension leave my body, too. *Unreal*. Is this woman actually turning my giant slab of difficult into a friendly conversation? As I breathe back in, I am suffused with her jasmine and vanilla scent. The memories start to come easier.

"I was...young. *Really* young." The qualifier feels necessary. "Nash Quinn recruited me for Quantumm Corp before I finished my junior year at Fordham. He had a huge project starting with Eurail and wanted me to be a co-project director on it."

"Project director?" Her stare bulges. "For all of Europe?"

I shrug. Her reply lands me in more familiar territory. While it's not new to compare an ambitious college student with a decent brain to a genius superhero, I've still heard every dazed gush composed on the subject. "I was very close to dropping out and accepting."

She gives my hair a reproving tug. "Always in such a hurry."

"Hurrying had nothing to do with it."

"No?"

"No. The zeroes he kept adding to the offer, on the other hand..."

"Zeroes don't help everything, Cassian."

"No. But they get attention—and *that* helps everything."

Her face tightens. I want to feel shitty for dumping the brutality of it like that, but I don't. Isn't the truth what we're in this room for? Wasn't it what defined us from the start—when the zeroes I threw at her father earned me the attention needed to get her here? Zeroes I would've increased in a second, if that was what it took.

Voicing it crosses my mind, until I see the recognition

take quiet—and troubling—hold in her eyes. In her world, wealth has done nothing but corrupt people. In mine, it has been the door to supporting them. Her way isn't totally right, but neither is mine. Maybe it's another reason fate has pulled a few favors with the universe to rope us together—and why I hope, beyond logic or sanity, that the knots just keep adding up.

"So." She neutralizes her expression once more. "You were young..."

"And right out of college. *Yes*," I assure, answering the approval in her gaze, "that *did* happen, in every sense of the word. Wore the cap and gown, shook all the necessary hands..."

Her head tilts. "Your maimanne stepped in with some 'tactful' prodding?"

I snort. "Prodding's one way of saying it."

"She went for the castration angle?"

"Worse."

"*Worse?*"

"Threatened never to make my favorite lemon bars again." Though I almost break a grin with the knowledge that my castration would be that troubling to her.

"That must have all been before Prim."

Sarcasm etches her words—on the surface. Nothing about them is tossed casually. I wonder how long she's waited to utter them—and guess it was nearly from the moment she and Prim met. That was nearly two months ago, but I remember that walking-on-cacti moment as if it were yesterday. Prim, so suspicious she looked jealous. Ella, so uncomfortable she looked guilty. They've tiptoed into friendlier airspace since, but I could be doing more to de-ice the waters.

"For the record, Prim's lemon bars don't approach Mom's." Now I do insert a chuckle. "And Prim will be the first to admit that to you." Wrap my hands around hers, lowering them between my chest and her knees. "What Prim *hasn't* been so forthcoming about is that she and I have never been with each other—nor will we ever be."

She huffs out a skeptical laugh. "Désonnum, Cassian...but many believe unicorns exist too, and—"

"She was Lily's best friend."

As I hope, that stills her. As I dread, that means revisiting more of the past—a reckoning I've ignored for too long. Every pound of my heart reconfirms that much. "I met her as I was getting to know Lily." Though imagine that, the beginning *does* feel like the best place to start. "Nash wanted me on the Eurail project the second I graduated. Flew me to Utrecht, in the Netherlands, the day after I walked for my diploma. For the next month, we were at Eurail HQ during the days and buried in meeting debriefs every night, so Nash insisted I stay at the castle he was leasing instead of a hotel."

She lifts a knowing smile. "Hmm. Not a tough assignment."

"Unless you like toilets that actually work."

Her giggle is as genuine as my smirk. "You billionaires are so picky."

"Didn't have two euros to rub together back then." I illustrate the point by spreading my hands. "I was just a kid at my version of the Magic Kingdom. Modernizing communications and operations for one of the world's largest transportation entities...working with high-level engineering executives in every country in Europe..." I shake my head, kicking up a one-sided smile. "For the first time in my life, my wings didn't feel clipped."

She fingers back the hair from my forehead. "That was good?"

"That was fucking amazing."

She's quiet for a moment. "And it got even more amazing when you met Lily."

"Lily wasn't amazing." I'm unsure what shocks me harder: the speed or the vehemence of my rebuttal. Neither escapes Mishella either, blue crystals of curiosity in her eyes. "She was... enlightening. Intriguing. Maybe even confusing." Despite how my brows pull in, I recognize the words as therapeutic—to me *and* Ella. "No. That part came later."

"But at some point, you fell in love with her."

I grimace despite her leniency with the conviction. So easily—and justifiably—she could've turned it into accusation. Used my own honesty against me.

And you...loved her?

Yes, Ella...I loved her.

I'd surrendered the confession in the middle of Bryant Park, minutes after she'd learned about Lily the wrong way. Even if that night hadn't ended with my ass in an ambulance and Ella's sobs in my ears, the lesson from it was clear. Delaying the truth, even with the excuse of making it "easier" for someone, is just as idiotic as lying. In the end, it'll eventually bite you in the ass.

"Yes," I finally state. "I fell in love with her—though at the beginning, it wasn't that at all." My forehead falls atop her knuckles. "It didn't come close to what happened with you."

I don't break the pose. Pray that some magical osmosis takes over and bleeds the truth from my brain straight into her. Right. And unicorns *are* real. If *I* were her, only one thought would be permeating my mind at this moment. *This asshole sounds like a greeting card—and believes every stupid word of it.*

And there's the shittiest rub.

I do believe every word. To the depths of my fucking soul.

"So...what was it?" Her insecurity rasps every syllable, confirming my qualms and stabbing my gut. At this point, my greeting card might as well be printed on toilet paper.

So prove that it's not.

Wade into the quicksand.

Give her your truth.

"At first, more than anything, it was just...curiosity."

The word is accurate but sounds lame. Relief floods in when she rocks her head again, looking like I've just conveyed aliens are real and living in relics of a city beneath the Atlantic. "About what?"

I should've expected the question—but my mouth opens on nothing but air for a long second. "I was a kid from a shoebox apartment in Jersey. Farthest I'd ever been in my life to that point was the Canadian side of Niagara Falls. So getting to *see* a real European castle, much less find myself living in one..." I stop to pull in a breath—and make a new stab for all the right words. "Very quickly, it started to feel like a dream. A damn good one."

"And Lily became part of that."

"To an extent...probably...yes. I mean, she sure as hell *looked* the part..." My voice trails as the remembrance takes over. In those early days, Lily *was* every inch the princess, with her porcelain skin, dark hair, and tentative smile—when she decided the situation warranted a smile. "But..."

"But what?"

Belatedly, I realize how thick my silence has gotten. Silence—the gift Lily keeps giving. Once upon a time, I called it her "glamorous stillness." Once upon a time...when I was a Jersey apartment kid suddenly living in a castle. "But dreams are different things to different people." I surprise myself by looking up. Looking *there*. Making sure the maw of that shattered window is stamped hard into my psyche. "If you fall asleep in the tower, you'll dream of clouds and flying. If you curl up in the dungeon, you see monsters in your sleep."

More silence. But just a moment of it.

"And Nash Quinn kept his daughter in the dungeon?"

Harsh laugh. "Nash Quinn would have built a stairway to the clouds for Lily if she asked."

Ella sighs. The sound is filled with instant understanding— and unique sorrow. "So she chose the dungeon."

I lift a stunned stare. Smack it away with a fresh dose of *duh, dumbshit*. Will I ever get used to the dichotomy of this woman? Do I *want* to? Her ability to figure people out like an ancient seer, though things like automatic tellers, flavored water, and Twitter fascinate her like a child discovering its own toes... I really *am* reduced to a card-carrying dumbshit—and proud of it. Beautiful sorceress. Bewitching girl...

"Yeah." I release a long breath too. "She did."

One of her hands lifts again to my nape. Soothes with rhythmic motions through the ends of my hair, into the tight muscles beneath. "And there was nothing your friend could do about it."

"Which tore him apart."

"Which tore *you* apart."

I let my grimace serve as a *yes*—before my mind fills with more scenes from those days. Five years. They sometimes feel like five decades—and sometimes, like now, feel like five minutes. "Nash wasn't just my first real-world boss. He was the first major business figure who believed in me, mentored me. Lily was the only thing he had left of his wife, who died when Lily was a girl. Watching him grieve about her, even after spending millions on her..."

"But things weren't what she needed." Her caresses continue, matching the quiet calm of her voice. "Help was what she needed."

"Yeah." I remain a block of tension, refusing even a thought about any pleasure from her touch. Punishing myself for everything, even now. "Help we couldn't identify." I jab a growl into it. "You hear all the talk about depression...all the signs, all the stats...but when it's staring you in the face, you hit the damn denial button. Call it ten thousand other things. Make up excuses for it..."

"Try to save it?"

I jerk up my head. Search her face. "Was that wrong?"

Her brows lower. Her lips purse. "Wrong?" she replies. "Do you mean following your nature? Being true to who you are?"

I feel my own gaze narrow. "What the hell does that have to do with—"

The music of her laugh cuts me short. "Oh, Cassian. It has everything to do with...everything." She slides her fingers along my jaw. "You are a warrior. You fought to excel in school and then in business. In the middle of the two, you battled even your mother—though I wager you have fought on her behalf as well, depending on when your brother was not around any longer."

I jerk to my feet. It does nothing to dispel the rocks she's dumped down my limbs. "Damon has nothing to do with this."

"Forgive me, my love—but bullshit." Ironically, she finishes by looking like a Madonna. Shifted forward on the chaise, angling more of the chandelier's light over the golden waves on her head, she caps the moment by spreading her hands, palms up. "But we shall burn his back for now."

"You mean...back burner him?"

"Exactly." She returns the hands to her lap. Twists them just softly enough that I'm reminded of the truth here—that she's really struggling through all this as much as I am.

Screw the Madonna. If I'm a goddamn Conan, then she's my valiant Xena. If she's getting through it, then I can too.

"For a while," I go on, "it was...idyllic. A gorgeous bubble. I worked hard with Nash and loved passionately with his daughter. We finished on Eurail, but another contract came through from the Dutch government, ensuring Lily and I could stay on in Utrecht for another three months." I fold my arms while facing the ruined window once more. Am drawn to the jagged frame as if it's a magic mirror, revealing the depths of time instead of a regular reflection. "We were so young," I grate. "And, in the custom of ignorant youth since the beginning of time, thought it would be that perfect forever. Or maybe we were so desperate to believe it, we just did."

"Which is why you proposed."

I drop my arms. Past the buzz swarming my head like pissed-off cicadas, my palms burn from the stab of my fingernails.

Did I expect her to come to other conclusion?

No.

But did I expect this corner of the memories to hurt so damn much?

Same answer, shittier version.

But I've been through worse. Like the first time I lived through this crap. Months and months of it, instead of a few bitter minutes.

Words finally choke their way up. "Let's define 'proposed.'"

A rustle. A change in the air behind me. Though Ella

doesn't move beyond that, I can picture her stance now. Proud but pensive. Elegant hands clasped high against her waist, as regal as the royalty she served back in her kingdom. The "trap" I thought I was saving her from—a call I now question with every new second that passes. Every new corner of my past now exposed by her light.

Every dark, dirty corner...

"I do not understand."

Just like a queen, her voice is velvet girded by steel. Just like the beggar at her palace, I shuffle through a turn back at her.

"Yeah. Of course you don't."

"What are you trying to say?" Exasperation bites her words. "All right, you loved her. Then you married her—"

"Yes." I jog up my head another notch. "I loved her. I married her. But I never proposed." Hard breath. One more. "I wasn't given that choice."

CHAPTER THREE

MISHELLA

There's an intent here. Something he dreads saying so much, he cannot frame the words for it. Something his stare pleads with me to figure out, resulting in a stalemate of frustration because I cannot. I know my tight glower and leaden huff do not help—but despite his obvious assumption, the answer is *not* as clear as a spot on the floor between us. If it is, then it was created with invisible ink, and I have yet to locate the black light for revelation.

I didn't propose. I wasn't given that choice.

I am tempted to call bullshit again.

He formed those feelings for Lily Quinn of his own volition—perhaps encouraged by his mentor, but certainly not forced. Even a girl from a sheltered past on a tiny island can deduce that. Besides, had Cassian not bid for Lily's hand, there were likely five hundred others waiting in line to do so.

So what had been different? Why was Cassian "expected" to marry Lily without taking the steps expected from a social echelon he had worked so hard to become a part of? I have sneaked glances at enough of his daily mail to know. The magazines, newsletters, and social notices of the American upper crust are unique journals, chronicling day-long spa visits, tiny-sized food, and "casual parties" that took weeks to plan and thousands to fund. Events like engagements approach the status of national holiday celebrations. The wedding plans of someone like Lily Quinn would have boosted the family's social and financial clout...

Unless those plans had to be made in a hurry.

"Creator's toes." The spot blares to clarity. "She—Lily—she was—"

"Pregnant." *Now* the explanation flows from him without effort, even murmured like a prayer. But is it a prayer of gratitude or shame? The dazed cast of his gaze does not supply any definition. "With my baby."

I pull in a breath. Am not shocked that the air shakes in my chest. Imagining him as a father-to-be is the easiest—and hardest—thing in the world. Watching his protective ways with Prim and Mallory makes it simple to envision him doing the same with his own child—but in my mind's eye, that child has no other mother than me. The force of the fantasy weakens my knees. "So Nash made you marry her."

"Nash didn't make me do shit." His nostrils flare and his lips thin. "She told me the day after Christmas, during a trip back here to see her parents. The day after *that*, we hit the jewelry store and then the courthouse. Her stepmother was understandably horrified, but Nash yanked the curtain on our masquerade pretty fast."

"And then what?"

"And then he couldn't wait to welcome me into the family."

"And were you happy too?"

"I was delirious." He issues it as if confessing to murder—likely reading the little "Baby Daddy Cassian" scenario that burns across my face by now and knowing the words will be its ice bath. But he has not brought me up here for an evening of wine and roses. For two months, I have not been allowed into this turret for a reason—and I have held no illusions it would be a pleasant one to hear. "In my mind, the bubble had just received steel plating," he explains further. "I was on top of my professional game, now running the European division of Quantumm for Nash. Lily and I started looking for a home. We had a child on the way. Life was damn good."

"But even steel plates can be blown back." It is the logical response, as my gaze follows his back over to the destroyed window pane. When he descends into his unnatural stillness once more, I prod, "*Cassian*. What happened?"

His head angles to one side. The light catches the whisky tint in his hair as it teases at his forehead, though it cannot illuminate the new darkness in his eyes. In an instant, he is not here with me anymore. Distant memories claim him...as well as their ruthless stamp of grief. "Not what happened," he grates. "It's what *didn't* happen." His eyes slide closed. "The person who should've been most thrilled about the baby...wasn't."

The obvious answer makes no sense—but is finally the one I blurt. "Lily?"

His silence serves as confirmation. I cut into it with a gasp.

"But...she loved you in return, right? Why would she not be thrilled to—"

His bite of laughter is a shocking interruption. "Why the hell wasn't Lily thrilled about *anything* in her life?"

I cease fighting the liquid in my legs. Slump back to the chaise, mind spinning, working to fill in his spotty portrait of the woman who captivated him...who carried his child. But the image keeps popping back like a Picasso, cubes of images in places they do not belong.

"Now I really do not understand."

"Of course you don't."

His reiteration is much different than the first time. It accepts my truth, only this time with sadness instead of fight.

"Why did she not welcome the child?" I ask it after a long pause, sensing we both need a mental walk in the midst of this emotional run. Or perhaps sensing the climb we have ahead.

Cassian drops his head. Drags it back up—with his jaw defined by a full clench. "Because she had to stop drinking."

His bitter bite on the last word has the same effect on my psyche. "Oh," I stammer. "I—I see." In reality, I am not certain I do—perhaps I have overplayed his vehemence?—though the tension through every muscle of his body is unlike any I have seen before, even when he confronted the thugs in Bryant Park who tried assaulting me. In the park, he was furious, clenched... empowered. Right now, he is helpless, tight...

Haunted.

He labors through another dark huff. "Wasn't long after that, I gave in to an epiphany of my own." Presses his lips into that murder-confession grimace again. "I wasn't sure *I* could handle her...or even knew her...without all of it."

"Without all of..." I feel my features tighten. "Without the *drinking*?"

He flinches as if I've stabbed him—though his eyes, instead of thick with pain, are hollow with loss. He has been to this space before, at least in his soul. But if this is the first time he has ever done it verbally...

I flinch now too.

Suddenly, the locked door at the bottom of the stairs makes total sense. He did not want to do this. Hated even thinking about it. But he is doing it now...for me. With me.

I reach toward him, filled with gratitude.

He whirls from me, shrinking in shame.

Though it tears me apart, I respect his move. Let him hold on to it.

For now.

"I...hadn't realized." He grunts it with barely any volume. "How much booze she'd been getting down every day. Sneaking it in...even on days when I was with her all the time. I just thought she had shifting moods..." His hand digs raggedly through his hair. "*Dammit.* I was such an idiot."

"No," I rasp. "No, Cassian. She was probably just that dev—" *Devious* is definitely *not* the best word choice right now. "Just that smooth."

His hand fists against his nape. "When her 'morning sickness' developed into a fever and strange visions, I insisted we go to the doctor. He was the one who told me she was going through alcohol DTs. Nash helped me get her into a confidential rehab program, specific for pregnant women... but she checked herself out after two weeks. She said she was better. Focused. That the only thing that mattered to her was the baby."

"What did you do?"

"The only thing I could." He releases the fist, though the hard ropes of his shoulders still strain against his shirt. "I believed her. Trusted that she'd really hit her bottom in that facility and was ready to climb back up for the sake of our family."

"Hit her...bottom." Once more I echo him in a stutter, but it seems the only sane way to properly process this. Like the night I first learned about Lily and her significance in his life, my gut has been hollowed out and then kicked in—by a horse named shock.

He was going to be a father.

Sweet Creator.

What if he still *is* one?

"Everyone in recovery has a different bottom. And regrettably, nobody knows what theirs is...until they've hit it."

He turns back around, stiffly and slowly, though his gaze sharpens once seeing me again. I cannot even think about hiding all my feelings. There are too many now, clamoring on top of each other.

"And you thought Lily had gotten to hers," I finally rasp. "But she started drinking again?"

Something passes over his face. Not a shadow. Something darker. "No."

Double take. "No?"

"That was when she started taking the drugs."

CASSIAN

"By the Creator."

I resteel my nerves as the words practically gasp from her—because I know what's going to come next. After the astonishment, there'll be the sap and the sympathy. *The fucking pity.* The look I have hated on anyone's face who knows this story. The expression I haven't even thought of on hers— because just thinking of it there is enough to set off a nuclear bomb in my blood.

I can't let it happen.

I refuse.

"Stop." I dictate it as her posture surges forward, already writing me an advance check of the shit. "Just stop the fucking cart right there."

For one exhilarating second, a furious scowl replaces her

sorrow. Then she's all mush again. "Stop...what?"

"The cart full of your pity." I fold my arms. "The weeping wagon, feeling 'awful' for the poor husband of the drug addict." My teeth clench hard enough to hurt. "It takes two to make a baby. I was not a goddamn victim in the situation."

"Hmm." It's her base coat expression, used when she wants to start with neutrality but color the meaning into something else. This time, it's a reprise of her anger, given in a swift jump of her brows—to which I respond by crunching my own.

"I watch over my own, dammit."

"I am well aware of that." Her posture straightens, fused with the same fusion of strength and serenity that bowled me over when meeting her the first time, back on Arcadia. Just like then, I'm flooded by gratitude—but unlike then, it's for a different reason. In that reception hall in the Palais Arcadia, my soul knew she was different...remarkable. This time, my mind confirms it too.

Which should scare me.

And does.

For a disgusting ton of reasons. But right now, I can only address the first.

She deserves the rest of this story.

Every damn, ugly detail.

I glance upward. *Hey big guy...could use a little help in the fortitude department.* But the Almighty isn't fond of my endearment right now, even if I did borrow it from Mom...

Until He drives me to my knees again.

Using the one weapon He knows I won't refuse.

My sweet little Arcadian.

"Come here, Cassian." When she gestures to the floor

next to the chaise, I drop down without second thought. Let her twine our hands together in the middle of her lap. I gaze at the union of our fingers, her slender tapers wrapped against my long logs, and soak in every fortifying drop of the sight.

Thanks. This time, I know the "big guy" has heard. I've found my strength. Now I'll find the words. Somehow.

"To this day, I have no idea what the shit even was," I begin. "Even the coroner said it was a designer mix...a pharmaceutical cocktail intended to make her feel pretty damn good. Well... her idea of good." I stare across the room—and swear I can still see Lily there, a smile finally lighting her face, the day she walked into this little room for the first time. I would have done anything to keep that look on her face forever—and I sure as hell tried. "For a while, the bubble had finally returned," I rasp. "And it was more breathtaking than before...probably more so, since I actually thought she'd gotten her shit together after just two weeks in rehab."

Her fingers twist tighter around mine. "You believed the best in her," she murmurs. "Because that is what you do when you love someone."

Dammit. Her words are as good as a tether—in the exact moment I long to break away. *Not. Happening.* "Yeah," I snap, letting the frustration speak. "That's why they call love blind."

She yanks my hand harder—forcing me to whip my head up, directly impaled by the conviction of her huge blue stare. "Being blind just means you get sharper in other ways." I bark out a scoff, but she uses her other hand to snare fingers into my hair. "How do you explain all the ways you know *me*? All the ways you can simply read me, anticipate me?"

I lower my head. Lean in until our gazes are just inches apart, and I'm lost in the perfect warmth of her touch, her closeness. "Magic is easy to see when it's just there, sorceress."

Her face dissolves with emotion. She's so breathtaking, I'm almost glad I decided to finally do this. *Almost.*

"So what finally happened?" Her prod is suffused with a conflict of tenderness and toughness. She's beginning to see the quicksand, in all its vile shades—and realize that the "storage space" I originally passed this room off as holds a larger chunk of chaos. But her gaze is still steady. She's determined to cross the bog with me—no matter how dirty she gets in the process.

I haul in a long breath. This isn't the time to dwell on the thousand layers of my gratitude for her, though that's exactly what I long to do.

Instead, I simply show her—with the only thing she still wants. The truth.

"For a while, as I said, things got better." So far so good—but I'm still at the easy part. "We started making plans for a real wedding, to take place as soon as the baby came. Continued looking for a place we could call our own, with a nursery for the baby." A laugh escapes. "Hell. We must have looked at a thousand apartments in two weeks."

"Instead you found a mansion named Temptation."

My humor mellows into a smile. "For which we had Prim to thank. Or blame. I'm still debating which."

My sarcasm finds an appreciative target. She stops stroking my knuckles long enough for a delicate snort. "You said she was Lily's best friend?"

"Since prep school," I supply. "Yes. In case you can't tell, Prim's not one of those heiresses who likes coloring inside the lines."

Second target hit. As I expected, the "heiress" bombshell detonates, turning Ella's gaze into the expanse of summer skies. She's always had the color; now she has the size. "Prim?" she challenges. "Prim *Smith*, with the dreadlocks and the pierced nose and the no-bra policy? *That* Prim...is..."

"The daughter of Houston Smith, owner and CEO of Starstruck Entertainment, Five-Star Foods, and Starbright Tech. She and her brother, Houston the Second, are currently worth close to fifteen billion apiece."

I lift a finger, nudging her jaw closed. As soon as I pull it away, her mouth drops again. "But she is...she is..."

"My cook?" I hitch a shoulder up and down. "Not exactly. Well, not officially."

"What does *that* mean?"

I feel my smile disappear. "She likes it here, Ella."

She has no trouble slamming her lips back together now. "I wonder why."

"Because she just does," I growl. "You think she can be herself, in all that Bohemian glory, in a crowd of billionaires' daughters in Dallas?"

Her eyes close as she exhales, betraying some inner command she levels for composure. "If Dallas is anything like the court of Arcadia, I imagine not." When she looks at me again, her features return to open serenity. "So...she helped you pick this place out?"

"Helped Lily," I clarify. "By the time I was able to get away from the office and come look, she was pretty passionate about wanting it." My lips lift again, just at the corners, at the memory of how excited Lily had been that day. "I bid on it at once." Then paid cash, at a price significantly higher than the Realtor's ask—desperately hoping it would keep Lily that happy forever.

Dumbshit.

As if life hadn't taught me in heaping piles already, *hope* and *happy* and *forever* didn't belong in the same sentence together.

"We closed on the sale and were moved in by the following week." I push to keep the words coming, hoping it'll help the difficult part, like warming up during a workout. But sometimes, workouts just feel like shit. "It wasn't until a few weeks later, when Lily suddenly couldn't find her 'prenatal vitamins,' that Prim and I suspected something was up."

"Why?"

"She freaked about it as if the jar were plated in gold and all the pills were diamonds." I shake my head slowly, remembering that surreal night—well, early morning. "It was about two a.m. She woke everyone up, including the newly hired housekeeping staff—whom she immediately accused of stealing the pills for themselves. When Prim pointed out that both women were already grandmothers and had no need for prenatal vitamins, Lily swung the accusation *her* way."

"Oh, my." A burst of air leaves Ella, as if she's been holding it in on my account. Her gaze probes across my face. "What did Prim do? What did *you* do?"

"The only thing we could. Made her some hot cocoa, rubbed her feet...somehow got her calmed enough to fall asleep. Then we compared notes—and weren't surprised to learn we shared the same suspicion."

Everything about her goes still. "That Lily's vitamins were not really vitamins."

"Yeah." I grimace. Hard. It's the first time in at least three years that I've heard it put into words, and it feels like running full-speed onto a splintered lance. "But we still couldn't be sure. Those suspicions felt like more than suspicions—but accusing my pregnant wife of disguising her designer drugs as prenatal vitamins..." I drag a hand through my hair. "I'm a driven man, especially when it comes to finding the truth, but..."

But what?

The words hang in the air, unspoken but damning. Just like their answer.

But even I draw the line between being a bastard and an asshole.

No. That's not it. I've had no trouble embracing my inner asshole since I was a kid—on the day Damon decided to embrace his.

"This time, I wasn't ready for the truth."

Yeah. *There* it is.

Fuck.

Fuck.

"And was it?" And dammit, why does her voice have to be the silk in this filth, towing despite the quicksand calling as a perfect escape? "The truth?" she persists. "Was that what was happening? What Lily was really doing?"

I should nod. Get it over with—slog through this sludge, face the crap on the other side—but my neck is too busy helping my spine stay straight. "Prim and I compared notes, confirmed our instincts matched—but neither of us had the stomach for the dirty work, so I found someone. Hired him to keep tabs on Lily for a week."

"*Tabs.*" Her eyes bug a little. "You mean to follow her? Everywhere?"

I nod. "Interesting fellow...by the name of Conchobar Hodgkins."

Her gaze jumps wider. "Hodge?" Resettles at once, as the logic takes hold. Though he's now one of the steadiest fixtures in my life, I know virtually nothing about his before he arrived that day. Probably a good thing.

Looks like the same thought hits Ella before she presses, "So what did he find out?"

My hand tightens into hers. "That our intuitions were all correct."

"By the powers." Her free hand, threading into my hair, shakes almost as hard as her whisper. "But...why? *How* could she have—"

"Endangered her life, as well as that of our unborn child?" I shirk from her touch. It feels too good, and I have no fucking right to feel good right now. "Because that wasn't how she saw it." I rise. Turn around. Order myself to peer at every jagged edge jutting from the window frame—to let it gouge me open, along with everything I've confessed—to finally let in the pain too. Doesn't work. My psyche clings to the safety of distance. "Her depression sucked the control from her," I grate. "And the only times she ever *was* in control were when she drank."

"And when you took the liquor away..."

"She turned to something else."

"Oh, *Cassian*." It's rough with emotion as she gains her feet too—though feels my need for distance and keeps hers. "What...did you do next?"

"At first? Nothing." My shoulders drop. "Not the best choice, I know...but I was tired, Ella. So fucking tired of it all. The rehab she ran from. The chemicals she ran *to*. The secrets she kept. The lies she told." Another step closer to the window... as another confession burns at my lips. The most hideous one of all. "I spent a few days just wallowing. Wondering if her 'love' for me was just another one of those lies. If she'd ever meant, even remembered, any feeling she'd professed for me. If our child and I were even worth fighting for."

Rasped words in Arcadian from the woman behind me—sounding like a prayer—before she murmurs, "And you confronted her with all that?"

"Damn straight." I don't rein any of my growl back. Replaying the story has brought all the ugliness back, but crossing the mire is my only hope of ever reaching the other side. I let it all in. The fury. The hurt. The digging, despairing, is-this-what-crazy-feels-like confusion.

"And...she was not amenable to listening."

"When she got home, she was already wasted." I jam my hands into the pockets of my track pants. Burn every inch of the window with my glare. "And wasn't really 'amenable' to anything except keeping her high. Her roll. Whatever the fuck it was."

"So she ran up here...and you followed."

The dread eats me from the floorboards themselves. Mows up my body, ravenous and ruthless, before tearing into my brain. "She never allowed anyone up here, even me. This room was her sanctuary. But that afternoon, I only assumed it was where she was hiding more drugs."

"Was she?"

"I don't know." I throw a glance around, feeling the corners of my eyes tighten. "But it wasn't for lack of trying." Burning memories. Heavy breaths. "I...went ballistic. Started tearing the room apart. It was either that or rip the walls out. She fought me. Screamed that the baby—our child—was sucking the life from her, and that I—" My throat clenches on the words. Tries to shove them down to my gut, where they're fried in bile before surging back as a sparse croak. "She said that I was Lucifer. A demon for planting my spawn inside her."

Another rasped Arcadian prayer. Determined steps, once more stopping far enough back to give me space...a blast zone for my memories. I hate it, that she knows such a thing is even necessary. I hate that she must stay away from me by even one fucking inch.

And yet—right now—I need it.

"And then she ran toward the window."

The pokers flare me wide open now. Scorch away the layers of time, bringing images to life in my head—razing me all over again with their horror.

"Yeah," I hear myself croak. "She ran toward the window."

A threadbare sigh. A hurting gasp. "And she did not stop."

Thundering blood. Hammering chest.

Fuck. *Fuck.*

"No. She did not stop."

CHAPTER FOUR

MISHELLA

"Cassian."

As soon as I lift my shaking hand to his rigid back, he plummets to his knees again.

This time, I fall with him.

Let him twist, crushing hard against me, grabbing me closer by fistfuls of my shirt, and smashing his face into my neck. I wrap my other arm beneath, holding him tightly, gulping hard when the tidal wave of his anguish knocks into me like a storm wave, robbing my breath. Still, he does not make a sound. I wonder if he even allows himself to breathe. I wonder if he is afraid to.

But then he does. In tight rushes that feel like seizures, gripping at me just as violently. In spurts of just two seconds each, he breathes in pain and exhales grief, mourning the woman he could not save...the child he would never know...the fury he has stuffed down for so long.

So long.

"No longer." The words are as much for him as me—for the thoughts I hear in him as well as me, for they are not a process of his mind. They are a cry from his soul—the light in him that fights to keep burning through the tears he refuses to shed. I clutch his nape with one hand and his waist with the other, lashing him to me before sending my spirit in to crouch over that flame...treasuring its strength and beauty. "Do not hide it any longer, Cassian. Any of it. You do not have to."

Creator of ours, author of all the energy that binds us, please carry my words to his spirit. His flame...

But once again, his frame stiffens to utter stillness. Even his chest and shoulders seize, betraying his refusal to even let air in. I swallow hard, knowing he will eventually have to. Dreading the moment he does.

CASSIAN

I can't breathe. *I won't.* I refuse.

Why can't I just subsist on her now?

Isn't this all I need?

Her softness, making me forget all the shattered edges. Her scent, fresh jasmine, banishing the stigma of this old room, these forgotten books, these tired memories. Her voice, strong but silken, banishing the dirge of death that's played for so long in my psyche.

No longer.

Her promise.

Isn't it all I need? Why can't it be all I need? The key to moving on...

But it isn't.

Because I have to breathe again. Have to be reminded I'm still alive, dammit. That I lived on, and Lily didn't.

My baby...didn't.

Was murdered by the woman with my ring on her finger. Who couldn't have looked at it, just once, and believed in what it represented. Chosen me. Chosen our child. Chosen our life.

Which turned *life* into a very different word for me, for so long...

until I journeyed halfway around the world and walked into a reception hall in a tiny island's palace...

and remembered what life was supposed to feel like.

Which means *I* now have a choice.

To dwell in the death that has turned living into simply existing or to turn forward, into life...

Into letting Mishella all the way in?

I have to make the decision.

Now.

And I do.

CHAPTER FIVE

MISHELLA

Cassian Court is not a man known for his indecisive ways. I have known it since the night he scaled a trellis outside my bedroom balcony and tilted my world's axis with our first kiss. I likely knew it before then. I certainly have been reminded of it, in about a thousand different ways, since arriving in New York...

But never as vividly as in this moment. This instance, such a perfect crash of my body and spirit that it will be imprinted on my mind forever.

Body. My legs still tingling, after he swept from our embrace to his feet, hauling me up too. My fingers still stinging from his conquering grip. My blood still pumping from our rush down from the turret.

Spirit. Whirling from trying to figure out his purpose. Rejoicing from realizing that it does not matter—that I would trust him if he dragged me down to the first floor, through the basement, and into the fires of hell. And now sobbing—when he slams his bedroom door shut, locks his gaze into mine, and gives me the full force of *his* trust.

And his tears.

Shining and heavy—as he frames my face with both his hands.

Hot and salty—as he angles my mouth higher and then smashes his over it.

Then takes me harder.

And deeper.

And does not stop.

We sob and moan and tangle into each other, taking and giving grief and sorrow and loss...and hope and need and possibility. And life. Its pulse through us. Its power inside us.

Its magnificence because of us.

And suddenly, I understand more. I see the gift of this, of *him*. That I saw from the moment he first burst his light into my world. His beauty was only the beginning—how every woman in that palais room was *not* a puddle from his princely perfect features and godlike body is beyond my logic—there was the sheer power of his very presence. The fierce force of his will over the air molecules themselves...

So what has he *ever* seen in me that is worth forty million dollars?

What on earth did Cassian crave from our "arrangement" that could add up to half of what he has brought to me?

Until now, the Creator has been cryptic about the answer.

Until now...in this moment when I see so much of this man. See *into* this man. See exactly why it was not just his choice but his *need* to keep the details about Lily from me. He was terrified of having to relive them all for himself—*by* himself—because he was sure of never finding someone willing to walk those memories with him. Someone to give the darkest part of himself to, who would still be there when he was done. Probably not knowing if he even could.

But loving me enough to try.

Trusting enough to let me in.

Once more, the magnitude of his gift slams me like a wave. No...a tsunami. It soars my adoration for him into galaxies I never dreamed...starscapes that give me the will to pull back from his lips, if only far enough to gaze again into the dark forests of his eyes. I sweep back the thick blond strands from them, locking my gaze into his, and suck in his breath as my own before uttering words I have told him before—but never meant so deeply.

"Cassian. You are not alone."

The shadows in the forests ignite. Blaze with fire so beautiful, it makes me gasp again. The flames grow swiftly, spreading across his face and igniting me with the intensity of a thousand feelings.

And I see more of the answer. So much more.

This was what he could not write into the contract. What he had to disguise behind a forty-million-dollar deal with my parents that put *them* on the hook for new economic advantages on Arcadia and six months of access to my body. What *I* received from the whole thing was the one thing I longed for more than any other: freedom from being sold off into an arranged marriage.

Which makes the irony of this moment even more insane.

The last thing on my mind is freedom.

I can think of no other desire but a thousand tethers to him. They would be but physical markers of the bonds inside me, already twined into him like platinum cables. Enduring. Unending. Sealed by the surety of him in my soul...

A soul I throw open to him now, letting him in to learn it, know it, taste it, feel it—all the same ways I let his mouth reclaim mine. I open thoroughly, giving him the length of my tongue, the cavern of my mouth, every sigh in my throat. I hold nothing back, flowing it all to him, giving my gratitude in return for his anguish, my passion in answer to his pain, my hunger as a call to his lust.

And still, I want more.

He does too. I feel it in his tongue's deepening thrusts, his chest's violent moans, and then—*oh yes*—in the hands raking down, cupping my backside, commanding my body to slot perfectly against his. His throbbing shaft spreads my trembling core, even through our clothes. I break our kiss, only to set my outcry free, afraid my arousal will make me bite through his lips. Not that it still isn't a possibility...

Especially when he wheels around, still carrying me, and rams me against the door we have just walked through. Air leaves me in a stunned rush, captured again by his mouth's dominant force, sucking everything from me but the need to hold him, the longing to let him in deeper...to be anything and everything he needs right now.

Even if all he needs is to lose himself in my body.

Maybe it is all *I* need right now, too. An excuse to abandon the anguish. To forget the loss. To celebrate life instead of mourn for it. To break free into perfection, connection, completion. Passion as perfect as the heart of a flame...

Our flame.

His shoulders flex as he hitches my thighs higher around his waist, angling my buttocks down...driving his groin the same direction. He plummets his mouth back in, forcing my tongue to accept his hot, ravenous licks. Our noses collide. Our foreheads crash. He rolls his hips, eliciting my shudder as his cock rubs new parts of me—echoed in the powerful quake overtaking his body. My tissues expand, softening as he grows against me...and then pulls back to stare deeply into me.

And once more, it all bursts between us.

Magic.

Awareness.

Desire.

Revelation.

Everything that has always been so good and right for us—only better now. Drenched in a new light. Awash in a sunburst made possible only by razing the forest that has blocked it. The sorrow, pain, self-doubts, and fears left behind in the blood on a shattered windowpane, by a woman without the courage to live for her family instead of dying for her addiction.

Not anymore.

I lift my arms, gripping Cassian by his nape, sending those two words from my psyche into his. But his eyes slam shut anyway. I lift my fingers into his hair and twist. Hard.

"*Cassian.* Look. At. Me."

He growls in protest. Digs his own grip in harder, making me wince—but I do not relent my own hold. A leaden gulp expands his throat.

He opens his eyes.

"She does not win anymore." I may but whisper it, though will gladly proclaim it from the tops of the turrets if he demands. I promise it again with the grit in my teeth and determination in my eyes. "She does not *get* to win anymore, Cassian."

His jaw compresses. The harsh lines in his face almost look like pain—but in every spike of green glass in his gaze, I behold the truth. In order to banish death, he has moved beyond pain—and now struggles with something more excruciating.

Redemption.

He tautens again, seized by the wraiths that would hold him back from it. So many ghosts—many of them dispatched from his own spirit.

"Ella." He shudders, gripped by a motion bordering on a sob. If only the universe would be merciful and grant him that.

I wrap him closer. Bloody the lining of my soul to give him every layer of love it holds. "I am here."

"I know."

But does he? His voice is a grate, his body a coil. He is held back, caught in an invisible cage—and I cannot stretch far enough through the bars to reach him.

"I am *here*, Cassian." I slant up, sliding against him. I lift my mouth, nearly pleading for his kiss—and that, at least, he heeds. His tongue lunges back inside, conquering and sliding and possessing, wrenching a moan up my throat. The need to serve him. To heal him.

To redeem him.

His mouth becomes insistent, never stopping. His body surges tighter, never relenting. Over and over he works his cock against my core, a groan consuming his chest as a sigh possesses mine.

"Ella." He husks it against my lips. "Fuck. My beautiful Ella."

"No," I protest, voice sliding on sandpaper. "*You* are the beautiful one." And I am overwhelmed by it...

Hands tangled in his thick, silky hair...

Skin on fire from his hard, straining muscles...

Eyes pierced by tears, from the crystalline truth in his. The purity of his freedom.

Surely he sees it now...recognizes what he has accomplished. The empire he has shaped, the spires he has built, the fortune he has amassed...none took half the courage of what he did tonight, in facing the ghost of Lily once more. In grieving everything she took right out that window with her.

He leans in. Kisses the drops from my cheeks. Takes their salt back to my lips, only kneading our mouths at first but quickly demanding more. Then more. Parting me. Invading me. Filling me. Taking everything from me...

But then giving all of it back. As something new. Something more.

More.

A desire that shakes me. A craving that commands me.

Yes...

A lust that possesses me.

I feel the urgency in him too. In the buttocks beneath my heels, clenching to power the surges of his hips. In the urgency of his hands, cupping me below, spreading me...preparing me. And in the throb of his flesh, so huge that I wonder how he has not ripped through his track pants because of it.

We tear apart, if only to confirm our raging feelings on each other's face. To validate this connection as reality, not some elysium of fables and fantasies, of dreams we cannot possibly be living. Of need we cannot possibly be feeling.

He is so real. And I am so damn glad.

I show him so—with my surrender. Widen my legs and crash my head back, submitting as openly as possible with my back against the door and my legs around his waist. In return, primitive thunder erupts from his chest—before he lunges his head, biting the side of my neck.

"*Faisi vive Créacu.*" It is the first time I have ever uttered the filthy Arcadian phrase—but it is also the first time my body has ever known such a fever. The jab of pain from his teeth becomes a javelin, stabbing down, embedding into the fruit of my sex. I fracture into a thousand slices of arousal—hot and wet, fervid and frantic, possessed and obsessed, swept by a force that drives my hands into new explorations over his body. I stab up under his shirt, exploring the striations of his back and spine and shoulders before dipping again beneath his pants and clutching him by those perfect, muscled spheres...

Dear, sweet Creator.

And he calls *me* the sorceress? There is magic in his backside. It absorbs my attention to the exclusion of all else, especially as its taut muscles contract and then expand beneath my touch...

I need him.

"I need this."

Only one other trio of words have meant more from his sinfully curved lips. These three make mine smile as much, though not for long. In seconds, I am forming a wide *O* of new lust as he twists at the drawstring of my black cotton capris hard enough to tear its mooring wider. Then again and again and again, until the front of the garment is not there anymore—and my naked flesh is instead exposed in the gap.

I gasp heavily.

Cassian snarls, heavier. Someone likes that I obeyed intuition and interpreted his order for "something more comfortable" to mean the exclusion of panties.

As the snarl sharpens to a grunt, he dips his hand in. Fully palms my mons.

"I need this." The repetition is definitely not like its predecessor. He wields it now as conqueror, not requestor. "I need this, Ella. Here. Now. Like this."

Liquid, delirious nod. I hope he does not demand something more verbal. I am usually eager for the "conversation," reveling in what his filthy words do to every inch of my body, but right now, that ravaging wolf's growl has me soaking the finger he pumps up into my intimate tunnel. The reason is clear. Though the bed is steps away, he wants to continue suspending time: to fuck me against the wall like a warrior of old, being welcomed home by his willing concubine.

Will the concubine in the room please moan in approval?

All too easily, the sound tumbles from me. Cassian responds by ramming his finger in deeper—before joining another to it. I cry out now, needy and mindless. By the *Creator*, the angels surely dipped the man's fingers in an extra pool of magic. The things he does to me with them. The dark, perfect desires they elicit...

"I love your little cries, woman," he utters into my hair. "But none of them have contained a proper *yes*."

My throat twists on a frustrated sound. He *cannot* expect more. Not right now. Not with all the quivering, amazing sensations he keeps spreading through my body...the stars in my skin, the fire in my breaths, the lighting in my womb...the thunder in my thoughts. I can barely think, let alone speak.

"Ella."

"Yes." I finally force it out. "Yes, dammit. I need you like this too."

His mouth finds mine again. The rolling movement makes me open, expecting a tender expression of his thanks, but that is when he reminds me of one key fact.

Warriors do not care about etiquette.

The thought crashes in as his lips do. He plunges brutally, takes thoroughly—claims every doubt from my mind about what his soul needs, as well as his body. A return to control. A renewal of power. A reaffirmation of life. A rededication to the magic we have together. The power we make together.

"Oh." The revelation strikes in a rush, rushing the word up from my heart despite the fuzz in my head. "Oh...Cassian." I re-anchor my hands to the sculpted mounds of his shoulders. The motion is more than just physical. I need him to see—to *know*—that now more than ever, he is my strength. My inspiration. My beacon, illuminating the path out of the cynicism and distrust with which I have lived so long. In helping him heal, I am finding a new way to live. To love.

"Yes."

The new whisper is not just for him. It is an affirmation to the truth in my heart. "Yes...please..."

"Ella." His rasp vibrates through him. He has heard the change in my voice. Understands it.

"Take me." I stab his biceps with my nails. "And let me take you too."

He relatches his hold to my buttocks. Secures me higher against the wall, pinning me in place...preparing me to receive the full force of his pleasure. I shiver and let him feel it. Gasp and let him hear it. Level my head so he can see fully into my eyes—and know how he can claim every inch of my body—but in return, I want every ounce of his pain.

Because together, we shall turn it into something beautiful.

CASSIAN

This. Hurts.

Two words that wouldn't even be a flash in my mind if my dick has the sole vote in the matter. Everything between my legs, from the tightness in my balls to the weight of my shaft, powers straight into the *hell yes* zone, flexing and ready and aching in all the best ways possible.

This, right here, is the best part of any fuck. Staring down at a woman spread and wet for me...open and compliant for me...under my complete command...

But this isn't any other fuck.

Ella Santelle isn't any other woman.

And I know, once my body slides fully inside hers, it is only the beginning of my unraveling. The first layer of many she'll rip free from the cells of my being, until I'm only a collection of naked nuclei, again showing her everything I am...everything the world doesn't get to see. Everything *I* haven't even seen in so damn long that I have no idea what it'll look like. But I sure as shit remember what it feels like.

It's going to hurt.

Even more than it does now.

"Cassian. *Please.*"

God*damn*, it's going to hurt.

But denying her is like refusing to breathe. The fabric of my flesh has been created for hers. Every drop of my sweat has been chemically calibrated to her scent. Every tremble of her body becomes an earthquake in mine. She is my custom-created gift from the universe. The other side of me.

The perfect parts of me.

I choose that perfection now. Follow it as the light to reach at the end of this terror, letting it beam through my mind and guide my body.

A couple of shoves at my pants, and my cock is free. A pump of my fist, lubricating my length with the hot liquid at my tip, and I am ready. Holy fuck, *beyond* ready.

Yeah, for all of it.

Even the pain.

Though at the moment, only pleasure is my ruler.

"Fuck." It erupts from my locked teeth as her sheath closes over me. Draws me into her tight core, kneading my dick until I shake from the bliss. I widen my stance and clench my ass, letting gravity do some of the work, gripping into her hips in order to set the driving rhythm I know she loves.

"Ohhhhh." She sighs, transforming it into one of the most erotic sounds I've ever heard. "Creator's toes..."

I drop a short but hard kiss on her mouth. "You really thinking about toes right now, armeau?"

Her attempt at a laugh is adorable—and carnal. "No," she rasps. "Only you." *Harder.* "Every thought...is *you*, Cassian. Every sensation. *Everything...*"

I drag my gaze open far enough to look at her. Exult in how her pupils dilate every time her pussy rams over me. Bask in the beauty of her parted lips, the bounce of her long curls, even the golden sheen that forms over the column of her neck...

Christ, *yes*. Even her neck turns me on.

"Everything." I don't hold back the selfish need from it now. Make it damn clear that on my lips, the word isn't an offer. It is a decree. The core of what I exact, in exchange for what her very presence exacts from me.

"Yes." Her response is high and hot, filling me with celebration.

"You'll take it all from me."

"Yes." Higher. Hotter. "I want it all." Her nails rake my arms. Her eyes are stars gone supernova.

I spread her ass cheeks. Grind into her harder. Faster. "Every inch of my cock."

"Yes."

"Filling your perfect cunt."

"*Yes.*"

I stretch my fingers in. Toy with the puckered rim of her most forbidden entrance. "And here." I press in, my touch as unyielding as my voice. "You'll take me here too."

Her gaze flares. Instantly ingests the meaning behind mine. A trust for a trust. Revelation for revelation. My opening up...for hers.

"Push out." I'm just as clear as before. It's not a request. "It'll widen you, armeau." Deeper still, until I feel her compliance, the muscles expanding around my fingertip. "And it'll feel so damn good."

That I'm not certain she believes—until I recalibrate, timing both invasions with each other, giving her double the stimulation with every drop of her delectable body. Once more, her mouth opens in astonishment—only now, it's infused with something besides straight confusion. Tiny valleys begin to pinch her forehead. Little gasps become more strident huffs. Soon, they are finished with high-pitched cries...and then pleading moans.

"Oh...my...*Creator.*" Her stare is now a wash of sultry need. Her pussy eagerly milks my cock. Her clit is stiff, popped out from its hood to rub up against my lower abdomen. I take a moment to revel in it all—both her tunnels tight around me, her wet sex rubbing and marking me—before even trying to form a reply.

She beats me to it. "More." Locks her sexier-than-shit gaze to me, baring the grit of her teeth just a little. "*More.*"

I want to refuse. She's not ready for this—not without lube aside from the juices from her pussy—but she wiggles, freely taking my finger deeper into her virgin entrance.

"Fuck." I roll the digit, working to stretch her, while

scraping a bite to the edge of her jaw. "*Fuck me.* Gorgeous... sorceress."

She leans up, returning the favor by clamping teeth over my ear. "Abra...cadabra."

And isn't that the goddamn truth. How can I deny her now? How can I resist her *ever*? How can I stop my cock from shuttling harder up her channel and my finger from pounding deeper into her ass, when she's the sexiest creature I have ever held in my arms...allowed to blast into my soul?

"I'm going...to hurt you."

A last-ditch effort at a protest. Do I even mean it? Could I stop if she protested completely? Pull out and admit that her scent, floral and fuckable, hasn't thoroughly bewitched me? That her heat, clutching and captivating, hasn't milked all logical thought from me? Deep inside, somewhere, I still hear the answer, and it's yes. But dear sweet God, I pray it's no.

"Then hurt me."

Thank. God.

"*Dammit.*" I'm inside her to the hilt, making her gasp with every plunge into her tight, hot holes. She scores into my back with both hands, creating craters for my sweat with her grip.

"Cassian! *Oh!*"

Her spell wraps me deeper. Thighs smacking. Nipples tightening. Pussy tightening. Ass clenching.

"Am I...hurting you?"

"Y-Yes."

Good.

"Fuck."

"No!" She tears one hand up to my head. Forces my cheek against hers, our skin rubbing slick together. "Do not...stop. Oh...Cassian...please..." Her voice vibrates with the tone she reserves only for me—the notes that say she just heard what nobody else can in *my* voice. "It is all right. It is *all right.*"

"Not...yet."

My throat goes dry, turning the words into a pair of bricks that would be ideal window destroyers. *Ideal analogies for the Daily Double, anyone?* Showing her the shattered glass in the turret was tonight's easy part—and I can only make this next part happen because of her. *With* her.

Instead of searching for the words to accommodate it, I put action to it. Pump more violently into her until her body rides the wood at her back like a rag doll. Dear *fuck.* So beautiful.

She lets out a sharp yelp. Clamps her legs higher around my waist, angling me deeper inside her. I groan and intensify the pace. The door audibly rattles. We'll both be bruised tomorrow, and I gloat in the knowledge...welcome the pain. It's nothing compared to the different version of the shit about to hit me from inside.

"Cassian."

Sweet, fucking hell. She's still using *that* voice, turning my name into something between a prayer and a poem. I've never adored her more. I've never hated her more. I'm about to break, and it's all her fault.

"God*dammit.*" I trap her tighter. Drive in deeper. *Not deep enough.*

"Oh...Cassian."

"*Not...yet.*" I dictate it in a growl, even as I fight the force of the storm. Sweat cascades down my spine, between my ass cheeks. My balls pull in, kissing that delicate space of her body above the entrance where my finger plunges. Her neck is slick against my forehead. My flesh fills her body, but she surrounds my soul, making it safe to let the tempest roil closer. To let the wave crash in...

"Cassian."

"Not yet!"

Please...fucking God...not yet.

"Cassian! By the Creator, I am going to—"

A scream is her punctuation, as her walls crash over my cock in spasms of completion. My balls declare mutiny over my spirit, punching lightning up my cock. I detonate so hard and fast inside her, my own bellow is delayed by long, speechless seconds. But once my groan hits, it lasts forever—or so I pray and pray and *pray,* knowing that once it is done, my defenses will be annihilated.

And they are.

I pull out in a harsh yank. Manage to get her safely on her feet, though I am unsure of attesting the same for myself. My limbs are liquid, my strength drained—

And that's just the fucking start.

The physical liability is just the crack in the dam—through which my grief has every excuse and reason to flow.

Driving me to run. To escape, locking myself in the bathroom.

Only it's no escape at all.

In here, naked and cold and by myself, the anguish has even more room to spread—to attack.

Driving me to battle back, roaring in sorrow...

Mindlessly violent.

CHAPTER SIX

MISHELLA

The last time I paced a hospital hallway floor, it was in dress heels.

Doing it in flats does not make the ordeal less nauseating.

The tension on Doyle Knight's face tells me he agrees. All right, there is *always* tension on Doyle's face, but this is strain of a different ilk, the kind only possible when a man is brother-close to another. Doyle's history with Cassian is still mostly a mystery, but I have glimpsed enough to know that tonight's outcome shocks him as thoroughly as it has me.

I steal glances at the man. If Cassian is a golden sorcerer, Doyle could be his comrade in darker shades of allure, with those bronze tiger eyes, cascading umber hair, and vigilant demeanor—that does not betray a shred of his inner thoughts. *Maddening.* Where I can all but complete sentences for Cassian, all I can read in Doyle is rigid stress, polished off with anger.

But at what? Or whom?

My stomach clenches from contemplating the answer.

Before my mind resonates with one of Vylet's favorite expressions.

Suck it up, buttercup.

A smile edges my lips. Even from thousands of miles away,

my best friend knows when I need her corny motivations the most.

"Doyle." I turn, shoulders back and arms set, before the resolve leaves me. Buttercup is doing well so far. "If you must say something to me, just say it."

The man unfurls his long legs from the chair in the corner. Drops the issue of *Cardiology Today* he has been pretending to read. "Yeah," he mutters. "You're right." Steps over, hands in the back pockets of his faded jeans—until he comes close enough to scoop up both of mine. "I'm sorry I didn't get this out sooner, Mishella."

Forget the nausea. Pure pain stabs everything south of my ribs. "Get wh-what out?"

"Thank you."

Head snap. "Thank me?"

"Yeah."

"You—you are not...mad at me?"

He mirrors my gape. Well, the Doyle version of it, which equates to one arched brow and a quirk at the same end of his mouth. "For thinking on your feet the second shit-for-brains put his hand through the shower door?" His brows hunch, nearly in proportion to mine. "Come on, Mishella. You're the reason twinkle toes hadn't lost a gallon of blood by the time we got him here."

I swallow. He deserves the truth, despite how hard it is to form the words. "I...do not think it was an accident, Doyle."

All right, they are not *the* words I intended—but they are not lies. All too vividly, everything plays out in my mind again: a string of moments that seemed a crazy collision at the time, thanks to the confusion stabbed through every one of them.

Our climaxes, cataclysmic...perfect.

The sag in my body. The expectation of the same in his.

Instead, his jolt of tension while sliding from me. His gentleness, alarmingly stiff after the lust he had just unfurled on me, while easing me back to the floor.

His rushed yanks on his pants, as if newly ashamed of his nakedness.

The harsh stab of his hand through his hair.

The terrifying swiftness of his turn.

The stunning speed of his retreat into the bathroom.

Calling after him—to think the closed door had suddenly become the slab over a crypt. Then his silence, so deep and dark...

Before the burst of his tormented bellow.

Then the crash of the shower's door.

I slam my eyes shut. Issue an internal plea to the Creator to take the rest of the recall away. He sends Doyle as my savior. The man's chuff borders on a growl, though his tone is actually an easy slide as he goes on, "Who the hell's calling it an accident besides the press?" Gets in a short shrug. "Nobody who knows the man, I can tell you that. I've seen Cassian Court nearly every day for the last three years. He's never tripped on a damn shoelace, let alone his own feet in that football stadium of a bathroom. No way did he 'slip' into that glass door, no matter what he ordered me to believe."

He has more to say. The drumming of his fingers on his thigh betrays that much. I wait through the heavy silence until he lowers a boom I have half expected.

"I was also informed about the field trip he took you on. Up to Turret Two." A fresh shrug follows. "The fallout wasn't difficult to figure out."

"Oh." I cannot fight off my uneasy squirm—which leads to more displaced nerves. Am I upset he knows about "the field trip" or that he knows the secret of Turret Two, period? And why do both feel like a weird, intimate invasion—access to a piece of Cassian that has felt like it was strictly mine? Which has to be the silliest line of reasoning I have ever known...

"So. What's it like?"

My stare hones in on his. "What's what like?"

Another pause. Something strange flashes across his face. A hint of...*emotion*? "The room." His lips form into a tense line before I can determine that. "*That* room," he clarifies. "Where Lily sent his heart to hell on a platter."

My brow furrows. "You...you have never been up there?"

He flashes another odd expression. Okay...*not* full emotion. Something different. Deeper. "Nope. That's invitation-only territory."

I fold my arms. Smirk darkly. "And you have never figured out the Prim Smith password?"

Quick shrug. "It's okay. Her jurisdiction is earned. Besides, she keeps the room completely pristine—her choice, not Cas's—though I know he appreciates it."

"So *he* is up there all the time too?"

"He's never been before last night." His steady gray gaze confirms it. "At least not in the three years since he brought me on. Still doesn't mean he doesn't appreciate it."

"Three years." I contemplate that while echoing the information. "So...you were not there when it happened?" At this point, there is no need to define "it."

"No," Doyle replies. "I was hired a little over a year after. He was about to take Court Enterprises public and decided a valet might be a good idea at last."

My eyes widen. "A *valet*?"

A wry shrug. "He actually told the agency he wanted a personal trainer."

I bite my lip, but a laugh spurts anyway. "Of course he did."

"The man doesn't like doing things the traditional way." He turns the shrug into a snort. Slides both hands back into his pockets. "In case you can't tell."

"I have lived on a remote rock for the last twenty-two years, Doyle—not under it."

"Touché."

I refrain from preening. It is the closest thing to open approval I am likely to get from the man—and though I acknowledge it with a gracious incline of my head, there is no stopping the thoughts still whirling within. Nor the confusion about why we are here.

Why we are *really* here.

Frustration takes hold. Pushes out a breath from my pursed lips.

Finally, however secretly, I admit it.

Despite all of his confessions last night, I still do not have all the pieces of this.

Of him.

Nor should you want to...remember?

But I do. *I love him.* Whether fate will allow me to keep doing that for four months, four weeks, or four *hours*, it is a thorn in my psyche not to have *all* of him. To have gone through all of last night, having discovered the awful secret of Turret Two, but know that part of him is still trapped in that damn tower. Is lashed down to the anger, fear, and dysfunction that drove Lily to take such a huge part of him...

But that she was not the first.

I suspected it when we were still in the turret. Had it confirmed during every moment of our passion, even after the walls tumbled from his composure and he finally exposed the complete truth of the pain Lily had dealt. Something else remained. A deeper pain, with a thicker scab to rip free. Cassian had hovered over it, longing to break it open for me...

Until he could not.

And that stiffness gripped him again. Pulled him from my body and then out of the room, back into its darkness...

Until he fought back.

Railed against it by driving a fist through a giant pane of glass.

Why, Cassian?

What ghost tortures you worse than the woman who murdered herself and your child?

CASSIAN

"Good gravy. You *are* one gigantic chunk of stubborn, aren't you?"

I turn over my extended left hand, adding a growl to my glower. "Just give me the goddamn shirt."

"Mr. Court—"

"I've been putting on my own clothes for a long damn time. Give. Me. The. Shirt."

She huffs. Flings the fabric at me, deciding to add an eye roll—doubling it up as an excuse to once-over my bare torso. I'd chuckle if I weren't so perplexed. The nurses in this place must be required to take a secret online training course: *How to Give Court Shit and Get Away with It.* The drill sergeant who tended my ass two months ago must have aced it. This little blonde, reminding me of the lead "Bella" from that girl a capella movie Mishella made me watch last week, must have *written* it.

She indulges a sweetly sadistic smirk as I fumble into the shirt—fighting rockets of pain launched by my stitched and bandaged hand. "So how's that feeling, Cool Hand Court?"

"Awww, come on." I grit it while noticing the shirt is inside out. Too late. Already halfway done. "No fair buttering me up with the best of King Cool."

"You call that butter?" She adds a sharp *psssh*. "*Cool Hand* was just Newman's warmup for Butch Cassidy. You know that, right?"

I finally jab my head out the shirt's neck hole. "Guess I just need a Sundance Kid."

"He's right outside." She nods toward the door while swiping a finger across her smart pad. Enters some information with efficient taps. "Certainly likes to play the part, doesn't he? Strong, silent, grouchy?"

My lips quirk. "Doyle enjoys accessing his inner outlaw."

"Hmmph." But the flags of color across her cheeks negate it. Oh, yeah. Another female munches dust because of my friend's brooding sexuality. Seems the best explanation—aside from the sadistic angle—for why she makes me work for the follow-up information.

"Is there...anyone with him?"

The *hmmph* gets a repeat—accented by another smirk. "Well, listen to you, mister. Trying to keep it smooth with the hotshot businessman vibe while panting for your woman?"

"She's not..."

But hell, how I savor the words.

My woman.

As if on cue, the door opens. Mishella's worried, wonderful face appears.

My woman.

It hits me harder than before—sounding just as right. Feeling even better in my head.

Just as quickly, she retreats back by a step. "Désonnum," she murmurs to a capella queen, before quickly translating. "I am so sorry. They told me everything was finished—"

"And it is." I extend my left hand. "Come here, armeau."

I need you.

I pull her close, inhaling the rich vanilla in her hair. "I... missed you."

But you know what that really means, right?

She tilts her head up, her tiny smile confirming that she does. Smooths a hand over my chest, flattening it above my heart—which passes at least ten seconds in double time, drawn at once to the magic of her touch. "Are you all right?"

"Of course." I dip my head, rolling my forehead along hers. "Biggest dumb fuck on the planet, but all right—thanks to you."

She draws a few inches away—and raises rebuking eyebrows. Since the "incident" happened while she stood a few feet outside the bathroom door, I didn't even try to pass it off as an accident to her. The expectancy in her eyes—as well as my nurse friend's cynical glance—convey that she's not doubling down on my hand either. *Shit.* That means the gig is up with Doyle too.

"As long as you're getting fun with the status report," the nurse turns and declares, "you can add 'lucky cool hand' to the list."

Ella frowns, confused. "Huh?"

I crack the hint of a smile. Might as well now, since it won't be easy once the anesthetic, though just a local, has worn off. "I think she's telling me to be grateful."

"That's exactly what I'm telling him." The woman nods at

Mishella. "He doesn't have a millimeter of nerve damage—a miracle given where that hand has been tonight."

"She doesn't know the half of it." I lick the curve of Ella's ear after whispering into it, savoring her body's little tremors of reply. Her nipples pucker too. At last, a positive to the idiot move I made. There was no time for her to put on a bra—which means there *definitely* wasn't a moment for underwear...

As soon as my hand dips between her delectable ass cheeks, she steps away. Clears her throat. "Do...errmm...do we need to know about any follow-up?"

A capella turns back, offering an easy smile and a stack of papers still warm from the printer in the corner. "Dr. Yago will be in to get you set with all that. He did a great job. The stitches are tight and clean. The pharmacy has already filled the prescriptions for pain meds and antibiotics, and the instruction sheets will explain how to take everything, as well as possible side effects. Mr. Court doesn't have any drug allergies, so it should all be pretty straightforward."

"Mr. Court is also sitting right here."

My grumble doesn't daunt either of them. Ella catches my hand on its journey back to her ass, beaming a big smile of her own. "Thank you for everything, Kristine." Of *course* she already knows the woman by first name. "I mean that from the bottom of my heart. I know he can be an...interesting...patient."

Kristine's head falls back as her laugh breaks free. "I've certainly had worse."

"All right, all right," I bark, mostly just irked that my attention has been torn from her ass by the starlight of her own laughter. "When the hell can I get out of here?"

Kristine rolls her eyes again. "Behave, Butch Cassidy."

Unbelievably, I do. This isn't the Hail Mary pass I want

to pin the game on. As final paperwork is distributed, Yago himself comes in, already puffed-up about being *the* doctor attending me tonight. I focus on being friendly but formal— and letting Mishella shine instead.

And hell, how she does.

"*Merderim mahaleur*, Dr. Yago," she murmurs. "In my language, it means thank you very much. You have given a true gift with your time tonight."

Yago, who must be close to my age but looks like a hipster psych major who's just strolled in from a night of beat poetry in the Village, parts his dark beard with a smug smile. "The gift is all mine. How fortuitous the timing. I wasn't supposed to be here but hopped on the chance for the extra shift after plans fell through for a night in the Village with some friends."

Well, hell.

I don't dare look the man's way now, despite feeling the expectant weight of his scrutiny. More accurately, of Ella. Oh, he's assessing, all right—watching the signs, silently determining what Ella is to me. *Go ahead, Hipster. Look your fill.* If he doesn't get the clue by watching my gaze, glued solidly to her, I'll be ecstatic to provide a more blatant demonstration.

"Well, Kristine says the stitches look wonderful." Ella uses the voice that first hypnotized me in the halls of Palais Arcadia, filled with such sweet sincerity. Stupidly, I'd first written off the allure to being in a storybook castle and breathing Mediterranean air—but here, surrounded by plain green walls and antiseptic odor, Yago is clearly, dangerously, close to falling for the same count. "Truly, doctor, we are grateful for a professional so good at his work."

"Work he is well compensated for, armeau." Shockingly, I get it out without growling.

To his credit, Yago laughs softly. "Mr. Court is right." Squares his shoulders toward me, though dips his head in deference. "It is an honor to have been of service, sir. I assure you, that hand will be back in fighting shape very soon." He jabs a quick upper cut. "I guarantee you, John Cena's already watching his six."

Christ.

"John who?"

Before Yago can decide whether to be charmed or confused by Ella's question, I roll to my feet. "Thank you, doctor. I'm sure you have other people to examine now." Five seconds after we step out into the hall, I add in a mutter, "*Other* than the woman on my arm."

Mishella stops. Huffs. Veers toward an alcove containing a drinking fountain and a wall-mounted defibrillator, her princess swiftly turning to lioness. "This is not *his* fault, Mr. Court."

Mr. Court.

Shit.

Clenched jaw. Deep breath in. Back out. In again. "Fine," I mutter. "You're right. I'm just—"

"In pain?"

No.

Yes.

But the ice picks in my hand and arm have nothing to do with it. Ella's fist, clutching the front of my T-shirt, betrays how thoroughly she knows it too. Her whisper, pleading my name into the inches between us, drills it in even further.

She wants in.

A few hours ago, I even vowed that was where she'd be. The silos wouldn't exist with her. And goddammit, I meant it.

Really, asshole? Because you've chosen a twisted way of showing it.

I still can't explain, even to myself, what happened in those moments after our passion in the bedroom—only that the flood I'd expected came as a firestorm instead. It was acid rain from the corners of my psyche, turning into radioactive fury once hitting the light of my conscience.

That's the extent of what I *logically* get.

What my soul declares is something else entirely. A dictate demanding action. Right now.

"They told me Doyle was out here."

Ella answers my searching stare with a little nose wrinkle. I haven't answered her question—and she's had more of that than I intended tonight—but right now, logistics must supersede the chaos. Untangling it for her means setting it straight for myself. Staring at the ceiling for an hour, with my ass parked on an ER gurney, has given me insight into the best place for that—but I'm going to need a car for it.

"I'm right here." Doyle strides up. "Figured one trip in my truck was probably enough for you tonight, so I called for Scott and the Jag to get—"

"Your truck." The recognition jolts like good espresso. His fifteen-year-old Ford, a subtle middle finger to all the other creature comforts of being on my payroll, is usually the eyesore I put up with. Right now, it's my answer. If it's a slow news day and the paparazzi *are* looking for the Jag—sometimes I doubt the wisdom in having the fucker custom-designed—they'll be duped.

"Shit." Doyle reacts to my incisive stare—at the keys in his hand. "What the hell, Cas?"

I extend my hand, palm up. "Wouldn't ask if it wasn't important."

"Would not ask what?" Ella's stare goes summer sky wide, triangulating from my face to Doyle's to the keys. "What on *earth* are you—" She sputters her way out of my interrupting kiss. "Cassian Cameron Jonathan Court. You will entertain delusions about going nowhere but *home* right now!"

"Don't try the puppy eyes on *me*." Doyle whisks up both hands. "I'm on her side."

I advance on him by a step. "Give me the damn keys."

He slams the collection of metal into my left hand. "You crash it, you're dead."

"Too late." Ella pushes forward so furiously, the curls fan a little off her shoulders. "I have already decided to murder him." Wheels on me with no mercy. "What in Creator's name are you—"

"*Ella*." The snarl in my voice isn't what softens her. It's the choke I add to the end. "I can't explain. Not right now." I cup her face, hating how my bandages scrape her soft skin—and make her wince again. "Not yet."

My emphasis on the final word beams a little hope into her eyes—before she rams them shut. When she reopens them, exhaling hard, I feel my own face tighten. The hope is still there, but so is all her stress and exhaustion. I can't remember her looking this tired, even after a week at my bedside after the shooting or on the morning I showed up at her family's villa on Arcadia with the contract that would irrevocably change our relationship.

And me.

Everything about this woman has changed me.

And dammit, I can't backslide now. Can't become that person frozen in the graveyard of my heart, so afraid of disturbing the ghosts that I'm unable to move...to live.

I just need to tell that to the ghosts.

Especially the most tenacious one.

"All right." Ella finally pushes it out on a resigned sigh. "Do what you must." Mutters something under her breath mentioning stars and faith and terrified saints. The little monologue becomes sexy with shocking speed, forcing me to step back before everyone in the hallway gets to take a camping trip courtesy of the tent in my jogging pants.

"I won't be long."

"I shall burn your feet with that."

"Huh?" Doyle mutters.

"Hold my feet to the fire?" I circle her waist, yanking her close once more. Pain pinballs up my arm because of it, but I'm beyond caring. *My woman.* The more it rides over the repeat button in my mind, the more incredible it sounds—and the more I wonder if it wasn't in there all the time, from the moment I met her.

The more right it sounds...

The faster I need to get *myself* right—

For her.

When our lips ease away from each other's, I keep her close, needing to capture every facet of sapphire life from those huge eyes. Needing all the fortitude her nearness can bring before I have to let it go for one of the shittiest mornings of my life.

★ ★ ★

I arrive at the cemetery a good hour before dawn. I remain in the truck, getting used to returning emails on my phone with my left thumb instead of my right, while waiting on the groundskeepers to arrive. That goes well for a while, until it's clear that Singapore has gotten wise to the fact that I'm awake and online and messages start flooding in.

And the photo album on my phone beckons like fun new candy.

No. Even better—now that the folder is filled with pictures of a certain Arcadian sorceress.

The throb in my body eases.

The weight on my mind feels lighter.

The smile on my lips is huge.

Suddenly, the morning becomes a tribute to her. The sunrise streams through the trees in textures of gold and umber, like her incredible hair. Birds call to each other, pure and free, like the music of her laughter. And the brightening blue in the sky is always, *always* the magic of her eyes. Eyes that always give me so much. Believe so completely in me.

Giving me the guts to finally rev the Ford's engine and follow the groundskeepers through the cemetery's wooden gates.

It's a small and unassuming place, though my belly would be just as tight a knot if driving into fucking Woodlawn, past Jay Gould and Joseph Pulitzer. No bullshit like any of this for me. In the "personal affairs" I've been ordered by an army of lawyers to have in order, I've dictated specific instructions about where to put my carcass when the world decides it's done with me—and in the ground is *not* it. I've already served enough years in a dark, dirty box. It was called a New Jersey tenement.

But that's not the piece of the past I'm here to visit.

Today, it's all about the asshole buried in the knoll ahead.

Though his plot is marked by a simple stone plate in the

ground, I've long since memorized its location. No surprise, since I've been visiting the fucking thing for nearly the last fifteen years.

The words on the plaque are simple.

Damon Matthew Marcus Court
Beloved Son – Cherished Brother

The dates beneath aren't worth getting into. They mean nothing, since my brother's spirit was gone long before his body.

Since he let the drugs take it.

My stomach matches my arm for pain. My throat convulses, battling the heat of the sick, the surge of the anger.

Always the goddamn anger.

"Shit." It escapes me in a slow, burning hiss. I long to let my body drop the same way, just giving in to the weariness in my spirit, but I dig deep to keep my legs locked. *You don't get my surrender today, brother. You don't get my tears.*

"You shouldn't have even gotten the house call, asshole. You don't deserve it."

The wind picks up, giving brief reprieve from the muggy slush calling itself air.

My core remains ice, congealed by pure fury.

Just before the heat ambushes the backs of my eyes.

"God*damn* you, Damon."

I huff hard. Stab a foot into the grass, deep enough to reach the muck of mud beneath and lob a small heap of it over. Watching the stuff ooze like shit over my brother's name.

And instantly want to do it again.

"Mom isn't here to stop me, dickwad." I toe the ground, so tempted. "Nobody's here except me now because nobody else gets to hear this. Kind of like all those other things I reserved just for you, man. You remember, right? The secrets we saved just for 'the brotherhood'?" A harsh spurt gets past my lips, twisting into an unwilling smile. "Fuck. 'The brotherhood.' The secret handshake. That stupid rules and regulations book. The all-nighter we pulled working on it. You wrote it all down so Mom wouldn't find it on the computer's hard drive—on the back of your goddamn algebra homework." A laugh scorches out. "Can't believe you didn't think she'd see it after you racked up that F for not turning it in." Drop my head and shake it. "But after she bawled about the whole thing, she hugged us like we were going to disappear. Did *you* ever understand that shit?" Short shrug. "No. Me, neither. And *then* she drove us out to bum-fuck for a couple of Skyscraper cones at Cliff's...and you nearly puked on that shit, man." A scoff echoes on the air. It has to be just the wind, but warmth rushes my chest anyway. "No, asshole," I argue to the echoing chuckle in the air, "it was *you,* I'm sure of it. You ordered maple walnut and then inhaled that shit like—"

My throat clutches shut as the wind fully gusts.

I plummet to my ass in the grass.

And here I am, hurling smack at a ghost again.

"Why, Damon?" I straddle the marker. Beg for answers from it with fists clenched atop my thighs. "Goddammit, *why*?"

Did the crap in those needles and pills feel better than 'the brotherhood'? Than going for ice cream at Cliff's?

Those are the easy questions.

Meaning the hard ones are coming.

And grate from my lips as whispered chokes.

"Weren't Mom and I good enough for you, fucker? Dammit...weren't we worth fighting for? *Living* for?"

The wind sweeps across the knoll. Sighs through the grass, swishes through the trees.

Doesn't bring me any more phantom scoffs or laughs. And sure as hell no more answers.

In the silence, only one sensation remains.

The ice in my veins.

It pushes me to my feet again. Yanks me back from the cement square by a step, staring down at the marker with a brand-new recognition.

I no longer want to kick more mud.

Or hang on to more memories.

Or try to get out any more words, except the ones that well up right from the heart that, for the first time in so long, I can *feel* beating. Feeling.

Living.

"You know what, brother? Save your answer. I don't care what it is anymore." The words are snatched at once by the wind—fitting exactly what has happened to the ice in my veins and the loss in my heart. It's time now. All of it needs to be taken higher...transformed into freedom. "The thing is...I've found an answer of my own. Someone worth *my* fight. She's waiting for me right now, and she's ready to fight for me, too. Hell—" a smile spreads, and it feels fucking good "—she already has."

I breathe deeply. The sunshine seeps into my limbs, and the music of the new day fills my senses.

It's time for this. At last.

"You know what that means, Damon?" I step back over. Stoop once more. Lay a hand to the cool stone slab, letting the damp mud spread up between my fingers...letting it remind me...empower me.

"I'm not coming back anymore, brother. Because you sure as hell aren't."

CHAPTER SEVEN

MISHELLA

"Damn." Doyle mutters it as he and I ride Temptation's wrought-iron elevator from the art décor splendor of the building's lobby to the glass and dark-wood modernism that awaits six floors up.

"What?" My prompt is soft but stressed. Exhaustion bites at my bones, but no way can I relax before Cassian's return—from wherever.

From visiting yet more ghosts?

And *there* is the extra burn I did not need, even knowing Doyle will be a sympathetic audience if I need to vent. He probably sees through my thin façade anyway, though is merciful about bypassing the notice to go on, "Sometimes, it's worth it when Prim gets stressed."

I do not have to ask for elaboration. By the time we glide past the fourth floor, the aromas in the building provide it. Melted butter. Baked dough. At least three kinds of chocolate, and sugar in twice as many forms. By the time Doyle pushes open the door and we step out, my mouth craves an early breakfast feast of everything I smell.

Sure enough, we round the corner into the kitchen to find Prim kneading a mound of bread dough. Two more loaves cool nearby, next to four platters of cookies and frosted petit fours topped with candy decorations, nearly too exquisite to eat.

The woman peers up through a blond dreadlock, an escapee from the others knotted atop her head. She wears an oversize Dashboard Confessional T-shirt and bright-pink shorts, the same attire in which she tore into the living room as Doyle and I hustled Cassian out to the ER. Not a line of weariness mars her face. If not for the mini bakery surrounding her, I would think she'd gone back to bed after we left. I want to hate her for that but cannot summon the strength or the heart—in many ways, because of the new lens Cassian has given me to her. Temptation is not just the building in which the woman works. It is the home she has found.

It is a helpful conclusion—to an extent. I battle for a peaceful demeanor as Prim hurls her stare around Doyle *and* me before charging, "Where is he?"

"He's fine." Doyle cuts to the real root of her demand. "And he'll be back soon. I need one of those cookies. *Now.*"

Prim blocks his path with a stance that could stand up to even my soldier of a little brother. "You need to tell me where you let him go with a busted-to-hell hand. *Now.*"

"For fuck's sake. He's a grown man."

"He also had a...tumultuous night." The pause in her statement is due to glancing—correction: glaring—once more toward me.

"'Tumultuous.' Damn. Bread, cake, cookies, *and* the walking thesaurus." He fakes a step to the right before sliding left and snatching a cookie. "You *are* stressed."

"And I don't have a fucking right to be?"

"Didn't say that." A groan caps the comeback. "But I *will* say you make amazing cookies, woman. Shit, this is—"

"The woman *said* to get away from the cookies." The

warning comes from the newest arrival in the room: a scowling Hodge, whose flame for Prim is a secret to no one but the woman herself.

Now is clearly not the moment to turn that light on for her either. "Can everyone forget the damn cookies for a second? The man took out his shower door with his own hand. Did you really just let him leave the hospital and—"

"Prim." The interjection does not belong to Doyle *or* Hodge. Too tender. And female. "Honey. *Breathe.*" It is one of Mallory Court's favorite words, usually used to tease, though issued this time as a mandate. She lets Prim get through a minor fume before stating, "I'm quite certain Cassian is aware of what he did to his hand. I'm also certain he didn't just feel the need to go for a little coffee run."

Prim rolls her eyes. Pivots back to the bread dough, digging hard at it. "My coffee is better than any swill in the neighborhood anyway."

"And if you have some of it fresh, I'd love a cup." Mallory's smile is such a seamless stitch of regality and warmth, I wonder why she is not queen of some small island of her own. "Thank you," she murmurs after Prim sets a cup of the fragrant brew in front of her.

I feel nowhere near as elegant as another steaming cup is slid over—in front of me. It is plain hot water, accompanied by a small wire ball filled with my beloved blend of jasmine and mint teas. I look up, bewildered, into the golden gaze still bisected by the single dreadlock. Though those eyes no longer glower at me, they are a *long* way off from friendly.

"I...know how he can be," she finally mutters. Reaches and pats my hand—just once. The gesture, a Prim Smith version of an olive branch, diffuses the tension in the room faster than a puppy in a preschool. Accordingly, Hodge and Doyle make up like a perfect pair of four-year-olds, talking in grunts, fist bumps, and three-word sentences while fetching their own coffee and then vanishing.

In the stillness that falls, I am jittery. There is no explanation for it, as Mallory and I have always been all right with passing silences with each other. In just six weeks, we have had plenty of practice. The hours in the hospital, watching over Cassian after the shooting. After bringing him home, dealing with fidgety moments by tending the potted plants and flowers up on the terrace. Even our long minutes of strategic silence during *Scooby Doo* Monopoly...

But something about this is different.

Most notably, her.

The steadiness in how she pivots toward me. The focus in her stare. The way she seems to reach some hidden decision, only to sip her coffee with a knitted brow, as if trying to talk herself out of it.

"Mallory?" I almost talk *myself* out of murmuring it. The woman takes pride in her surety of words and meanings, as well as her commitment to them once declared. I am familiar with the trait, since it got solidly passed down to Cassian. Perhaps she does not want her vacillation to be called out—

"Mishella." Just as suddenly, she is the decisive queen again. Picks up my hand like a monarch going for her scepter and nods back at my tea. "Grab your drink. Let's go up to the terrace before it gets too hot."

I have gotten attached to many aspects of living at Temptation. The terrace tops that list, reminding me of many like it back on Arcadia. The view is much different, of course. The coastal bluffs and island trees have been replaced by a vista of buildings old and new. But like the Arcadian landscape, their appearance changes as the day goes on. Right now, just past daybreak, the air is still calm, though it vibrates with a low hum of anticipation of the day to come. The rumble of delivery trucks thrum in time with the shouts of a coxswain, driving her rowers faster on the river. A light breeze ruffles the potted ficus trees, bringing a riot of smells: sweat and steam, cinnamon pretzels and honey-roasted nuts, patchouli and incense, bagels and bacon, and about a hundred more.

Surprisingly, it is all as soothing as my tea, which refreshes my throat as I turn toward the padded seating area around a granite table with a bed of glass fire rocks in the center. I settle onto a couch, looking up as a hummingbird buzzes in for nectar from the tiny white flowers in the arbor overhead. Mallory lowers next to me, already drinking from her own cup with a reprise of that "decision that is not a decision" expression.

When she lifts her head, the look remains. Oh, her confidence is still there, firm in the set of her chin and the brace of her shoulders, but shadows still battle for control in the depths of her gaze. There is definitely something on her mind—and it is *not* about Monopoly strategy.

"So." She works her lips together. Pulls in a deep breath. "We know the only ones buying the 'stupid slip in the bathroom' line are the dumber members of the press."

I am not sure how to reply to that—or if she wants me to. Another sip of tea seems the best choice instead.

"So why don't we talk about what really happened."

A blush prickles my cheeks before I can leash the thoughts causing it. "I—I am not sure what you mean."

Because talking about what really *happened would mean discussing the orgasm your son gave me three minutes before stomping off in a mysterious rush and then removing his shower door with his fist.* Not that anyone did not discern that exact fact for themselves, once I frantically contacted Scott on the mansion intercom. The recall is a strange combination of vividness and blur...

Throwing on clothes—Cassian's T-shirt, my shorts—before letting Doyle into the room.

Struggling not to slip on the bathroom tiles, slick with blood and glass, as he rushed to help his friend.

Cassian rearing up, growling at the man to shut the hell up, because I had no idea what a "nine-one-one" was, let alone how to dial it.

And every step of the way, fighting the nausea and terror and fear of watching too much blood leave Cassian's body at once.

"Oh, dear." Mallory's mutter, despite its self-censure, is a welcome break to the memories. "I flashed the G-string again in public, didn't I?"

"Errrmm..." I actually *know* about G-strings, thanks to Kathryn and the lunch trip for the waxings from hell, but have no idea if Mallory is being literal or symbolic. To be safe, I sneak in a fast peek—which comes up fruitless. Her stylish summer blouse has a trendy bow below her waist, preventing any conjecture about anything she wears beneath the cute white culottes. "Pardon me?"

"Sorry, cutie." She sets down her coffee. Reaches for my hand with both of hers. "You're so damn bright, I sometimes forget..."

"Forget what?"

Her smile transforms into a full but soft chuckle. "That you're not as...worldly...as the other women my son has been involved with."

Ergh. It is a meaningless swat at a mosquito of vexation, despite knowing she meant her words as praise. Why the damn insect has continued to grow, I cannot explain, even after last night.

Wait.

Maybe *because* of it?

Knowing now who Lily was—exactly *what* she was to Cassian—swings a new spotlight onto the relationships Cassian has had in the four years since. Seven models, three CEOs, a couple of professional athletes, and a princess. Yes, I have looked up each one. Probably know more about them than *he* does—because I know exactly how long he was "involved" with them. *Involved.* The word is an easy grab for Mallory but chomps into my psyche and sucks blood, just like that mosquito. From the photos that made it to the internet, one would presume all those relationships were happy and romantic, comprised of dates to both high-profile events and low-profile retreats, marked by plenty of hand holding, cute kisses, and that dimple-framed smile a woman could become obsessed with all on its own.

Every relationship looking exactly like what *I* have with him...

Except that all of those women were fifty times more polished than me. Five hundred times more glamorous. A thousand times more elegant.

A million times *worldlier.*

And none of them lasted more than ten weeks.

So, yes...*ergh.*

"*Hey.*" Mallory shakes our joined hands like she's flicking a bullwhip. "In case you haven't noticed, Mishella, that's a *good* thing."

Her tenderness is my undoing. My nose wrinkles and my eyebrows arch. "And having a child around the house is a good thing too, yes? Until it paints the dog pink."

"What's wrong with a pink dog?"

"Maybe you should ask the dog."

She gives that two seconds of a scowl before her face firms into more thoughtful angles. Serious intent.

Very serious.

She spends at least half a minute ensuring I am fully aware of that point before speaking with just as much quiet tenacity. "He's never taken anyone else up into that tower before last night. Not even me."

Thank the Creator the wind has gone still. If it even whispers across the terrace again, I will be flat on the Italian stones at our feet. "Wh-What?"

She jogs her chin up. "He told you. About her. Lily. Didn't he?"

"Yes." Speaking it is probably unnecessary. Certainly, she can read it on my face already. That is the easy part. The questions that still remain—those are the hard part. When waiting for the answers about Lily, at least I knew what the questions *were*.

"Mallory..." It is my turn to lift a steady gaze. "Lily is not the only part of it all, is she? Of why Cassian lashed out last night?"

My hunch is confirmed when the woman's shoulders hunch with tension. The stress travels down her arms and into her grip. I soothe fingers over her knuckles, taking the right to be her strength as she has been mine.

"I met Kathryn Robbe not long after arriving here." I murmur it carefully, still not understanding completely why.

"She told me that Cassian has been battling...ghosts."

Her forehead furrows deeper. I backtrack, overriding my initial intuition. Careful is *not* the right call. Bandage. Wound. Whether removed slowly or quickly, the blood is going to be plentiful.

"Through these weeks, I have kept that in mind," I go on. "How she phrased it. *Ghosts.* Plural. Then last night, after he revealed everything about what Lily did, I thought...well... that..."

"The ghosts were she and the baby."

"Right."

She squeezes her eyes shut—exposing the glitter of fresh tears along her tawny lashes. "I'd already started thinking of names," she whispers. "Funny thing was, they were all girls. Madeline, Chloe, Elizabeth..." She shrugs and pushes out a laugh. "I was selfish. Never had the chance to do the girl thing. Imagined this perfect little person with Lily's dark hair and Cas's dimples...getting to do princesses and ponies and tea parties, you know?"

My throat squeezes around my breath. "Of course."

We sit with that sadness for long minutes, each dealing with broken hearts from imagining Cassian with his heart wrapped around the delicate pinky of his gorgeous, grinning daughter.

Suddenly, even more about him makes sense. His mantra of motivation and religion of a work ethic. His brutal physical workouts. Even the way he usually sets aside most cocktails before they are half-finished. Nothing that will even crack the unwavering dominion over his own emotions.

Unwavering—until last night.

Mallory and I collide into a hug. Seize each other like

buoys in a storm, letting our tears softly fall and our heartbreak quietly blend. "I am sorry," I finally blurt. "Mallory...so very sorry."

She presses her hand to my face. Lifts a watery smile and jerks in a sniff. "I know, cutie. Thank you."

I pull my bottom lip beneath my teeth as more understanding snaps together. "So...was that why he punched the door?" I venture. "Perhaps he started thinking about his baby again and was struggling with processing it?" Especially after everything he'd just revealed to me in the turret. "He has also just been more restless this last week..." I tilt my head, notching more deduction into place. "I had actually just thought it was an itchy gas pedal foot. He hates not taking life at less than mach five."

Mallory snickers. "You think?"

"So maybe he tried to drive what he could." Contemplative breath. "Flush the gunk from his engine while there was mentally time to do so."

I leave out my silent addendum—that if that is the case, I must share the blame for every stitch the doctors put into her son's hand. I think about the moments when I have been inches apart from Cassian but still felt as if he were oceans away, his psyche swimming at depths so dark, I feared he will never return. I do not tell her how I have halted my very breath, funneling even that force into begging his ghosts to release him back to me...

Never dreaming that spiritual rescue force included his own baby.

Mallory draws her posture straighter. "Logically, that makes sense," she offers. "But no, I don't think that was the case." She soothes my frown by patting my hand. "Believe me, Ella. Mothers just know these things. They know their children."

I fight the urge to pull my hand free. *They know those things when they care. When those children are more important than status, power, or the next political "agreement" to gain more of both.*

But I do not pull away. Despite that, my nerves snarl and my belly twists, as if Maimanne or Paipanne has actually just strolled out here. The self-doubts are worse than ever, compounded by a new element: second thoughts. Have I been unfair to both of them? Maybe remembered things wrong? Looked at their love through the lens of the teenager I once was, even the strong-willed woman I was genetically bound to become? Being by Mallory's side, witnessing all the forms her love for Cassian takes—even pulling her dictator over *his* dictator when it is necessary—has made me wonder about all the judgments I have cast.

Over the people who were entertaining bids for the chance to take your virginity?

But people who did not know any better. Who were part of a different world, a different time.

Which excuses *their behavior?*

I push the mute button on the deliberation. Refocus on Mallory. "Then what was it?" Not muted enough. The tension in my mind jabs into my tone. I compensate by gently taking her hand again. "What could have caused him to burst out as violently as that?"

The woman turns her head. Gazes toward the gray-blue ribbon of the Hudson. "If my gut is right...it has to do with more than Lily and the baby."

My spirit gives itself a quick fist bump. My premonition

from the hospital waiting room was accurate. There *is* someone *else* stalking Cassian's soul alongside Lily...

But the new tension across Mallory's face cuts my celebration short. As difficult as it is, I hold back at prodding. She is prepared to tell me more but needs to do it her own way. I see it clearly as another breeze flirts with the edges of the terrace, pushing her bangs away from her eyes. They are glittering with a new depth of emotion...a deeper surge of grief.

"How much has Cassian shared with you...about Damon?"

"Damon?" For a moment, the name does not connect. It is doubly hard because of the sorrow I feel so fully from her. Finally, it clicks. "His brother?"

A hard gulp vibrates in her throat. "Yes."

I force more clarity to mind—though it requires dredging unpleasant memories. *Unpleasant?* That is the diplomatic description for that night, the one that will not stop taunting as one of the hardest of my life. First, being thrown out of Turret Two by Prim—followed by a confrontation with Cassian I can only define by borrowing an expression from Vylet's dictionary.

Balls to the walls; here comes the brawl.

Though his balls had ended up nowhere near the walls, I had desperately longed to put them there—especially after he cracked open the door about Damon but slammed it again. I took the shutdown personally. *Too* personally. Viewed the situation past blinders that were like solid oak doors, likening myself to nothing but his "fuck friend" and "booty call." Though I now see everything about the situation more clearly—obviously, we both let our fears do the talking—I have been reluctant about reentering that space again.

Reluctant? Try *terrified.*

But what in my life, in the two months since I first clasped hands with Cassian Court, has *not* been terrifying?

And what, among all those fears, has not been worth pushing past?

Suck it up, buttercup.

"Cassian mentioned him once." I add a soft smile to the revelation. "He was relaying a story about a trip you three took to the coast. Something about a hotel with thin walls and loud neighbors..."

Mallory laughs and then sighs, staring toward the river again. "Oh, yes. *That* one."

"Indeed." I tap a finger on the air. "And he was good about remembering the arm farts too."

"Dear God." She drops her head into her hands. "How could *anyone* forget the arm farts?" A new laugh—that dissolves into a sob. "Oh, God. That was so long ago." Pulls a knee up, settling her pain-lined face atop it. "Yet it was just yesterday, wasn't it?"

Heavy sigh. I let her hear it, hoping she feels my empathy in it too. Not the *sympathy*—like her son, Mallory Court is a person who will suffer the pity of no one—but as my offering of understanding for the yesterday she pleads for. Those days in which the waters she gazed at were the Atlantic Ocean and she held *both* her boys in her arms...

"Mallory." I wait through the moment in which her face contorts harder, like a woman facing a firing squad. "What happened to him? To Damon?"

Finger by finger, she extricates her hand from mine. Slides it beneath the other, between her chin and her knee. The trajectory of her gaze does not change, extending toward the river's far shore...though I sense the intent of it does. Her eyes, clear and dry as blown green glass, reflect it. She can revisit the pain but not relive it.

"He was always my dreamer," she murmurs at last. "Cassian was the doer...like me. Impatient, impertinent, impossibly stubborn. Didn't want to 'talk' about his shit. Just wanted to punch through it."

I slide a wry smirk. "*What* a revelation."

After a conspiratorial wink, she returns to the thoughtful repose. "But my Damon... I worried about him a lot, especially after his father left. Which, just for the record, was a damn good thing." Her lips compress. "Larry Court could charm the wings off an angel, about his only talent outside of counting cards. When he finally decided he liked being big man in Atlantic City more than being big man for his kids, he was gone—and frankly, I couldn't shut the door hard enough on his worthless ass."

"Though it was hard for a bit?" I discern it from the fresh tension in her jaw.

"For more than a bit." Her head lifts a little with the pull of her inhalation. As she resettles it, her shoulders hunch. "Cassian was too young to remember or care—just five years old and reveling in kindergarten—but Damon was seven, nearly eight. He took it hard. Blamed himself for a few years. When he got old enough to realize it wasn't him, he started blaming me. And once puberty hit..."

She whooshes out breath with slow but rough emphasis.

"Oh dear," I mutter.

"About says it all." Her fingers wrap harder around the tops of her knees. "Though *oh shit* fits too."

I hum in agreement. All too clearly, I remember what a different creature Saynt became when his tempestuous teenage hormones kicked in. Seemingly overnight, my sweet little brother turned into a textbook Heathcliff, minus the moors.

"What happened at that point?" I ask quietly.

A heavy moment passes.

Another, even heavier.

Mallory surges to her feet. Like Cassian, she must deal with the force of her tension by doing something; *anything*. "Like all clichéd stories of teenage boy angst—"

"It was about a girl."

She halts, providing an instant *yes*. "At first," she confirms. "But when said girl decided she was no longer into him, a buddy helped him deal with the breakup by getting him high."

My hands coil in my lap. "Oh...shit."

"You *are* a fast learner."

"Did he get addicted to it?"

"The pot?" She bursts with a sharp laugh. "Oh God, Ella. If he'd stopped at the pot, I would have been happy. Not thrilled but happy."

My jaw drops with slow-motion heartbreak. "He—he tried *other* things?"

She wraps her arms around herself. Paces to the terrace ledge. Drums her fingers on the lip of a planter before reaching and plucking dead heads from a burgeoning hydrangea. The doer has gone sonic with her doing. *Ohhhh shit.*

"Mishella...what *didn't* he try?"

My head dips, weighted by the claim. "By the powers."

"That sounds about right too—since the boy had hallucinations about possessing superpowers when he was amped." She circles back around, one foot balanced on its heel, her face a mask of neutrality. Now I see where Cassian has gotten his talent for erecting instant emotional walls.

"There were the other delusions too, of course—like the time he thought he was Snoopy battling the Red Baron and bicycled around Cassian's school barking at all the kids. Another when he swore he was the reincarnation of Freddie Mercury and strutted up the street belting *Don't Stop Me Now*."

Her foot drops. So does the façade of indifference. She drops her head—but not before I catch the violent shiver of her chin. "I put up with all of it, hoping he'd wake up the next day and feel like such crap, he'd beg me to get him into rehab." A shaky breath goes in but does not leave. "But I waited too long—and knew it the night he went at Cassian with a kitchen knife, thinking his little brother had been hired by the Russian mob to assassinate him..."

"Creator's teeth."

My gasp is well-timed. At the same moment, she exhales as if setting down a huge weight. Not a surprise, though the start of a revelation. Has Mallory been carrying that awful memory all by herself over the years? Cassian knows, of course—but he was a small boy when it happened, unable to process all of it fully or properly. Talk about a giant thumb into the modeling clay of his psyche...hardening into the man he is today, now making so much more sense to me. His unshakable devotion to Mallory. His fierce loyalty to the Temptation Manor "family" who serves and loves him. And his protectiveness of me, intense as a sun guarding a planet in a cosmic storm.

"Wh-What did you do then?" I finally rasp.

Mallory kicks at the deck with her toe. "Only thing I *could* do. Told him to get clean or get out—and that if he ever came again at Cas like that, tweaked or not, I'd call the police." The wind whips her hair against her face. She ducks her head, letting it happen, her mind and heart seemingly lost in a dark, spinning whirl. "It was the hardest thing I've ever had to do in my life."

The gust wanes as quickly as it rose. In the following silence, my soul battles my body. I yearn to rush and embrace Mallory again, to match her tears with the burst of my heartache, but sense her composure is only bound by pins of glass. If even the wind touches her now, her worst nightmare will come true. She will shatter.

"What happened after that?" I abhor that I must ask it—but it is not an option. Once more I remember Cassian's face from last night, right after we exploded in passion together—sweeping from fulfillment to torment in the space of seconds. But the recall no longer confuses me. Dredging up everything about Lily was just the first stop on his soul's world tour of pain. And if the story about his brother ends where I think it shall...

"Damon took off, of course." Her all-business mask is resecured as she jerks up her head and sets her shoulders—another move so much like Cassian, I wonder who borrowed it from whom. "Cas and I dealt with it the only way we knew how. Moved on, one day at a time." The edges of her gaze tighten, emulating her son even more. "I took advantage of some free social programs to get Cas some counseling about it, though I was never sure how much of it stuck. Whenever I asked him about the sessions, he only shrugged and told me shrinks were like strippers—teasing at answers but never giving them."

I concentrate on not swallowing my tongue. "And he was *how* old?"

"Too old." It is clear the words—and their allegory—are not new for her. "He's been too old for it all since the day he was born."

I tip my head toward the sky. Not really necessary, for

the accuracy of her words is as obvious as stating Cassian has green eyes, deep dimples, and one ear lobe a little lower than the other. He is an old man in a demigod's body—knowledge that wrenches my heart and simmers my blood in the same jolt. "Did Damon ever come back?" I finally ask. "Try to get in touch?"

I hesitate at assuming the worst, though Cassian implied it when first telling me about his brother. *This isn't something I want to talk about anymore, Ella.*

Mallory confirms the exact same meaning, making my heart squeeze and my eyes sting, as her proud shield tumbles.

"The next time I saw my boy, I was standing in the morgue...identifying him on a steel table."

I push fingers to my quivering lips. I have expected this truth, simply not the image it was delivered on. "H-How did you tell Cassian?"

"He...already knew." She slowly shakes her head. "The little bastard just...did. He even had dinner ready when I got home. Said he knew I'd be in no mood to cook." Her cheekbones tighten, gaunt from the effort of containing her emotions. "Boiled hot dogs and burned Tater Tots." Finally, her tears brim over. "I ate every damn bite—and then threw it up in the kitchen sink later, when listening to him trying to muffle his sobs by running the shower."

I cannot hold back any longer either. With wet tracks pouring down my face, I hurry to her. Hold her as tightly as she grips me, letting our sorrow flow once more, emulating the morning in which it has struck: in quiet gusts created by a somber river.

Until someone behind me softly clears their throat.

I angle back, the mirror image of Mallory's move,

welcoming the chance to smile again. "Prim. Thank you for coming up." Presumably to inform me Cassian is home—or at least that is what I infer, before noticing the furrows in her brow. "Is everything all right?" I charge. "Where is he?"

"Not home yet," she replies. Dips hands into the pockets of her apron, always worn during her baking sprints. "And I *am* sorry to intrude—"

"You're never an intrusion." Mallory's insistence, true to her queenly grace, threads reprimand with encouragement.

Prim, no slouch in the two-messages-in-one department, answers with a smile that is half *thank you* and half *fuck you*. "Well, when this kept clanging like the bells of Notre Dame"— she pulls my cell out of her left pocket—"I thought it best to come find you."

As if on cue, the device chimes in her hand. Then again. I take it from her, my frown intensifying. "That is the text bell from my parents."

"Well, they're damn near nine-one-one'ing you, girl."

It is the first time Prim has approached casual conversation with me—a bittersweet win since there is not a second to enjoy it. Not with Maimanne or Paipanne, perhaps both, turning my phone into a dinging arcade and my chest into a jam worse than the Lincoln Tunnel at rush hour.

Tension that only worsens as I scroll the confusing barrage of bubbles down the screen.

What in Creator's name is going on?

What on earth have you done, young lady?

Could you have at least smiled for this? Even once?

Why are you not controlling this bedlam?

Where are you?

Why are you ignoring your father and me?

Mishella DaLysse--this is a complete disgrace.

We will not be able to show our faces in court.

There are at least two dozen more, spewing the same thing in different syntax. Two more pop up before I am finished reading, so I give up.

Mallory's face copies my perplexity. "They're timestamped over the last fifteen minutes."

Prim nods. "The bell choir started a few minutes after you came up here."

I drop back onto the couch, letting Mallory keep my device. "But what does it all mean?"

Mallory's lips tense. Still barely moving them, gaze still glued to the screen, mutters, "Do they always talk to you like this?"

Pandora's Box. Huge, pretty bow.

That I completely ignore.

Boxes cannot be concerns right now. My parents need to be—only I have no idea where to begin answering them. "What are they babbling about?" I ricochet a stare between Mallory and Prim. "I have no idea what they are even—"

The phone shrills with another sound. The *Cake by the Ocean* ringtone. A familiar face lights up the screen on my device. Dark sherry hair in a trendy style, with eyes nearly the same color. A warm smile, reflecting the fun we had during our first lunch outing nearly a month ago. Since then, those lunches have become weekly occurrences. Undoubtedly, Kathryn Robbe has become my closest friend in New York—to the point that I know she is an avid night owl and hates facing the world, me included, before nine on any day.

So why is she calling at quarter to seven?

I nod my thanks to Mallory and punch the phone's green button. "Bon *sabah*, my friend."

"Hey." It is breathless and hitchy and slightly impatient, not the usual "and good morning to *you*, dear *arkami*." I am almost tempted to ask her what marathon she is warming up for but have a strange feeling sarcasm is not on her breakfast menu.

"Errmm..." I extend it through the hurried rustlings coming from her end. "To what do I owe the pleasure of your voice before the strike of nine?"

"To what do you—" The rustlings stop. "Oh, God. Someone's listening to us, aren't they? Do you think they've gotten your private number already? But Cas bought it for you, right? He's more careful than that. *Much* more careful."

"Kate." I feel my brows drop. "What on earth are you about?"

A strange pause. As in, the kind of wordless stillness I expect from Cassian, not Kate.

"You really don't know, do you?"

"Know what?"

"About the explosion you and Cas are causing."

"The expl—" I surge to my feet. Swoop my stare in a full circle, admitting to nobody that I actually expect to see a plume of smoke somewhere on the horizon. "And where, exactly, would this apocalypse be?"

Early morning no-man's land or not, she has earned herself the sarcasm. To my delight *and* dread, her riposte rides the same bandwagon. "Do you have a web browser open?"

I pull my phone away long enough to tap on the internet function. "In about ten seconds." The little wheel rotates, taunting me for three seconds longer than that. "Where do I go?"

"Anywhere."

Nothing proves her more right than the list of trending subjects for the day.

After scrolling through the first screen of them, I succumb to sitting down once more.

As my stomach turns into a tempest, my lungs morph into twin Kraken and my limbs become ice luges...

And I realize, at last, why my parents are texting as if the end of the world has started.

For a moment, I completely commiserate.

Just when Mallory has given me the key to Cassian's final door, the entire world has stomped into our way. Tapped on the dominoes—when we have barely had time to line up a decent stack of our own.

"Holy saints." I tap the first link in the list on my screen. Correction: the first link appearing not to take blatant advantage of the others. Vy had a distinct term for it. *Click bait.* The definition takes on new meaning when one's own name is that lure.

When the page bursts into view, my head spins despite my backside on the cushion and my feet on the ground.

There is more than just a story here.

There are pictures—indeed painting a thousand words—

each one "angled" with a total fallacy.

I am tempted to swear by the saints again. *No.* This calls for my inner Vy—with her sidekick, Miss Screw Priority.

"Dammit to hell."

CASSIAN

"Dammit to hell."

I stomp on the Ford's brake after rounding the corner—and spotting the mob of reporters from half a block away. The feat isn't hard, considering they've brought all the big equipment, including telephoto lenses and video cameras. I even spot a few on-camera reporters getting sound levels checked.

Fuck. That'll be the only easy bite I'll get out of this newly lobbed pie at my balls—for that's exactly where the bastards have aimed. I've always appeared at enough high-profile events and been generous with quotes from the lobby of Court Towers that the press gives me Temptation as a haven. On one hand, I can count how many times they've violated the boundary. The first was after Lily's funeral, when the entire world wanted a piece of my grief. The next two were responses to the media version of booty calls, answering leads from "unknown sources" inside Temptation itself. Both times, I was "seeing" models who had high-profile marketing deals pending. Prim had ridden me hard about the first and become a full girl bear about the second. *You know, asshole, we'd all be better off if you'd think with the big head instead of the small one.*

I groan softly. What will she say this time? And how the hell will I debate the point? Technically, she's right. I wasn't thinking wholly with the gray matter upstairs when redrafting that contract back on Arcadia. How could I have, after knowing what Ella's elegant curves felt like beneath my touch...what the first bloom of her passion tasted like beneath my lips?

Ella.

"Christ."

I say it and choke on it at the same time.

Did *she* make the media booty call?

"She doesn't even know how to call nine-one-one," I counter in a growl.

Then who? And why?

I stab the Bluetooth at my ear. Bark the speed dial number for Prim but end the call two seconds later. Whatever the hell has gone down, I'm not sure what started it, why it's ballooned, or what we're facing because of it—including these shifty bastards tapping into cell signals, if not full calls.

Waking up the phone has fired up its screen—where an unread text from Kate waits. Does *she* know anything?

I flip on the truck's hazards, duck my head, and quickly read.

I've got your package. Nice ribbon. Waiting in
the usual place. Avoid the tunnel. It's packed.

One side of my mouth hitches up. *Devious, wonderful woman.* It's all code, betraying she *is* more ahead of this than I am, and here's the tow rope to help me get caught up.

The first line is the simplest. *Package* and *ribbon* equate to *gift,* translated into the Arcadian armeau—what Mishella Santelle has sure as hell been to me since the start.

The usual place takes a second longer. It could mean a number of our favorite dive bars around Manhattan, though that's weak—it's barely ten in the morning. While Kate enjoys trying to drink me under the table, the only time we indulged this early was the day I buried Lily.

The last line lends the final insight. *The tunnel* is Scott's nickname for the underground delivery entrance into Temptation, accessed by the alley on the north side of the building—and a secret from the press until six months ago, when I started dating Amelie Hampton. The diva was just mildly annoying about her agenda at first—until she started responding to social invitations on behalf of us both, as well as hinting about the tunnel to a few key members of the Manhattan paparazzi corps. Three months after that, when I broke things off with Amelie, the clickers backed off. I was no longer juicy prey.

Looks like I'm back on the menu.

Which means someone, somewhere, finally grabbed a clue that I came home from Arcadia with more than a new contract and a case of the island's fruit wine.

"Mishella." I let it stalk up my throat like the raging, possessive lion with which I suddenly sympathize. The agony of my hand fades beneath its ferocious fire.

Because if I'm back on the media menu...

She's in the middle of their merciless fire.

Fuck.

CHAPTER EIGHT

MISHELLA

There have definitely been days in my life that fit the category of challenging. Perhaps a little crazy. And one—the day I began by signing six months of my life over to Cassian and ended by stepping onto the tarmac at Teterboro—even surreal.

But insane?

I never considered any of those days as true insanity. Not in its purest form. Not like now. Not with the thought that sometime between leaving the hospital with Doyle and sinking to the living room couch now, I have fallen into a reality so bizarre, it must be insanity.

I reach out. Desperately and gratefully, curl my hand into Kate's. Since arriving an hour ago—and enduring the gauntlet of reporters to do so—she has not been just my life ring in this turbulent ocean. She has been the life*boat*. Proving good to her word, she left the apartment attached to her Upper East Side gynecology office and came right over, without makeup or formal clothes, to keep me breathing through this wild storm.

"*Breathe*, Mishella."

Literally breathing.

Reluctantly, I comply with her order.

My next action is easier. I snap an order at Doyle, knowing he already forgives the tone in light of the insanity. "Turn it up, Doyle."

It being the huge television monitor over the sleek wood mantel. The reasoning for my command? The now-familiar face that consumes the screen, accompanied by a smaller window in the upper-right corner—with my picture in it.

A muscle thuds in the man's cheek. He may forgive me for the tone, but the action itself is clearly another issue. "You think that's really—"

"*Turn it up.*"

The other side of his jaw clenches. "*Mishella.* Don't do this to yourself—or Cas."

"*Cas* is not here!" I push Kate's hand away, leaving her to trade another anxious look with Doyle. Beneath my breath, seethe out, "Where the *hell* is he?"

Kate checks her phone. "Still no response to my text."

Doyle checks his. "But the GPS on the truck still shows it a half block away."

"So what the hell?" Kate voices it for us all, which does not stop me from jiggling both knees, fighting the acid-dipped nettles in all my nerve endings. Kate finally leans over, attempting to calm me while raising expectant brows at Doyle. "Give a girl a hand here, Knight. Turn up the damn volume."

With a resigned sigh, Doyle complies. We are just in time for the start of the woman's broadcast. She beams teeth like stadium lights, highlighted even more by her candy-apple lipstick. Her voice fills the room with equally sticky sweetness. "And good morning once again, everyone. I'm Chantal Dunne."

Chantal Dunne. I do not know the woman, but in the last hour, she has become my gut punch of a nemesis. The well-known anchor of the Top Global News Network's *People and Places* segment, with her doll-like eyes, freckle-sprayed nose, and trendy but prim dress, is the perfect package for delivering three minutes of half truths and speculation every half hour. After all, who would dare question the veracity of such a cute little ginger?

The question—and its obvious, sickening answer—have turned into the lead ball now lodged beneath my ribs.

The woman lifts a conspiratorial smile before beginning her segment. "I've got just one question for everyone. Are you ready to be taken to court again?"

"Fuck. Me." Doyle slams his ankle to the opposite knee. "The woman can't even come up with a different lead-in than last hour?"

"The interns were busy playing beer pong." Mallory gives a delicate smirk. "At least she's not running for office."

"Not yet," Doyle mumbles.

"Bite your tongue," Kate adds.

On the screen, the window with my face changes to a montage of images, no less shocking than they were during the first broadcast. In one, Cassian and I are holding hands by candlelight over a private table at Daniel, both of us in elegant black cocktail wear. In the next, from the same meal, he's feeding me a handcrafted wafer slathered with caviar. In the third, we are both in denim and dark T-shirts, taking playful pictures of each other with the costumed characters beneath the iconic Times Square billboards.

The next one makes me grit my teeth harder. It is from this past weekend, when we escaped out on his friend's yacht on the harbor. We had felt free and alone with the sun, the wind, and the water and took full advantage of the situation— not to the point of impropriety but certainly pushing decorum to the naughty edge. Those moments explode to life on the screen now: shots of us cuddling, kissing, and even groping beneath each other's clothes in our hunger to have each other...

I want to throw up.

Private moments. Intimate memories.

The world sees them all now.

Narrated with gusto by a smirking Chantal Dunne.

"Could there be another salacious scandal rocking the halls of Temptation Manor this week?" she drawls. "As many in New York's social elite are already aware, Cassian Court returned from a 'business trip' to the beautiful island of Arcadia with more than just some new business deals and a few seashells. Rumor has it that the gorgeous god of a billionaire, fresh from separating from socialite bombshell Amelie Hampton, fell hard at first sight for an Arcadian local, Mishella Santelle."

Doyle humphs. "At least they got part of it right."

Next to me, Kate emits a wistful sigh. When a twinge in my belly compels me to glance over, she murmurs, "Was it like that? He really 'fell hard at first sight'?"

Despite the sliceable stress in the air, a smile emerges. I hear the ache in her voice but also know I owe her more than a lie. "No. It was *not* like that." I squeeze her hand. "*I* fell first."

And one day, a god of your own is going to fall in front of you, Kate Robbe.

She sees that message in my eyes—evidenced by the little *pssshh* that bursts off her lips. "I'm just happy you make *him* happy, lady."

Chantal Dunne makes it impossible for us to indulge any more feel-good moments—especially after new photos flash to the screen beside her.

"Wall Street's prince of passion flew the foreign beauty back to New York himself nearly two months ago, where they appeared in public together shortly thereafter, at the Manhattan Literary Guild's annual formal gala."

I cringe. There is no other word for it. Viewing the images of Cassian in his finery from that night only makes me remember how most of them ended up: as a blood-stained heap on the floor of the ambulance before the paramedics slammed the doors and took him from me. Shivering, even in the summer humidity, as the sirens started to wail...threatening to drown the echoes in my head of the song that he had whispered...

'Cause you're a sky, you're a sky full of stars...

I'm gonna give you my heart...

"Following the gala, Mishella remained by Cassian's side, getting tight with Mama Court by nursing him through minor surgery to repair a high school sports injury..."

Doyle grunts again. Thumps the air with a triumphant fist. "Thank fuck those nondisclosure agreements held with the first responders and nurses."

"But a *sports* injury?" Kate flings a grimace. "Really?"

"Model United Nations is a sport." Doyle spreads his fingers upward. "Right?"

"Cassian wasn't benched for long," Chantal continues, seeming to relish when the "sexy date" pictures are re-cued to the feed. "And couldn't wait to start upping his batting average with Mishella by playing charming tour guide all over the Big Apple."

"And again with the sports." Kate groans. "You see the slippery slope, Mr. Knight?"

Doyle grunts. "Meh."

I wish I could laugh at their repartee—but wonder if they haven't thrown it out for the sake of distraction to begin with. We all know what TGN has in store for the world now.

"But now, it appears that Cassian has had enough of charming—and that Mishella may have had enough of *him*." Chantal braces both hands on the edge of her glass and chrome desk. Colored lighting turns the glass cutouts pink, matching the nail polish adorning her almond-shaped fingernails. "Though the couple seemed to begin the evening right, coming home early from a date at the Met Cloisters in upper New York—"

"By the *Creator*. How do they know all this?"

"—things took a more dramatic turn a few hours later, when there was a flurry of activity inside the Temptation Manor complex, on the Upper West Side."

"And how the hell did they know *that*?" Mallory exclaims. "And where's their proof?"

Doyle's gaze tightens. "They don't know it. They're bluffing. Filling."

"In other words, lying," Kate huffs.

Doyle nods. "If they had the footage or images, they'd use them."

I want to feel better about that—at least the monsters really cannot get inside Temptation—except that I know exactly what is coming next.

The attacks worse than the photos from the yacht.

Sure enough, the feed cycles to a picture of me, being helped by Scott and Doyle into Cassian's custom limo—or so that is the *truth* of the matter, as *we* know it. Without context, the image takes on a different meaning, especially because my exhaustion makes me look ready to stab someone. The photo is usurped by a shot of Cassian, appearing as if *he* has the blade in his belly. His eyes are rammed tight, his jaw clenched beneath his thick stubble. He holds his shredded hand in front of him—only with all the blood and the poor quality of the image, it is difficult to determine what his injury truly is. I am positive the picture was taken upon his arrival to the emergency room, when Doyle and I were flanking him, though both of us have been completely cropped from the shot.

Surprise, surprise.

Chantal leans toward the camera, once more giving her viewers that "just between us" expression. "Within minutes, Cassian was rushed to the hospital, covered in blood and clearly in pain. *People and Places* has learned he was treated for 'numerous lacerations' and was not a pleasant patient at all."

"Because it was the middle of the night and the doctor was an overcultured prig!" I push to my feet, wondering where a convenient shower door can be had to put *my* hand through. No. I shall put Chantal Dunne's hand through it instead, then see how "pleasant" a patient the woman is.

To my dismay, she goes on, both hands intact. "Mishella did show up at the emergency room but left a few hours later, appearing tired and worn out. Onlookers wondered if trouble had indeed come knocking at Temptation and whether it was she or Cassian who'd answered the door."

I twist my hands against each other in my lap. "Tired and worn out is usually what happens when one has been up all night."

"*Breathe.*" Kate wraps an arm around me. Rubs my shoulder. "She's after ratings, and she's getting there on your back. Don't hand her the reins and the crop."

A final photo appears, showing a different angle of my departure from the hospital. I duck my head, unable to look anymore. Could the angle and lighting have been more unflattering?

ANGEL PAYNE

"Though Cassian was nowhere to be seen, his custom Jag XJL was on hand for enchanted carriage duties back to the manor. Mishella was escorted on the ride by Cas's personal valet, who looked none too happy about being assigned to babysitting duty."

Thankfully, the first reaction to that comes from Mallory—in the form of a nasal scoff. "None too *happy*? Imagine *that*."

Kate gives the humor an acerbic snort. "Now we *know* the interns were beer ponging instead of researching."

Before she finishes, Doyle is back on his feet and stabbing the remote, banishing Chantal to the land of mute once more. "Since when is this kind of crap considered *news*?"

"Since when are you supposed to be watching it?"

The interjection, coming from the landing behind us, has me pushing from Kate, exploding to my feet, and then scrambling over the back of the couch. On the other side, I stumble and nearly fall the final two steps—but at last I am back in his arms, inhaling the cotton of his shirt, the grit of the street, and the lingering iodine from the ER, along with his perfect, unmistakable musk. He accepts my weight with a discernible grunt, making me all too aware of the pain he must be in, but when I shift away, he jerks me back, refusing to let go. His left hand tangles in my hair. His right strokes up my back, the bulk of the bandages lifting my shirt and abrading my skin.

It feels...wonderful.

And freeing.

The relief of his return means I can now get truly mad. The dive feels pretty good, erupting enough so I can push back a little—far enough to smack the center of his chest.

"Where the hell have you—" My voice strangles when watching dust slough off his shirt. I drop my gaze, stunned to see the dirt is caked over the rest of him. "Cassian...where the *hell* have you been?"

At first, his answer is only a harsh breath through his nose. His elegant mouth finally twists, erupting with another pained sound as he tugs out Doyle's truck keys, mistakenly using his right hand.

"For the love of the Creator." I hiss it when the dolt makes things worse by tossing the keys to Doyle. "He is less than ten feet away."

"And this is just a bandage on some stitches, favori, not a full cast."

"Yeah, well..." Kay spurts a little giggle. "Those Model United Nations injuries can have hidden complications."

"Huh?"

"Forget it." Doyle gives him a ruthless once-over. "You look like shit."

"Thanks, honey."

"Dare I ask what you did with Dora?"

"Who?" I shoot a sharp look between them.

"His truck," Cassian explains. He keeps his hand in my hair, fingertips making small circles against my scalp. "She's fine," he assures Doyle. "Parked her about half a block up, in front of the renovated Victorian."

Doyle scowls. So does Mallory. Kate and I—and even Prim, who has entered with a huge plate of her handiwork from the baking binge—add our probing stares. Vocalizing the question behind all those looks is another challenge. Doyle rises to our rescue. "Wait. So how did you get in?"

Cassian's jaw firms. "Over the back garden wall."

"What the—"

"*Over* the—"

"How the—"

Mallory, Prim, and Kate cut short their triplicate of shock as I wrench free from his hold—yearning to pummel him once again. *Much* harder. "You did *what*?"

"He got it done." Doyle chuffs. "*Nice.*"

"Shut. Up." Maybe I will start by smacking on *him*. The idea still appeals, even when I wheel back to Cassian and fight not to sway at the new hit of his golden beauty. The effect is given a punch of holy-shit-wow by the rugged mess of his hair, the tawny grit of his stubble, and the smudges of dirt up and down his clothes. Now, I even notice the small tear in one of his pants legs and the blood on the knee beneath. *Dammit.* I need to throttle him. I long to kiss him. And more.

"Sorry, armeau." But he does not mean a syllable of it. At least not for the stupidity for which I stand here seething at him. He is even more brazen when stomping farther into the room. "Shutting up is *not* on the action plan for anyone today."

Doyle powers the television all the way down. Straightens into a battle stance that matches Cassian's...too damn perfectly. "*That's* what I'm talking about."

"What?" I rush forward. Once more, my glare is a frantic metronome from one to the other of them. "*What* is he talking about?"

CASSIAN

I inhale. Exhale. It all feels like fire in my lungs, without a chance of escape. Doesn't matter. I don't even want one— though answering her has just turned into hell's own battle because of it.

Challenge accepted. With pleasure.

A minute ago, the task wouldn't have been so daunting. But those sixty seconds ago, all I functioned on was the adrenaline that got me over the back wall, riding an inner locomotive of pissed off and determined. It was stoked to life during the minutes I sat in Doyle's truck, trying to get a step ahead of this mess by Googling myself on my phone. Sure enough, gossip blog posts flared up the feed, with the promise of assorted hashtags and memes to follow.

I'd pounded the dashboard, thinking of Ella's reaction to the shit storm—Kate had beaten me back here, meaning *someone* was already aware of it—and in frustration, hated myself for not being the one by her side instead. Despising those goddamn reporters for delaying me from getting here sooner. Making me sneak into my own home...

It had been just a taste.

A tiny bite of the outrage upon which my psyche has just gorged, walking in at the end of Chantal Dunne's "news" report—a story TGN has clearly ordered their vulture editors to hold on to, waiting for the most succulent moment to stab into the meat. And the fact that the meat is still alive? Writhes and twists with every one of their slices, her generous face crunching, her sweet body tensing, her pain like a panicked creature in the very air, struggling beneath their ruthless blade?

That's not their concern. It never is.

Which has turned *them* into *my* concern.

Blazing my course brutally clear.

Unsnap my sheath. And show them the size of *my* knife.

I power the resolution to my gaze and then my grip, clutching Ella back against me—hating myself once more for a move as asshole as TGN's. But there's a difference to my action. My knife is pointed out, not in. And I'm sure as hell ready to start using it.

"Dammit, Ella." I rasp it against her forehead. "I'm so sorry...about all of this."

Her body sags enough that I know she won't resist again—thank fuck—though she tugs her head back enough to pierce me with all the crystalline facets of her brilliant gaze. "Because *you* were the one responsible for any of it?"

"Because I was the one responsible for *all* of it." Despite the press of our bodies, I hold her tighter. Pain races up my arm, but the agony's worth it. The completion I feel with her near... *God help me.* Even with our clothes on, the mesh of our forms feels like a union...a oneness I've never had with anyone. No, not even Lily. The constant poison in Lily's body killed off that possibility.

"All right." Ella draws out both words while arching a dubious brow. "So *you* were the one who held those photographers at gunpoint, forcing them to follow us all over town?"

I twist my lips. "I'm the big game their news director wanted to bag, making *him* pull out the gun."

"Damned expensive gun."

Kate's comment earns her Doyle's defined nod. "The pictures in Times Square were a freebie—but paying off the restaurant staff and the boat dock crews..." He snorts and shakes his head. "Hell, even having tip-off assets inside the damn hospital..."

"*Fuck.*"

It spews before I can stop it, though nothing would've changed it with any forethought. I'm torn between grabbing Ella closer and fully pushing her away. God*damn*. Will I protect her best by giving her up?

Not. An. Option.

"Cassian Cameron Jonathan. In case you haven't noticed, there's a lady in your arms."

"And an army of media after my balls, Mother." At once, my body tautens as if the statement isn't just allegory. My tension spears into Ella, turning her into a stiff plank too. To Doyle I command, "Call the office of Presbyterian's CEO and set up a meeting. That ER will be investigated, and I *will* have the snitch fired." I leave out the part about hoping it's that asshole Yago. "After that, pull Daniel Boulud's number from my database too. I think he's traveling right now, but he'll take my call. I didn't just pay for a great Beaujolais and roasted duck last week. The discretion of his staff—"

"Hasn't been an issue before." Doyle steps around the couch, calmly assuming what I like to call his "bodyguard battle stance." He's never used it on me before, though. It's... weird. "Nor should we assume it's an issue now. More likely, the rat at the restaurant was a new hire at the valet stand, not yet properly trained. Those are independent companies who hire a lot of college kids."

"So you're saying my privacy was sold for someone's weed money?"

"No. I'm saying somebody wasn't given proper training, and—"

"And I don't give a shit." My roar makes everyone step back but him. Yeah, even Ella—which fires up my self-hatred all over again. *Fucking. Great.* It's not even noon, and so far today I've not-so-subtly insulted a few medical professionals, called my dead brother a selfish asshole, and watched the woman I love be turned into a trending hashtag under *#billionairebangtoys.*

And now I get to watch that woman look at me like the proverbial second head has sprouted from my neck. And maybe it has. Since I unlocked the door to that damn turret and climbed into that room again, it feels like another person has clamored to burst free from me—a goddamn beast, prowling that cage along with Lily's restless ghost, only one message imprinted on its mind.

You didn't do enough.

You didn't protect her.

You didn't make the hard choices that would've saved her.

I breathe hard, listening to every heaving breath and snarling word from the monster now. If that means he's had to manifest into another head off my neck, then so be it. My regular one will be happy to channel the message too, just so everyone hears it—especially me.

"I want heads on platters, Doyle. Is that fucking clear? I'll have a stack of pink slips on my desk by next Monday—and right next to them, apology letters addressed personally to Mishella."

Doyle stiffens. Draws back a harsh breath, teeth locked—but in the moment I'm sure he'll haul a crossbow out of his jeans, I am cut down by harsher opposition.

The breathtaking blonde at my side.

"By all the bloody powers in heaven." Mishella reclaims the step I blew her back by, delivering a new slap to the center of my chest—only this time, she's not I'm-grateful-you're-alive pissed. This is I-may-just-kill-you-myself pissed. "You *are* joking...yes?"

I slash a glare down. Jolt one brow up. "I've never been more serious in my fucking life."

Her nose scrunches. Her lips part, unveiling the tight lock

of her teeth. "No," she seethes. "You are *not*."

Rough inhalation. A forest fire raging in my bloodstream. "Mishella. For Christ's sake—"

"No." She whomps my chest again. "*No*, Cassian, for *my* sake, you need to take a giant chilled pickle and—"

"Chill *pill*?" Kate supplies the guess.

"That too," Ella snaps. "I really do not care *how* it happens—but you make it fucking so, Mr. Court." She halts, letting the stunning impact of the dictate in. And this time, it *is* stunning. I'm close to certain nobody in this room has heard that special English word from her before, except me—and I can count the occasions *I* have on one hand, since I remember them clearly. The F-word is a delicious damn thing when the woman's begging me to actually do it to her...

Memories that turn it into fifteen kinds of hot temptation now.

Yeah. It's official. I'm whipped for this woman.

No damn use fighting it.

Instead, I suck back more air. Hold up both hands—in grudging surrender.

"All right. Fine. I'm listening, armeau."

Rough air puffs Doyle's lips. "Annnd hell really has frozen over."

"Shut up," I snarl.

Ella steps between my arms. Slides her hands up to my sternum, my shoulders, the sides of my face. Though I swallow hard, half the stress drains from my body. I'm not sure that it hasn't gone away...simply that now, it's understood. In her sorceress eyes and magical touch, I feel that. I *know* it.

"I have...an interesting idea," she finally murmurs.

One side of my mouth quirks—as one half of my soul

willingly dances its way over to her. "Heads on pikes instead of pink slips on my desk? *Ow.*" At least her dual tweaks on my ears distract from the hot needles in my hand. Even if they didn't, the cyan glow of her eyes would be worth it.

"Instead of retaliation...why should we not try recompensation?"

"Huh?" Doyle mutters.

"Recompen—what?" Kate is louder about her confusion.

Ella circles both hands to my nape. Sets her chin so our gazes fully meet. "Why do we not give them what they want, Cassian? Work *with* them, not against them. Together."

I dig the fingers of my good hand into the top of her arm. "You're serious."

She presses closer. With her head rocked back, still meeting every burning scrutiny of my gaze with gorgeous serenity of her own, she whispers. "Yes. I *am.*"

"In that case, you're also crazy."

She rises slowly on tiptoe, taking my bottom lip between both her own. So damn soft. So fucking sexy. "Probably."

I dip my head, unable to resist the perfect taste of her...the incredible, insane waltz to which her soul has invited mine. "In that case, Miss Santelle...you're also on."

CHAPTER NINE

MISHELLA

My consciousness crawls out of the haze of sleep, into the strange place a brain goes when awakened by thoughts or circumstances beyond its norm.

In this case, both are true.

Before my eyes are open, I know I am not in my usual bed at Temptation. The body heat and soft snores of the man wrapped around me, smelling like cedar soap and sandalwood shampoo, supplies that clue before my eyes are open. I crack my gaze open by a little, smile by a little more, and then burrow closer to Cassian, wondering how I gave this up for six long weeks. *Being* in this bed has not been the same as *waking up* in this bed, even if this still does not officially qualify as such an occasion. We have only been asleep for a few hours, after all...

What time is *it?*

Trying to gauge the hour by the light through the windows is fruitless. Summer showers were predicted and have arrived, spattering drops against the window beyond the Roman shades and turning his bedroom into a collection of misty brown and gray. I peer around, conducting a slow study of the space that has become so familiar. The stark lines of the modern furnishings are mellowed by fixtures in graceful curls, cushions in soft fabrics, and the clothes Cassian tossed before taking thirty seconds of a shower—the door repaired by Hodge before we were even finished at the hospital—and then falling into bed, his pain meds having finally kicked in.

I sigh quietly...and wish the same peace would make its way to my mind.

Instead, my thoughts are awake and ablaze in flashing, rioting colors.

Green. Gold. Red.

Green. Gold. Red.

Go. Slow. Stop.

Then again and again and again, taunting stoplights on the street race inside my mind. *I need to go. Just let me floor it...*

I push out a small huff, though it softens to a smile the moment a memory takes over. My first hour in the city. Cassian and I still on our way home in the Jag. The streets whizzing by, a kaleidoscope of amazing sights, sounds, color, humanity. And the streetlights, enrapturing me...

So when the lights turn red, everyone just stops? *What if someone does not agree to that?*

My smile grows as I recall Cassian's reaction. He'd given that special laugh, from deep in his chest...as if I had just given *him* the largest delight of our journey. Now, I know that I likely did—and that this man sat there, entertaining the possibility of being that one to *not* agree. That if he so wished, every light on our route would have indeed been green.

Cassian Court.

The man who has brought endless possibilities to my life. *To my heart.*

The confession is not new—though the fit of it in my psyche is. It presses a fascinating weight to my chest as I circle my stare back to him.

Unbelievable.

He takes my breath away even when lost to sleep, though it is in different ways than his "Mr. Court" mode. Stripped out of dark Prada and custom Ferragamo, the Bluetooth gone from his ear, he is like a massive lion freed from the zoo, allowed to laze in all his tawny glory...and latent danger.

I love him.

And there it is. The largest part of the danger. *I love him*— to frightening reaches of my heart and terrifying corners of my soul. But it took him lying in the Bryant Park bushes, bleeding from the three bullets in his body because of defending *me*, for fate to clonk me over the head with that truth, as well as its peculiar gift of an aftermath.

Hiding does not take away the fear.

And only makes the vulnerability worse.

I refuse to accept weakness about something that has brought me such strength—someone I want to give strength *to*. No moment coalesced those conclusions more than standing with Cassian in the living room this morning and embracing him in the spirit of that bright, amazing courage.

You're serious.

Yes. I am.

In that case, you're also crazy.

A new smile lifts my lips from the memory. "I am crazy about *you*, Cassian Court."

I confess it as quietly as I can, but the vibrations tickle the valley between his biceps. His snore cuts short. "Huh?" he mumbles, inciting my tiny giggle. The boyish sound, together with the dark-gold waves tousling his forehead, make me brush a kiss across the spot I have tantalized.

"Go back to sleep, beastie."

Though his eyes do not open, a scowl compresses his face. A growl works up his throat. "The fuck, woman? *Beastie?*"

I laugh again. "It is an endearment."

"Hmmph. You mean like 'stud muffin' or 'schnookums'?"

I trace a finger along the plateau of his collarbone and then the perfect hill of his shoulder. "I *mean* like 'beastie'—as in, you remind me of a lazing lion." I explore the sleek lines of muscle down his arm, reveling in how they tighten slightly beneath my touch. "You are beautiful...but sort of lethal."

His sulk changes. His eyes form assessing slits. "*Sort of?*"

"Well, you will not be chomping off anyone's head in the near future."

"And that's good?"

The incredulity in his tone makes me slap his bicep. He snickers, still watching me from a narrowed but smoldering gaze. By the *powers*. In Vy's terminology, the man is wicked hot.

"For the record, Mr. Court, that is very good."

He slides a sensual smirk. Clearly, the painkillers are still working, and I am glad—perhaps even tempted to take advantage of his diminished guard and dig in about where he disappeared in Doyle's truck this morning—but he still looks in need of more slumber, and that is more important than prying about what cannot be changed.

"Well, I hope all those spared skulls are grateful." He resettles, pushing his head closer to mine on the pillow. "And in my not-so-humble opinion, should still be writing you letters."

"Letters?" I retort. "What on earth for?"

"Thank-you notes." The sheets rustle as he slides his lower body closer, hooking an ankle around one of mine. "They owe you. For taming the lion."

I teasingly purse my lips. "That was the lion's choice, not mine."

"Bullshit." He growls low, nudging my nose with his. "The lion knows who holds his balls in her hand."

"Your balls are nowhere near my hand."

"That can be rectified."

Another laugh spills free. "Now I think the lion's painkillers are talking."

His leg yanks on mine. Aligns our bodies even tighter, slotting the bulge between his thighs into the cushion between mine. I shudder through a gasp. He savors it with a stare as mysterious as rainforest depths, capturing his lower lip beneath his teeth. *So hot.* "I'm not completely numb, favori."

"Oh...my," I whisper. "Well, clearly...ahhhh!" The cry bursts out as his fingers slip in, grazing one of my nipples through my bra.

"What are you still doing in this?" He slides that touch down, pushing at the waistline of my panties. "And these?"

By the Creator's angels. His caresses make me feel like crystal artwork, a treasure adored. My lungs hitch. My blood trembles in every inch of my veins. "The lion tamer has to have a costume."

His throat rumbles roughly as he slides even lower, palming my backside. "Well, this sure as hell isn't the one for public consumption."

I fight not to rub up against him. "For the lion's eyes only."

"Fucking right."

I swallow hard. Force rational thought to return. "But as long as we have broached upon that subject..."

"Of your costume?" He swirls enticing circles across both my cheeks. "Or my eyes on it? Or my fingers underneath it?"

"Of what I am wearing on top of it."

"Huh?"

"T-Tomorrow m-morning." I forgive myself the stammering. Right now, with him stroking up the valley between my buttocks, it is a miracle I can think, let alone speak. "For the interview. With—with Chantal Dunne."

His hand stops. His nose flares, blows out a lengthy snort. "Even painkillers won't make me amenable to the subject of her right now, armeau."

I scoot my head back a little. Look up at him through my lashes—on purpose. "But you agreed to sit down with her, in front of the cameras, for me." My hand lifts to thread adoring fingers through his hair. The stuff is so thick, it is still damp next to his scalp. "I am...beyond grateful, Cassian."

He dips his forehead against mine. "For the light in those eyes, I'd give Chantal Dunne an interview on Mars."

"The TGN studios are much closer," I deadpan.

"Thank fuck, because my navy Tom Ford is going to be a sauna tomorrow."

Puzzled frown. "So why are you wearing it?"

"Because it goes best with my cobalt tie, and *that* goes best with the dress you picked out." He flashes a cockier version of the lip-tug grin. "Yeah, I spied on you picking it out in the other room before I showered."

Groan.

I let out a real one while rolling to my back. Instead of shaking off his hold, the move just drags him up and over, until I am returning his probing stare with a glower. "*Spied* is right," I accuse. "You were *not* supposed to—"

"Listen to everything you were muttering at the same time?"

At least the assertion unseats his grip on my ass, forcing his hand up to stop the face palm I prepare to indulge. I battle him with a not-so-ladylike grunt.

"I—I do not know what you—"

"Yes, you do." His voice is lenient, but his grip is not, locking my arm into the pillow next to my head, his thumb digging into my palm. "Things like 'what the hell was I thinking' and 'all these dresses make me look like a cow' and 'Cassian will have me on the next plane home after this.'" His thumb pinches deeper. "Sounding familiar, beautiful?"

At first, he receives only my peeved hiss. *His* face is like a lake from a European postcard: breathtaking and serene. Dammit.

"The idea was mine!" I debate. "You remember *that*, yes?"

"Of course I do."

"So I had *no* bloody right to feel so nervous about it." The past-tense reference is useless. Just thinking about it *now* turns my stomach into an emulation of the designer fountain in the Court Towers lobby, with bile and nerves instead of chrome and water.

"Bullshit." Cassian leans down, pinning me tighter with the pressure of his whole body. "You had every goddamn right. You still do." Impales me with even deeper intensity in his gaze. "You think I was kidding when I called the idea crazy?" he charges. "Chantal Dunne is a hell's hare in bunny's clothing— fluffy on the outside, vicious on the inside. Think Barbie meets Maleficent, marinated in a subtle Nurse Ratched."

"Huh?"

He snorts. "I have to stop picking spy thrillers on movie nights. But for now"—he moves his hold to the side of my neck, brushing a thumb along my jaw—"I'm in this with you, Ella. All the way. Though the idea may be crazy, it's also brilliant." The kiss he presses is quick but intense, sending tingles down to my toes. "Now, we just need to make sure it's *really* brilliant."

I twist my head a little. Dip a frown. "'*Really* brilliant.' I hope that comes with an instruction manual?"

"Not a word of one." He releases a long breath. "But we'll write it the best way possible. Together."

I counter him with a deep inhalation. "All right." Give him the steady trust of my gaze. "How do we start?"

"By recognizing where Chantal will start," he asserts. "Beer pong or not, her staff has undoubtedly been ordered to do their homework on us."

My belly floods with fresh anxiety. Brims over, sluicing a chill through my bloodstream. "H-Homework? About what?"

His touch still reassures, but his brow furrows. "I don't know yet. Doyle and *his* team are doing what they can to find out, but we likely won't know everything she's got until we're face-to-face with her on set tomorrow."

The chill becomes ice. "Everything she—" I push against him. "Cassian." Sit straight up, clutching a hand over the wild pounding of my heart. "Do you think she will find out...about the real terms of the contract?"

He pushes up. Then a little more. The sheet obeys gravity—and the thirst of my gaze—to slide away from the crests of his chest and the ladder of his abs, puddling between his thighs like a loincloth on an Italian statue of gold marble.

"Not if the people who know about it value their relationships with us—or their status at Arcadian court." His commitment to every word is engraved across the solemn angles of his face. I nod, believing him. Nobody on the short list of insiders who know about the contract terms, Mother and Father included, has any reason to spill the sordid fine print about our agreement. At least I hope...

"*Ella.*" He cups a hand around my shoulder. I look up, already craving the look on his face—the one saying he has listened to every thought in my head and now has the perfect answer for them. "It's going to be okay."

"You do not know that for sure!"

"I don't," he concedes. "But I *do* know she has no reason to even look there. That's not what she's after."

"Then...what *is* she after?"

His reaction is not what I first expect. The little jog of his head and the sly smile on his face are such a switch from his earnest scowl, I wonder if *my* mind has gotten looped instead of his—especially when he moves with such startling speed, my yelp of surprise springs from it.

And then...arousal.

A lot of it.

By the Creator.

I have heard it said that fear and lust balance on the same razor's edge, but I never believed it...not until now. Not until, in the space of three seconds, I am pulled from shivering in a sheet to falling against sculpted muscle, my nipples mashed to golden pecs, my hips held by forceful fingers, my thighs spread...

And fitted around the most glorious erection Cassian has ever had.

He pulls me closer with an effortless tug, calling to all my feminine instincts. I feel so small in his arms, though our new positioning places me slightly higher than him. The angle gives me a chance to explore the beauty of his upturned face— and enjoy the fit of his arousal, moistening my panties as he punches against my sensitized cleft.

Ohhhh....*my*.

How are we doing this? *Why* are we doing this? There are pressing things we must discuss. What were those things? I will remember...in a moment. I *have* to remember...

Cassian pushes his face up another inch. The edges of his lips curve, once more all Italian artwork god come to life, before he scrapes the curve of my chin with the edges of his teeth. *Rasping quivers. Heated vibrations. Melting limbs.* Oh, Creator help me...

What on *earth* did we need to talk about?

He finally speaks again, lips still along my skin. "I have an interesting idea about your answer."

"Oh, dear." I half laugh it, letting the sound husk from my throat. "You and me and our interesting ideas..."

"I think you'll like this one."

I run my hands up his arms. Over the bulges of his shoulders. Plunge them into his hair, savoring the thick softness between my fingers. "I certainly like how it has started."

His hands roam up my spine. The gauze of his bandage adds extra abrasion, making me writhe from the vibrations. "Why don't *we* figure out what she's after?" He answers my shot of a quizzical stare by deepening the smile. "All by ourselves. Right here. Right now."

I study him harder. Bring fingers down, stroking across the proud planes of his temples. "Hmmm. Your proposal is certainly interesting so far, Mr. Court."

His head tilts, lending him a smug air—a tactic I imagine him using on business partners in the boardroom. And why not? It is sure as hell working on *me*. My senses revel in him. My body tightens and pulses and aches for him.

"I'm very happy to hear that, Miss Santelle." His fingertips dance down the dip of my spine. Tease at the back of my panties. "Do you prefer Miss Santelle? Or may I call you Mishella?"

I rock backward by a little. "Excuse me?"

He dips his head the other direction. The boardroom rogue is still having his fun. "Well, which is it?" he charges. "Chantal *will* ask, you know."

Comprehension teases like the flick of a match. I let it spark the edges of my own lips. "Ah...yes. She probably will."

"And...?"

I lean back in, looping my arms around his neck. Engage his gaze from just inches away, playfully nibbling on his bottom lip. "I prefer to be called 'sweet armeau.' Or 'my precious Ella.'"

His gaze narrows. "Anyone in that studio calls you either, they'll be visiting our friend Yago in the ER."

I am tempted toward a feminine preen. Funnel it into a feigned gasp of scandal while lifting an invisible microphone between us. "Hmmm. This is quite an interesting side to you, Mr. Court." I jab the "microphone" toward him, adopting my best Chantal Dunne face, with wide eyes and overly pouting lips. "Normally, you take up pen and ledger for your battles. Care to comment for our viewers about accessing your inner warrior?"

He chuckles. Jabs his head up to bite into the flesh between my thumb and forefinger. "Warrior?" Soothes the damage with a seductive lick. "Why stop there, Chantal? Why not go with...caveman?"

"Hmmm." I barely maintain the teasing guise, especially as he loops that talented tongue between the bases of all my fingers. "Primeval over medieval. That is...an interesting choice."

He lifts a sultry stare through his gold lashes. "I like to eat what I hunt."

I swallow hard. My womb clenches. My breasts pebble. "Freshly...plucked?"

"Sure. That's good." He tugs on my hand. Kisses over my palm and onto my wrist, never setting me free from his tiger-bright stare. "But I prefer it finely prepared too. Heated up...to the perfect texture..."

My breath speeds up, slicing in and out, as he slides his mouth up to the inside of my elbow. Still I manage to chide, "Mr. Court, I think you are trying to distract me."

He works his way up to my shoulder. Suckles the curve of my skin. Fires up every nerve in my body. "From what?"

I frantically lick my lips. "I—I have a job to do..."

"So do I." His voice is more fire, descending to the upper swell of my breast. "Yet here I am—" the blaze spreads, as he explores beneath the cup with the tip of his tongue "—agreeing to answer any question you want to ask." He glances up, just once, before pushing back the lace-trimmed fabric. "And consider anything else you'd like to...present."

A long, high sigh swirls up my throat. Rasps out as he closes his Da Vinci lips over my aching nipple, swiftly turning it into a stiff red erection. "*Cassian.*"

"Hmmm?" Damn him. Still smooth and cool as marble.

"This—this is *not*—"

"The hottest sight I've ever seen?" He pushes aside the cup over my other breast. "The most magnificent pair of breasts in this whole city, pushed up and waiting for me to pleasure them?" He flashes a savoring grin before securing his teeth over that dusky nipple. "I beg to differ, armeau."

A miracle, this strength I suddenly gain to press my lips

into a chastising line. "We must prepare for tomorrow!"

He soothes the burn from his bite with a lavish lick. My opposite breast gets more attention from the fingers extending out of his bandage, twisting my hard peak to bring just the perfect pinch of pain. "Prepare away, sorceress. Don't let me stop you."

"*Wéchant brutan.*"

"Now you *really* can't let me stop you." He growls it into the valley between my throbbing swells. I let out a tight huff. Dammit. This man and his penchant for my language. I cannot even cap it with an insult because he likes those more.

"It means you really are a wicked beast."

"Not sure Chantal's team will uncover *that* one."

"Perhaps it shall be my little gift to her cause."

"And perhaps I'll spill my own secrets during the interview." He skates his touch back down by way of my ribs, riding the line between tickling and arousing, until bracing the small of my back with his bandaged hand while sliding beneath my panties with his other. "Like how I fantasized about touching you like this, damn near from the moment we met."

Another gasp. Everything under his fingers pulses. Flutters. Zings with a thousand points of feeling and life. "You—you would not dare." *Because then the cameras would show everything on my face too. That I longed for the same thing that very night...*

"Oh yeah?" He strokes in, past the flesh that shields my most tender button, flaring my desire in all the right places. *He knows me...* "Try me." Rolls his thumb, stirring my lust, spinning my mind. "Dear Christ, Ella, *please* try me. Make me declare to the world how I dreamed of what your body would feel like, smell like, taste like. How I went back to my suite in the palais after that reception and didn't leave the shower for nearly an hour. Then the next morning, too...and that night. I thought of you, over and over again, making myself come with thoughts of touching you...fucking you. Those next two days were sheer hell, wondering if I'd see you again—and dreading it. Knowing that the second I did, those fantasies would return, twice as hot as before. That I'd be rock hard for you all over again." With a gritted sound, he pulls his fingers away. Shoves the panel of my panties aside so his bare flesh can rub into my slit instead. "Just like this. *Exactly* like this."

"*Cassian.*" I shake and throb, mashing myself tighter against him. I am a ball of need, desperate for the purchase of all his rock-hard sinew and relentless force, thinking how correct he is about his first assertion. *Caveman*, not *warrior*. Chivalry and heraldry be damned. I need his possession, his hunger...his primeval lust—and all the things it draws out in me as response. Wild things. Hot things. All the aching, animal needs of the woman who imagines we are on a bed of pelts in some Paleolithic cave, the storm drenching a dirt jungle outside instead of an urban one.

"You wanted me too," he growls. "Didn't you?" He rolls his hips, making me feel every angle of his length...taunting my shivering pearl with his engorged crown. The heat of his pre-ejaculate blends with my aroused cream, swirling an aphrodisiac scent between our slick bodies. "I saw it on your face, favori...every time we saw each other again. In the way your eyes changed, turning from daylight to midnight...so goddamn beautiful..."

I grip into the flexed tension of his shoulders. Fit my face into the muscled column of his neck. "And I saw it on *your* face. The tension in your jaw. The way the very air changed around you..."

"Because it did. The way I wanted you...the intensity it reached... It was a fucking cosmic shift." His chest churns with a harsh breath. "Christ, Ella. It still is." He grips me harder. Dictates the rhythm of our bodies, making my slit ride his shaft at a torturously slow pace. But I do not fight him. The effort would get me nowhere. I concentrate instead on the power beneath his movements...the strength, like twisted steel, of his solid will, his corded body. I let it flow through me too, the physical high becoming a spiritual rush, rocketing my mind and soul as it twists into every fiber of my clenching, convulsing sex. "You change my atmosphere, sorceress. You *are* my atmosphere."

His words pull tears to my eyes. Bring my face around so I can suck in breaths that are filled with his too. We gasp and hover and tease, the inches between our mouths like the anticipation between our bodies. I am heavy against him... around him. Mewling as he lifts me a little higher, working the edges of my entrance against his hot tip. Gasping as he teases back, shuttling through my wet folds instead. Dear powers that be, how can he keep doing this? Where is his self-control coming from? When the man is determined, even horse-strength painkillers cannot keep him down. Literally.

I angle back a little. Splay fingers through his stubble, bracing the elegant line of his cheek before rasping, "I love you so much, Cassian."

His smile transforms into something different. An expression I cannot identify nor remember ever seeing on his face before. It is...vehement. Almost violent. It terrifies me. Penetrates me.

Right before his body does.

I cry out, stretched and blazed and full of him. Every nerve

ANGEL PAYNE

of my intimate channel is turned into throbbing, thundering sensation—and then dissolved into nothing as he pierces more than just my sex. He permeates my being. Ravages every inhibition and fear, splitting me open, burned alive from the inside out.

"*Faisi vive Créacu!*"

"Ella. *Fuck.*"

"Yes." It is all I can blurt in English now, unable to wrap my mind around the extra step of translation. I let the stream of Arcadian come, gasping words both flirty and filthy against his lips as he digs fingers into my waist, forcing my flesh to take more of his. He is so deep. So huge. So hot and perfect inside me. "Yes!"

"Maybe this is the secret *I'll* spill to Chantal tomorrow." His gaze is as sultry as his voice. "You think I should tell everyone how wet this cunt gets for me? How tight these walls grip my cock, milking the come straight up from my balls?"

I gasp and throw my head back, letting him trail the words down my neck, into the valley between my exposed, erect breasts. The cocksure *bonsun*. He does not mean a word of the threat but knows just the idea of it makes me hotter and wetter for him by the minute. And Creator's toes, how I love every word he uses to phrase it.

"Should I tell everyone in that studio how you like to whimper for me, Ella? How sweet your tits get when you do? How they harden exactly like your clit as you beg me more and more for completion?"

"*Cassian.*" His litany has turned me delirious and wanton. I readily obey the furious pace he sets now, pumping up and down his incredible shaft, rejoicing in the clench of his jaw and the darkness in his eyes, blatant betrayals of how he will not be

173

able to hold on much longer either.

"Good girl." He flashes his teeth, lending a new layer to my arousal. He looks hungry. *Starving.* "My sweet, good girl. Beg me for it, armeau. Beg me to give it to you."

"Yes," I gasp. "I—I need it, Cassian. Hard and deep and—" I whine, unable to find the English anymore. "*Ardui,*" I plead. "*Faisi-bana-ardu. Joula-bana. Plait.* Plait!"

His lips peel back with a full snarl. "God*damn.* Yeah." Though unintentional, my native words set his beast even more free—to the point that he flips me over, pinning me to the mattress like a lion taking down its prey. With more wild intent, he throws both my knees over his shoulders. Nearly doubles my body back on itself as he fucks into me with long, savage, stabs of his full, beautiful cock.

So

good.

So

perfect.

"Ah!" I slam my head back once more. Flail my coiled fists into the padded headboard, letting them pound with every new, deep thrust of his magnificent body. "I'm...I'm going to..."

The scythe swoops down. I am cut deep, exposed and raw, open and orgasming—laid completely bare to the gaze, leonine and green, tearing over every inch of my face as the beautiful heat pulls me over, again and again. His stare devours me, gorging on the meat of my spasms, lapping the blood of my screams—

Until he is vanquished too.

As the blade sinks fully into him, he lunges and then stills. Our stares latch to each other as his cock expands and then spills, soaking me with the hot flood of his climax.

"Ella," he grits. "God*damn*."

"Yes," I whisper back.

"Take it." His hands brace my buttocks. Hold me in place as he continues coming. "All of it."

"Yes!"

He keeps emptying into me—and as he does, more than just my body clenches. My heart tightens, pushing at the walls of my chest, as I recognize an inescapable truth in the colliding green shards of his gaze. It is more than just his seed inside me. It is *him*...

As I am poured into him too.

More than just joined with him.

Filled by him.

More than simply in love with him.

Entwined with him.

And in an instant, I know why he didn't echo my declaration—why his gaze turned so strangely severe before he entered me. His soul already knew what mine has just caught up to. This is more than just "chemistry" or even the "love" we tried to honor it with.

This is an earthquake. A flood. A forest fire. An upheaval, altering the landscapes of our lives forever...

Backing my mind into one terrible, inescapable corner of conflict.

Our contract did not say forever.

So what, in Creator's name, do we do now?

CASSIAN

What the hell do we do now?

As hard as I try, the mute button on the question won't

stick—even after I've gotten towels to clean us up and then settled back to the pillows with her face tucked to my chest and our legs a tight tangle. Like a summer night after fireworks, the air in the room is blatantly quiet but prickled with expectancy. I savor both. Revel in *her*, damp and naked and soft against me...

And know, with every neuron in my brain and instinct in my spirit, that four more months will not purge this woman out of my system.

Four more *years*?

Drop in the bucket.

Four *decades*?

What the hell would that even look like? Feel like? I'd be almost seventy...

And burning just as much to sink my dick into her whenever I could. Living for the high, sweet cries she sets free, right before climaxing. Waiting for the perfect flutters of her cunt, clutching me as I fuck her to completion. Kissing her hard in order to open her eyes so I can watch her orgasm wash through them—and seeing myself reflected in the blue-diamond depths that mesmerized me the first moment we touched...

Wake up, dumbshit.

All the hearts and flowers and true love aside, you two haven't discussed a fucking thing past the end of the contract. Technically, she still owes you four more months of her ass in this city—and nothing more. After that, she won't just be down the hall or in the next room. All your amazing sexual chemistry aside, she's been promised she gets to go home—and then begin a life without *her worth being tied to a man. Yeah, even one she's in love with.*

Love.

Shit.

Is *that* what we're still calling it?

I'm afraid to ponder the answer to that—especially because the *first* part wasn't part of my own plan, either. Correction: *Plan*, capital *P*. The master strategy that has been my keel for almost five years, unwavering in guiding me toward every single hallmark of my success...

Success.

What the hell does *that* even mean right now? The goals I've always been so sure of—the stability, the respect, the power, the domination—all seem like shadows through rice paper. Fuzzy...and fragile.

So what the fuck do I do now?

What is real *anymore*?

"Hey."

The musical whisper tickles my chest, clanging me free from the dark meadows of my mind. I hum in soft gratitude before dipping a kiss onto Ella's forehead. "Hey."

"You all right?"

Snort. "Pretty sure that's my line, woman." I stroke into the dip of her waist—ordering my cock to stand down when observing the dark marks persisting on the silk of her skin. "After treating you like my caveman rag doll..."

She turns her face up, doing that delectable lip-biting thing. "In case you did not notice, the doll did *not* mind."

I let her make her way up, accepting the full pressure of her lips, letting her velvet tongue have its juicy way with mine for a long, wet kiss. *Fuck.* At once, my blood turns up the tempo on the drum machine, and I'm ready to show the doll how I want to keep time again.

"Ahhh Christ, armeau." With a dark moan, I brace her shoulders and set her back. "Any more of that, and you'll have me bargaining with God for an early Christmas."

"Christmas?" Her nose crunches. *So fucking adorable.* "Whatever for?"

I lift a lazy grin. "Because boys get to play all day with their toys on Christmas."

She flashes a mock glare. "Well, not on Arcadia."

I return a real one. "Bunch of buzz kills."

"We call it the Holiday. There are still decorations and toys for the children, and lavish parties given at the central villa of every region, with the biggest at the palais in Sancti— but during those celebrations, the children are expected to give back to their communities in some way. Many participate in plays or musical performances. Some paint ornaments that are displayed on the trees. Groups of the older children form teams and go out into their towns to help clear trails or maintain the natural forests and beaches."

"And what did you do?" I ask it quietly while finger-combing her hair with slow strokes.

She gives her bell-like laugh before teasing, "What do you think?"

I smirk. "Why can I readily imagine you in an elf's hat, with a hundred different organizational journals in your cute little hands?"

Her brows dance. "My Holiday journals were the rage. You should have seen them..."

"I can only imagine." I keep the laugh from it, unwilling to mar even one nuance of her glow. My nobility earns me a tighter twist in my gut. *Hell.* Watching her speak about Arcadia, with pride and affection brightening her eyes more by the second, only clarifies how much she likely longs to return already. Despite her parents' obsessive ambition, she has forged a meaningful life there. A vocation. A future.

But you can give her a future here.

Oh yeah? Doing what? Being *what?*

My girlfriend? My convenient little toy?

And how long will *that* last?

She can go to school. Get a dozen degrees in whatever subjects she wants. She's already obscenely smarter than half the college graduates I have met in the Court Enterprises HR department. Student visas are easy enough to renew, so she can stay as long as she wants—

No.

She can stay as long as you *want.*

And after it was all said and done, where the fuck would it get us?

Because as full as she fills my soul, there is no room for her in my life. There's no room for *anyone,* goddammit. The keel is balanced just fine without it. *I'm doing just fucking fine.*

"Cassian?"

"Hmmm?" I issue the answer at once. Her prompt hasn't startled this time; every awareness in my system has kept totally attuned to her. Treasuring every fucking second with her.

"What is it?"

I don't answer right away. I *do* wait for the better part of a minute, letting the beat of the rain inject some needed peace to my thoughts—and libido. "Just calming the beastie," I finally reply.

"So *now* we are all right with 'beastie'?"

"Perhaps." I buss her nose. "The cute and castration might have its purpose...in *this* case."

She retaliates by biting *my* nose. "Dare I ask what case might that be?"

"The case where I try to hold off from fucking you again."

"Oh." Biting still looks like her plan—in different ways. "But...where's the fun in that?"

Sure enough, she starts to undulate with purpose. As her elegant curves entice me in about a hundred new ways, she starts sliding a hand down my chest. Trails the notch bisecting my abs. Slips beneath the sheet, which is already a fucking party tent with a main pole that's all too happy about her approach...

Before she's halted. By my resolved clamp of a grip.

Determination I *almost* lose when she girl-growls with sexy-as-fuck force. Follows it with a kittenish snort. "Buzz kill."

I work to mellow her ire by pulling her wrist up to my lips. "Believe me, favori, the master of ceremonies will be just as ready for the show in a few minutes." I bask in the laugh, however reluctant, that earns me from her. Lower another kiss to her, this time with soft thoroughness, before letting my chest rise and fall on a long breath. "Right now...I think we need to talk."

Shit.

I really just went there.

And brace myself for the fallout.

Sheltered island girl or not, no way has the woman hung out with Kate Robbe a dozen times and not been educated about the importance of *we need to talk*. That truth is confirmed in the tiny knit of her brow before she pushes up and murmurs, "All right."

Like a lot of women in her place, she sets her chin bravely. But unlike a lot of those women, the stress over her eyes dissolves while its focus steadies. For a moment, I allow myself to be floored by that. Despite the anxiety she's learned from Kate, she's clearly chosen to listen to *me* first. To know that if I was going to "talk" with her like *that*, it wouldn't be with her thigh snuggled on my cock, her breasts pillowed against my chest, and a lot of my come still warm in her body.

After another deep breath, I decide to just dive in. "I think we should talk about last night."

Ella folds her hands atop my left pec. Rests her chin on them with a look that's damn near impish. "Before or after you ensured I would never look at the back of the bedroom door the same way again?"

I grunt while twirling her hair around a finger. Brilliant shades of sienna and strawberry flow across my skin, even in the room's watercolor light. "Well, get used to it—because you're moving back in here." I tug on the strand, mandating she pay even closer attention. "I'll not spend another night apart from you." Press my lips hard, debating about adding the rest. "We've wasted too much time already."

Debate over. For better or for worse.

At first, goddammit, it really feels like the latter. My chest knots as her whole face tightens and a grimace pushes at her skin like a swimmer trapped beneath ice.

She is everything except my ice.

Everything that has brought the sun back to my world.

The innocence I'd written off as lost. A wonderment I might have never had. And a fire, in my body and in my heart, I never knew I *could* have...

I need to tell her.

My sweet armeau...how do I even begin to tell you?

At the very least, I can get out what was on the original

agenda—yeah, from just five minutes ago—before she *had* to mention that heaven of penetrating her in two places at once. I've had less cataclysmic distractions, of course. Shit like hurricanes and emergency plane landings.

"Deal," she finally replies—attempting to bring her game face with a finishing smile. It climbs nowhere near her eyes, and I blame myself. Mentioning our ticking time clock was a moron-level call. "I shall be happy to be your roomie again."

I trail fingers to her face, making sure she feels the happiness in my touch. Press them in a little before pressing on. "Then you need to know that last night...how I behaved after we were together..."

She compels me to stop by forming her hand over mine. Pushes her cheek against our twined fingers. "Last night...was completely okay, Cassian."

I twist free from the hold. Straighten against the headboard. "You're *okay* with what happened?" She might as well have said two plus two equals sixteen. She couldn't have been "okay" with that bullshit. Someone like Amelie Hampton would be "okay" with it—because a bitch like that wouldn't have really cared in the first place. Because nobody, in a very long time, *has* cared...

Holy shit.

By punching out the damn shower, did I also cross the line of Mishella's patience? Is she letting me off the hook because she's too fed up to even *extend* the hook?

Christ. That makes as much sense as my warped mental bookkeeping. "Fed up" usually doesn't come with a suggestion to appear on national TV together—or to seal the deal by "rehearsing" with your cock between her legs.

You're getting as irrational as a girl, dammit. Pull it together and think.

That's the moment I look at her.

Really look.

And snap together the sweet understanding in her voice with the new, somber cast of her gaze. And here I was, thinking her eyes had darkened because of the twilight-tinged rain...

"Shit." I hiss it slowly through my teeth. It's not the damn rain.

"Do not be upset," she counters. "I was concerned. I did not know where you were or what you were doing. Your mother—"

"Just took it upon herself to spill the once-upon-a-time about Damon?"

"Since she thought it might explain why you drove your fist through a glass door instead of *talking* to me about it?" She jerks up, taking a swath of the sheet with her. "Then your answer is *yes*, Cassian—she thought 'spilling' was likely a good call."

I push up as well. Jack my head against the headboard, elevating my sight line enough to glare down my nose. "So you two had a nice little 'girl chat' about it all?"

Her nostrils flare. "'It *all*?'" She pulls up higher, canceling my advantage—which wasn't working anyway. "I did *not* share that you had left me naked and dazed in the very spot in which you just fucked me, if that is your insinuation." Yeah; *really* not working. "I *did* tell her that I was confused and concerned—and knew you were hurting because of something beyond what happened to Lily and your baby."

She concludes it with a rough breath, seeming to comprehend what a fucked-up mess it all is, now gathered together and spoken aloud. Her ire gives way to a stare that nearly implores—and impacts me like a hydrogen bomb.

With just as blinding a force, it explodes—and rains self-incrimination on me.

"Dammit, Ella." I reach for her. Not necessary. She's already on her way, face softening right before her body does, molding back against me...bringing the sun again.

"I'm sorry," I mutter into her hair. "You shouldn't have had to hear it from my mother."

She sighs against my chest. "But it is her story to tell too."

"Not if it rips her apart to tell it." I tug on her leg, fitting her tighter to me, and thank her for it by running soft fingertips along the crest of her thigh. "Having to talk about the loss of one's child..." Before I can help it, my hand stops. My fingers claw into her skin, directly proportionate to the sting behind both eyes. "Ah. *Fuck.*"

"Ssshhh." Her own fingers curl into my hair. Yank down my head until she can press my lips to the soft, warm comfort of hers. "Sssshhh. You have already been through that fire, all right?" Her fingers trace the tops of my eyebrows. "Is it any wonder you did not wish to do it a second time in the same night?"

I jerk back by a couple of inches. Palm the firm curve of her nape. "So you get it? I'm forgiven?"

"There is nothing to forgive, Cassian." Her tawny brows hunch in. "Your psyche tipped to overload, and you reacted the only way you have ever given yourself permission to, probably since the day Damon died. You ran and hid and then lashed out at something inanimate and painful." The brows arch up as she tips her head, gaze so clear it's like getting sliced by a pair of blue diamonds. "I wager there are still a few walls at your school and old apartments bearing a certain boy's fist imprint."

"Well, shit."

I grumble it after searching her stare again...truly wondering about the cutting diamonds. At the same time, she sets free a soft giggle.

"I am that right with the honey?"

"Right on the money." I yank her in for a quick kiss. "But yeah, you—*shit*." It bears repeating. Big-time. "You didn't tell Mom that part, did you?"

Her lips purse. "Only because I did not connect it until now."

"Good."

"She is your mother, Cassian. She likely knows."

I scowl harder. "You're probably right...dammit."

She soothes me with another small kiss—though the buss isn't enough. I spread my fingers into her hair while wrapping my bandaged hand around her waist, tangling our tongues and lips into a deeper, hotter connection before descending back to the pillows with her in tow. As the rain falls harder, we kiss and devour, taste and lick, adore and appreciate, until there's no air and we end up breathing the essence of each other...

The only air I need.

Several mind-blowing minutes later, she drags up and away, her lower lip caught beneath a smile that says she clearly questions her sanity in letting me go for even a few inches. I grin back, arrogant as fuck about the observation. And humble as hell.

A nuance that does *not* go unnoticed by *her*.

Tracing a deceptively casual line down the center of my chest, she releases her lip and raises her chin. "Cassian Cameron Jonathan..."

"Yyeesss, Mishella DaLysse?"

Somehow, she accepts the ribbing but maintains her

earnest authority. Her chin doesn't waver and is joined in the effort by a firmer set of her shoulders. She has no idea how the plan may backfire on her—how even her shoulders are enough to get me hard, especially when their golden angles are set as if her cleavage disappears into a satin ball gown instead of my chest.

I wrestle my gaze up to her face.

"I need you to think about something for me." Regal training or not, her tongue sneaks out to nervously wet her lips. *Goddammit.* So much for the refocus. "Just—just *think* about it, all right?"

I narrow my gaze. Consider the option of diffusing her effort once more with something in the key of smartass, but the seriousness is like a damn aura around her now. "You already know I will."

Her tongue retreats. From the set of her lips, it looks fitted to the back of her top teeth, giving her a look of determination I'm only used to confronting from opponents on the other side of conference negotiation tables. Only not with those shoulders—or that cleavage.

"The next time things like this surge inside of you..." She reaches for my bandaged hand. "Do not go punch a wall." Her fingers curve in, meshing with the exposed tips of my own. "*Or* a shower door."

I hook my forefinger in, latching it with hers. Give her a little finger shake of commitment. "I won't. I promise."

She doesn't let me go. "That's not all of it."

"Hell."

"*Listen* to me, Cassian. You cannot heft the world on your shoulders!" She dips her head because I do. "Though they are very *nice* shoulders, that is not the purpose for which they were designed."

"Whoa." I was right in saving the smartass. *Much* better here. "Are you slingin' bullshit on this barbecue, because *I* thought—"

"I know what you *thought*." She clearly doesn't enjoy the colorful visual. "But that is not we are discussing here."

"Ah." I drag it into a knowing drawl. "I suppose it's about *feelings*. Is that it?"

A huff rushes from her—as she sits up again, taking the damn sheet with her once more. Not that I'm complaining. Never in my life have I thanked myself more for spending insane money on imported Italian sheets. She has no idea that her areolas and nipples show perfectly through the diaphanous fabric—a view nearly as perfect as her nude flesh.

But not half as amazing as the sight of her untamed arousal.

Or a dose of her unreserved laughter.

Or a hit of her unpretentious honesty.

Or a slam of her unrestricted love.

Christ. All the ways this woman has filled my life...by stripping so much of it away. And dammit, like the naked emperor, I just want to strut around in more.

Enough to arrive at a decision so sudden, it's bewildering. But so right, it's terrifying. And exhilarating. And exonerating. A burden I haven't been able to shirk, the size of the damn globe she just accused me of toting, even after taking her to the turret and visiting Damon's grave...

But now, the weight is gone.

No.

Nearly gone.

"Mishella." I offer it now with no sarcasm or smirking, knowing she'll already hear the apology in it. What I don't expect her to hear—or to understand, since I'm as unnerved by it myself—is the husk roped around my tone. The guttural, practically critical, need...

"Y-Yes, Cassian?"

"I'll agree to give your suggestion some thought"—who the *hell* shoved two packs of cigarettes down my throat and lit them all at once?—"if you'll agree to consider one of mine in return."

A smile trembles across her lips. Just bringing her that small joy is worth the nicotine growl and the growing boulder in my gut. "You have a *suggestion*?" She even seems excited by that, making the boulder more a doorstop. "Well then...that sounds fair."

I fold my hands. Center them in my lap. It's the only way I'll keep from reaching to her and swaying her decision with the force of a kiss. It would be so damn easy—and so damn enjoyable...

"I'd like you to reconsider the terms of our contract."

The twinkle in her eyes dims. "The...the terms?" Her nose crinkles. "Which ones?"

Fuck it. I pull her back. Kiss her quickly but deeply. "Only one," I clarify. "The one about the length of your stay."

Her perplexity persists. "You...you do not wish for me to stay for six months?"

"No. I want you to stay longer."

CHAPTER TEN

MISHELLA

Heavy swallow. Another.

I dare any other woman in the building to react differently to the sight in front of me. By the looks of things, nobody will be taking me up on that. My caveman, newly transformed into a prince, has heated every drop of estrogen in the TGN studios to one status. Full boil. Yet as Cassian leads me down the hall to our private green room to await our call time to the set, elegant strides emphasized by the bespoke lines of his suit, he is as gracious as if he owns the whole bloody network—a gorgeous royal warmly greeting his subjects.

I have never been more proud to be on his arm.

Meaning I have never been more conflicted about what he proposed last night.

It is not easy to conceal the dilemma from my face, reflected by the little scowl on his once we are seated and offered coffee and pastries. We both decline everything except water, though the young production assistant hovers to double-check that a dozen more times. She swings her ponytail, taps on her smart pad, and fiddles with her headset, channeling the estrogen boil into looking efficient and in-charge.

The second she finally flits away, Cassian sinks back, settling his neck over the back of the loveseat in order to preserve the light makeup to which he's subjected himself for this. At the new angle, the bold perfection of his jaw and cheekbones are accentuated. The room's recessed lights capture the bronze tints in his lashes and the demigod gold in his hair, now slicked and styled so the ends curl deliciously around his ears. So classic and regal and beautiful...

And yours.

For even longer now...if you choose.

And why have I even hesitated about it?

I battle the all-too-clear answer to that...blaring straight up from my heart.

Because the time limit meant boundaries on other things too. Like hope and possibility—but also pain and disappointment.

Creator's mercy.

The man cannot stop turning my life into a jumble of utter confusion.

"Holy fuck." His mutter is aggravated but adorable, yanking me away from the brood. Gratefully, I indulge a giggle behind my hand. He captures my fingers as I lower them, using them to pull me a little closer. "If she asked one more time if I was comfortable..."

"Because you were making her anything but?"

"I was *nice.*"

"Yes, you were."

"So...that was a problem?"

Hiding my laugh is not even a choice now. I shake my head, careful not to smudge him with the goop they have piled on my own face. "Is the 'prince of passion' really asking me that?"

He grunts. "Well, the 'prince' is done with cruising the kingdom."

ANGEL PAYNE

"For now."

I lob it softly, threading in some humor just in case he has only ditched the Neanderthal bear on the outside. Sure enough, a low snarl prowls from his throat before he grits a reply.

"No, Ella. He's done for *good.*"

My chest immediately flips—only to fumble when my heart refuses to join the celebration. Because it is *not* one. His answer is as hazy as his proposition was—and is followed by no more explanation than what he gave then.

Well...*didn't* give.

"You—you want me to stay? Here in New York? Longer?"

"Yeah."

"How—how much longer?"

"I don't know, Ella."

"And do what here? Be what to you here?"

"I don't know the answer to that, either. I only know I fucking hate the idea of you leaving in October. I—I hate the idea of you leaving at all."

"But you cannot define what it would be like if I stayed."

"I can't define what it's like right now, let alone what it will be then. But I want us to find out...together."

"And that is what you want me to keep putting my life on hold for?"

"It's what I want you to believe in...possibly as a new life. To take a risk for. Just like I'm doing."

"By staying in your city—with your home, your business, and your family near?"

"That's unfair."

"More unfair than asking me to jump into a bottomless ocean?"

"Isn't that what love is? Dammit, I love you."

"And I love you. So much."

"So what's wrong? Why are you crying?"

"Oh, Cassian. Do you not see?"

"See what?"

"I do not want the whole ocean. I want the rock in the middle of it."

His eyes, now as tumultuous as a storm on that sea, betray how he replays the memory too. He drags in a heavy breath. Parts his lips as if to say something. With teeth locking visibly, forces it back.

My throat tightens. Clamps even tighter, gripped by defeat. *You cannot heft the world on your shoulders, Cassian.*

But am I not committing the exact same crime? Tamping down my burden and hiding it from him?

Time for the buttercup to truly suck it up.

"Cassian."

"Yeah?"

"You...are already my rock."

His hand twists tighter around mine. He lifts my knuckles to his lips—as the storm rages on in his eyes.

"I know."

He does not lower his gaze from mine, even when I know he must see what I need to say next—and do.

"Do you think—" Why is this so frightening, when bare honesty has always been our ultimate strength? "Well...could I ever be...yours too?"

He inhales hard once more. And just as he saw the words of my heart, I see the confession—and the confusion—of his.

"Climbing on rocks has always gotten me drowned, Ella."

Well.

Okay.

I think I get that whispered, despite the emotion closing like a noose in my throat. I can repay him with no less, after what he has clearly peeled back inside to surrender it to me.

Cassian.

You beautiful, stubborn, amazing, prideful, complex creature.

My rock? The description is laughable now—considering that the man sees himself as a whole bloody cliff. No. He does not "see" it. He demands it of himself. He is the shelter for his mother, the foundation for his empire, the crypt for his ghosts, and now even the strength for me—but never, *ever* will he see the chipped monolith needing extra support—sometimes even sanity—from leaning on another.

Will the mountain ever change?

Let himself be moved by the sea?

I do not hide those questions from him, either. Bare them to him, along with the corners of my soul that ask them, as our stares continue to mesh. Watch him absorb my honesty, wrestling with it in the darkness of his own psyche, before dropping his head to smash desperate lips to my skin again—this time, opening my palm for his kiss. My truth is not so rough to hide now. I let him see it all: the stars in my blood, the lightning in my skin, the quivers in my muscles...yes, even down there.

Especially there...

"Fuck." It is the barest grate from Cassian's lips.

"No shit." My slang makes us both chuckle, relieving our tension a little. Though Cassian sits up again, he remains all relaxed sexiness while looping an arm around my shoulders to keep me close.

"Thank you," he murmurs, drawing my arm across his lap and flowing his fingertips between my wrist and elbow.

I tilt my head up, full scowl in place. "Whatever for?" Replaying the morning so far only brings up my frantic indecision about the perfect shoes to match my Victoria Beckham sheath, our crawl to the studio in rush-hour traffic, and then forcing him to revisit the ocean of our emotional issues...

"For being brave enough to propose we do this. For finding the guts not to back down, no matter how many times you thought about it between yesterday and today. For making me so goddamn proud to walk in here with you on my arm." He dips his head, lining up his gaze directly with mine. His gaze, alive as spring yet sexy as summer, sweeps over my face as if fearing I shall disappear any moment. "For having a heart, a soul, and a spirit as wondrous as the beauty that first took my breath away."

Breath turned to nothing.

Awareness expanded to everything.

Heartbeats given wings, soaring and dizzy as a gull on the wind, as I return the unblinking intensity of his stare and wonder how in the world fate picked me to be blessed by this perfection of a man. I have racked my mind but cannot recall any deed from my childhood so miraculous to have earned the miracle of him. Perhaps I saved a hundred souls in my previous life. And the one before that. And the one before that. Cassian Court is the grand reward on my karma punch card.

Thank you, Creator on High. Thank you for him and all that he is. For all the good he chooses to see in me, and—

"Holy. *Shit*." I am fairly certain the Creator will forgive the interruption. If not, the complaint will need to be lodged personally with Cassian, for I am certainly not handling the task. I am not even capable of *beginning* it—not with the clog of sheer shock in my throat and the diamonds dazzling my vision.

As in, *diamonds.*

The cuff bracelet is formed of eight perfect rows of them, like stars captured and linked together. The effect is nothing short of eye-popping, a term I can absolutely assign to myself as Cassian pulls the piece all the way out of his jacket pocket. My breath shudders in and out as he pulls my wrist forward and then slips it on. It presses against my skin, almost a living thing in its decadent, extravagant knowingness. *You have never known anything like me. You are wet just from the feel of me.*

"Cassian. By the *Creator.*"

He lifts my arm. The diamonds catch the light, spraying crystalline specks around the room. "Doesn't compare to the woman wearing it—but now everyone watching this thing is going to know who she belongs to."

I refrain from pointing out the obvious—that the adoration in his eyes is enough for me and obvious to everyone else—choosing instead to indulge a moment of silly, girlish glee. "It is..."

"Dazzling," he murmurs. "Like you." His hand continues up my arm, trailing over the thin edge of black lace defining the cap sleeve of my dress. "And styled in an infinite circle... like my love."

Well, that seals it. I have certainly cashed out the karma punch card from the last *five* lives—as well as the five to follow.

The private sarcasm does nothing to help the emotions welling up around it and then punching through it. My head falls, dragged by the incredible weight of them, and I blink against the mist that turns the edges of my vision soggy. The jewels are dimmed because of it too—but the bracelet, for all its glory, could be a chain of daisies and gum wrappers for all I care.

The real treasure he has given me are his words. His honesty.

His willingness to try.

And if he is willing to try...

maybe I can too.

"Cassian..." It is just a rasp, but in the inches between our bowed heads, it is enough.

He lifts his head a fraction of a second before me. His gaze is bright, expectant. "Yeah?"

I lift a hand. Press it to the side of his face. Curl a watery smile as the light fractures once more off the bracelet, raining prisms over the hills of his lips, the nobility of his nose, the high plane of his forehead.

I am going to try for him.

I am going to stay for him.

And I am going to plunge through the fire of my fear and trepidation now—and tell him exactly that.

"Mr. Court!"

For a moment, I am sure the production assistant has kicked the door down. When the portal still swings on its hinges, switch to wondering where the fire must be—before she beams a grin as perky as her ponytail and spreads one hand up.

"What?" Cassian stands so swiftly, it is clear he wants to bite off something more than the word.

"Five minutes," the girl replies, cheerfully oblivious. "Are you ready?"

"Of course." When the girl continues hovering, he adds a

new snarl. "We'll be right there."

"Errrmm." She lowers the hand. Taps it nervously on her radio pack. "I'm supposed to bring you back to set *with* me..."

"Cassian." I stand and tug at his elbow. "It can wait."

"No"—a snap of movement, pulling me away and then blocking out the PA with his back—"it can't."

"But Chantal—"

"Can fill if she has to."

"And *that* is getting on her good side?"

"I'm already on her good side by agreeing to this in the first place." He presses closer, looping hands at both my elbows but wrapping my whole body with the force of his urgent attention. "Armeau. Let's finish this. Please."

I am helpless in his thrall. While my body responds to his pull from head to toe, my heart is captivated by his dog-with-a-bone need. "*Finish* it?" I cannot siphon the tease from my lips or my tone. "But we are only getting started."

The dog regresses into a puppy—bursting its way into his broad grin and his hard, thorough kiss. "Damn right we are."

As he scoops up my hand and leads the way to the studio, my heart leaps, ebullient and dazzled—and resolved to simply enjoy the moment before picking through the details of the future. For right now, the dangerous lion and the eager puppy are playing nicely...

And for right now, that is enough.

CASSIAN

Okay...I've had enough.

The impatience usually itches at me between the five and six-minute mark during on-camera interviews—but today, it's taken only half that time. Doesn't come as one speck of a shock, despite the fact that I'm actually enjoying myself.

No. "Enjoyment" isn't right.

I "enjoy" things like staff meetings, phone calls from Mom, and lurking at classic car shows with Hodge and Scott. Hell, I've even "enjoyed" a few interviews in the past—a *very* few—with those rare reporters who've seen me as more than a ratings spike or an inroad to a new scandal.

This is...something wholly different. A satisfaction I've never experienced before...bound to a matching rush of restlessness. The inexplicable wonder of watching my sorceress win a new convert to her fandom—while fighting my very definable urges for her.

Definable—to the point of pain.

Don't talk to the cock. Don't *talk to the cock.*

Right. Because ignoring the big guy on the playground is going to make him go away? Forgetting he's counting the goddamn minutes until you have Ella against your bedroom door again, dressed in nothing but that bracelet and her desire? Who the hell says you'll even make it back to Temptation? Why not order Scott to take the long way home—say, via Canada—and fuck her into three orgasms before you hit the border?

Yessss. Perfect...

Laughter stabs—and shatters—my fantasy. For the first time in my life, I'm actually grateful that Chantal Dunne giggles like a constipated parakeet. The outburst has saved my hard-on from being screenshotted across the world—at least for now.

The woman leans over and gazes as if Ella has just relayed a viable action plan for world peace. "So he really just slipped on the bathroom tile...and tumbled that hard into the shower door?"

Mishella dips her head, countering with a little laugh of her own. The actions seem authentic because they *are*. Not a word of what she's said to Chantal in the last five minutes is a lie; she's simply guided the reporter toward specific facts, letting her reach distinct conclusions—painting me mostly as a sex-obsessed Neanderthal.

Leading back to the whole I'm-enjoying-this-but-not-really thing.

Surprise fucking surprise. When it comes to Mishella Santelle, I *am* a sex-obsessed Neanderthal.

"Well..." She only enforces the point by tucking her lip under her teeth, funneling my attention back on her—more specifically, on that plush mouth of hers—in deliriously uncomfortable ways. "You know what they say about the power of forward momentum..."

"Oh, gawd!" The woman's screech tears the air again. "Well, I certainly *do*!"

Ella bats her eyes and pretends to hide a blush. It's a textbook just-between-us-girls move, and she pulls it off so gorgeously, half the guys in the studio clearly consider changing genders. "Well, just imagine that kind of...*thrust*...if thrown off-balance by certain...occurrences..."

"Oh, *no*!"

"Oh, yes." Ella meshes her laughter with Chantal's, though angles back toward me. She lays a protective hand over the bandages she helped me change this morning, adding a playful but gentle glance—sealing the deal on her subtle mastery of Chantal's narrative. *Those are all the details you get, missy. Now let my man and me have a little moment.*

To make the point clear, she coaxes my face down for a tender kiss—making sure to use the arm with her new bracelet on it. *Adorable minx.* I let my stare linger, imagining there's a matching cuff on the other arm and I'm about to hook them to an eyebolt—in the headboard of my bed.

Dear fuck.

I'm not a goddamned prude, by any stretch of the imagination—but balancing hard work with hard play has always been about exchanging pleasure with a woman, nothing more. *Absolutely* nothing more.

But *this* woman makes me want...

crave...

more.

Much more.

Her.

Belonging to me.

Controlled by me.

Needing me.

Begging me...

And, yeah. I'm actually thinking all this on national TV.

So maybe it's good that constipated parakeets exist—and have struck up a secret licensing deal with Chantal Dunne.

Three seconds more, and this moment would have been one for a million screen capture keys across the internet. The reporter saves me again, tossing her head back on the laughter while recentering herself in the hostess chair that's been custom-designed for her coloring, arm span, and leg extension. But as she braces elbows to both armrests and prepares to pivot off the juicy angle Ella's just gifted to her, my guard remains up. Way up. Chantal Dunne wants her Tweet-able, meme-able, screen capture-able moment. If it's not going to be the bulge in my crotch, she'll get it another way.

"Well, haven't you two little love bugs given us quite the juicy visuals this morning?"

Love bugs?

Ella slides her hand down from my face in order to rest it beneath her own chin, managing innocent and impish in the same sweep of a pose. A matching gleam forms in her eyes, reminding me of fairies—but not the cute twinkly kind. "Why Miss Dunne, you already *had* the juice after paying off half of New York to chronicle our first ten dates—including shots of this beautiful man in black tie, yachting whites, *and* Pikachu yellow." The evidence of her claim comes to life on the live feed monitors, with all the sneak photos of us once more worked into the broadcast, including the shot of me playing tourist in Times Square next to a Pokémon nearly as tall as me. Sure enough, jammed onto my head is a garish yellow cap with ears that match his. "What we have given you today, Chantal"—and suddenly, my fae sprite is the one angling across the coffee table, gorgeous body poised and huge stare intent—"is a full, delicious smoothie. Size. *Large.*"

Nope. *Not* Tinkerbell.

As the same realization wallops Chantal, freezing her posture and stiffening her smile, I borrow some boardroom techniques to refrain from a gloating grin. The fist bump's a tougher conceal, but the internet—and this show's massive viewer following—don't need to be focused on either. Ella and I are here to be bigger than that game. To *beat* the damn game. To showcase the desperation behind their innuendo, from the overtime on the paparazzi lenses to the "secret sources" in the hospital itself, betraying snippets of our lives that have added up to the giant zilch of their "truth."

But Chantal is nowhere near ready to cry no joy.

And shows us so, transforming her fawn in the headlights into a flying reindeer, tossing back her head on a laugh that's likely been rehearsed a thousand times in order to convey the perfect mix of "surprised humor" and "breezy confidence."

"Ohhh, Mishella. You are *adorable*. Picking up *all* the fun of the language already, hmmm?"

I've started yanking Ella back to my side, giving me the perfect angle for flashing a private but specific look over to Chantal. Fuck it, I glare. Hard. *Careful where you tread, dragon. You haven't begun to see* my *teeth and fire.*

For the edge of a second, the corners of the woman's eyes flinch. Target achieved. The rest of the world doesn't see it, but I don't care about them. I only care that ginger-glam girl knows exactly where her claws can and cannot go, especially as she recrosses her legs and addresses the main camera with practiced precision.

"Don't go far, everyone. We'll be right back with more of your favorite prince in pinstripes, Cassian Court, as well as his fascinating new paramour from exotic Arcadia, who promises to teach us all a little more about her special smoothies. Straws up, kids!"

As soon as the red light dies and someone shouts that the set is clear for a commercial break, the place erupts like an awakened beehive. An assistant checks the water glasses in front of us (still full), while another scurries to check on the tofu recipe specialist who'll be on after us (still ready). Three more hover around Chantal, primping hair and makeup that are already flawless. When one of the stylists approaches Ella, he's batted away like a giant bug. Once more, I hold back from saluting my woman with a fist bump.

My woman.

The certainty of it has never burned more deeply in my psyche than now, just as I've never been prouder to have her on my arm. While the manner in which our truth was dished to the world is still just a half-step away from a sex tape— undoubtedly, there are already a dozen Pikachu caps waiting on my desk as gag gifts—I'm damn glad we've been brought to the table and compelled to recognize the new truths about our "contract." Glad? Yeah, slight misnomer—as would be the horror from anyone on my legal team if they ever learned where I'd really stood when approaching Ella about "new terms" last night.

Funny thing is, I don't fucking care.

She's agreed to give it a try. Just a try—but it's enough, dammit. If she wants to charge me another forty million for that miracle, then so be it.

And yeah, I *am* choosing to call it a miracle. Something exists where it didn't before—I actually *want* to get up every morning—and isn't that what a miracle is?

Come to think of it, I kind of like the afternoons that come after those mornings too. And dear God, the magic into which Ella Santelle has turned all my nights...

The enchantment she has cast over my *life*...

The power she now has over my heart.

It's a recognition with damn shitty timing, because something tells me it's the most evident thing on my face as Chantal Dunne stares up through her lashes, her reindeer now still...and ruthlessly assessing.

Sharpening her antlers.

Someone shouts that we'll be back on the air in thirty seconds.

Chantal smooths her skirt. Swivels back toward us, rearranging the notecards in her lap, plastic smile on her lips. "All righty," she croons. "You two ready for a little more fun?"

Ella settles a little deeper into the crook of my arm. Cuddles there for a second, her smile remaining curved in sugar-sweet sincerity. But in her eyes, something has changed. Blazed to life like a pair of crystals activated by a sorceress's spell—and not one made of bird song and gum drops. Even Chantal recognizes the belladonna cast of it...the stabby things Tinkerbell's been sharpening too.

The things now carving edges to Ella's calm reply. "Something tells me your only idea of 'fun' is torturing puppies, Chantal—and neither Cassian nor I plan on fetching any balls for you. That being said...bring it on."

CHAPTER ELEVEN

MISHELLA

Funny, that a very real thought has struck me in the middle of a fake living room, overlooking a fake city, sipping water that came from fake mountain springs.

Bitches are the same no matter where one journeys in life.

Given a better haircut, a more flattering dress, and a few court etiquette lessons, Chantal Dunne is like every social-climbing *bamboo* of the Arcadian court. The word is not even my innocent idiom mash now. In Arcadia, we have no problem likening idiots to hollow, invasive plants. It has certainly made it easier to handle her, watering her stems with vapid comments that have become easy jumping boards for her own witty banter, though I am certain she considers the roots firmly in place, the plant prepared to bloom.

Cassian squeezes my shoulder. Flashes me a subtle wink. In addition to melting every cell in my blood at once, the moment conveys another important thing. He knows about bamboo too. We are unified. Chantal Dunne and her garden are getting no more fertilizer from us.

"And we're back!" chimes the woman herself, punctuating with a toss-toss of her hair that makes me cringe on behalf of all women with curls, especially me. "Along with more of my exclusive sit-down with Cassian Court and Mishella Santelle, surely the most alluring memento he's ever brought back to New York from his world travels." She beams a teasing look across the coffee table. "Better than a dorky T-shirt, eh, Cas?"

Cas.

I hook both hands around my knees, digging my grip in. I have only ever heard the nickname from Mallory and Kate: his mother and the woman who might as well be his sister. Chantal Dunne has no right even sniffing at that special category—but if she has no right, neither do I. It is Cassian's transgression to correct—and I am glad to see he looks ready to. While pulling in a long sip of the fake mountain stream, he eyes the reporter with an equal pretense of affability.

"Oh, she's far better than a T-shirt, Chantal." He winks again at me. "All my other T-shirts agree, since she looks damn good in them."

"Dear Creator." Until now, I have managed not to blush, despite the hot set lights. He certainly changes that.

"Oooo la la!" Chantal clips her index cards between two fingers in order to join the crew in approving applause. "Somebody has certainly bewitched the playboy!"

Cassian sobers his demeanor. Though setting down the water, he remains angled forward. Palming a knee with his good hand, he impales Chantal with the jade lance of his stare. "Playboy? That implies that I 'play,' Chantal. I've never 'played' with the women I see. Everyone knows where they stand, at all times."

Chantal's riposte worries me from the start. Not a second's worth of awkwardness, like what happened after I called out the slithery tactics of her research team. Her composure remains sleek—nearly as if Cassian has played right into her script.

"So that position applied to Amelie Hampton, as well?"
Or walked into her trap.

Shit. Shit. Shit.

If the same refrain has slammed Cassian, I—and everyone else—are not privy to it. "Of course it applied to Amelie." His brow simply furrows, as if Chantal has questioned whether his suit is custom-tailored or the sky is always blue. "And she was well aware of that."

Chantal dips a bewildered look to her note cards. "That so? Then why did she appear on this very show to claim you 'crushed her like a Mack truck' two months ago, by showing up at the New York Literacy Ball with Mishella instead of her?"

"The event at which she was as drunk as a punk?" I ignore the perplexity on the woman's face. I cannot simply sit back while the woman uses Amelie's sloshed escapades to skewer Cassian. "She had so much, she was able to waste some on the front of my dress—before throwing the glass at Cassian."

"Right before *you* walked out on him, Mishella."

Triumphant razors gleam in the woman's eyes. She rocks back a little, letting me wince through the suicide for which she's gleefully assisted.

And worsens.

"You walked out because Amelie started talking." Her head tilts as she dares going for the "best girlfriends" angle—at least to the viewers' eyes. "And she spilled the truth, the *whole* truth, about what happened to Lily Court."

She pushes forward again.

Just between us, Ella.

Reaches for one of my hands.

You can talk to me, Ella.

"Do. Not. Touch. Me."

I barely get it seethed before the witch leans closer, though any outside observer would interpret her as the compassionate friend to my emotional wreck. "It must have been so much to take in. A first wife with emotional instability and substance-abuse problems. All those trips Lily took to rehab—"

She's sliced into silence by the man who almost lunges across the table at her. "How the hell did you find that out?"

One corner of Chantal's mouth twitches. "Are you denying it?"

"I'm saying that those records are sealed and that someone broke the law giving them to you."

"Because you wanted to hide the extent of Lily's substance abuse?" The smirk is gone from her lips but lives on in her cutting gaze. "Because she was so desperate to stay high, she abused drugs even when pregnant with your child?"

My heart punches to my throat. Sticks there, in the moment Cassian pounds a fist to the table.

"Enough."

His snarl impacts Chantal as nothing more than a breeze. The note cards are coyly set aside. Her upper body slinks forward, calm and knowing as a she-snake. "Maybe you just want to hide the biggest kernel of it," she murmurs. "That the night Lily Court leapt to her death, she was *still* carrying your baby."

CASSIAN

"This interview is over."

My own words thrash the inside of my skull like ravens in a church: dark wings beating at stained glass, fury bashing the illusion of anything civilized and sane.

I watch my numb fingers tear the button of a microphone off my lapel. Next to me, Ella's doing the same thing, though uses the extra two seconds to hiss something down at Chantal. The black thrum in my head doesn't put all of it together until the words are out and the reporter is responding with nothing but a saint-on-stained-glass smile.

"Creator have mercy on your sorry, awful soul!"

As she sucks in breath, gathering strength for a follow-up, I grab at her elbow. Pull hard. The last thing this moment needs is a Tazmanian devil channeled through an Arcadian blonde, ripping things up worse than Chantal Dunne already has.

Chantal Dunne, who now has what *she* showed to work for today.

"Enjoy the glory while it lasts, Miss Dunne." *Your ass as at the center of my dartboard now.*

The thought powers into my steps as Doyle falls into step beside me, seemingly from nowhere, though I know he's just watched every second of what went down from the studio shadows. His cell is already at his ear, and he barks at the party on the other end to hold while he addresses me.

"Legal's been told to put everything else on hold and meet you in the conference room adjacent to your office."

"Good." Still without breaking stride, I scoop a hand to the small of Ella's back and hurry her the direction Doyle leads. Being in this building at all makes my skin fucking crawl; the sooner I can get her out of here, the better.

We rush around a corner into a utilitarian hall, where a stagehand nods at Doyle and then leads us to the freight elevator. It's ready, open, and empty, a detail for which I send D another quick nod of gratitude. Taking the public elevators

209

down to the lobby continuously packed with fans of the TGN shows would be like taking the Virgil express into hell right now. This catastrophe isn't over, not by the furthest stretch of imagination, and I don't allow myself a single delusion about that—or one moment's worth of an unguarded moment. Yeah, that includes even *thinking* about touching Ella more than this. Even the warmth of her hand is a risk, calling to the stupid caveman inside who clamors for an embrace, a kiss, the sweet goddamn nothingness of getting lost inside her...

Anything to help cope with the rage. The frustration. The pain. The self-recrimination.

I'm sorry, Lily. Goddammit, I'm so sorry.

For all the issues she was dealing with and the ways she kept me locked out of them, Lily didn't deserve to have her secrets exposed between commercials for dog food and fabric softener, with a tofu chef demo station waiting in the wings.

We didn't deserve it. Her or me—or our baby.

He'd almost be four by now. A toddler with Transformers and Legos.

Or she. A little princess with star wands...and Legos.

I chuff at my stupid joke.

Then pinch two fingers to my eyes, gritting back the hot sting behind them.

"Fuck." It grates out, as rusty and rough in my throat as the gears lowering us to the basement. "*Fuck.*" Then louder than the collision of the brakes when we arrive, finished by my swing of a punch to the iron wall.

Ella's quiet sob fills the ensuing silence. "Cassian..."

"Not now, Ella."

The door slides open. Scott is waiting with the Jag, even *his* face set in stoic lines. Well, hell. I've never seen the kid ditch his smile, even after Hurricane Sandy took out his parents' place.

Christ on ice. Was every goddamn person in the country watching *People and Places* this morning?

Apparently, yes.

I am the subject of nobody's pity.

Yeah. Fucking great life mantra—

Except for the day I'm the subject of *everyone's* pity.

"Cassian?"

I flinch from Ella's voice. Force myself free from her touch. Like either's going to stop the nightmare from reversing itself—all the disgusting details of Lily's death from being bled all over the tabloid media for the next week.

I need to move. *Have* to move. Be free to attack this clearly.

Be free of needing Ella so near.

Of being weakened by it.

My steps from the lift pound through the garage, punching hard on the cement walls. *Cement. Much better than stained glass.*

One by one, the ravens freeze and then die.

Thank fuck.

By the time I get to Doyle, I'm ready to hand them to him, laid out on the steel platter of my resolve.

"I need to know who's gotten access to Lily's files at both rehab facilities *and* the coroner's office. Do it quickly and quietly. They'll know we're coming but are banking on the legal avenues taking a little time."

Doyle jogs a quick nod. "Already on it."

I snort. "Of course you are."

"Just call me Kato. Or Stud. Doesn't matter."

"All right, *Stud.* Let's talk about alerting Holy Oak

cemetery that the media may be swarming Lily's grave—"

"Done."

"And making sure Nash Quinn is contacted—"

"Call's been placed. He's been in a meeting, but I told his people he needs to call you as soon as he's out."

"And coordinating extra security at the manor?"

"Next on my list."

I clap his shoulder. I know it's the only thanks he ever wants besides his paycheck but can't help my next comment from drawling out.

"At this rate, you're going to get a new truck whether you like it or not."

"May take you up on that, if you keep insisting on borrowing it, chief."

Like the good Kato he is, the keys are out of his pocket and in my hand before the words are done. It's not a move I try to hide, despite knowing the next trigger it'll pull—shooting out a bullet who rocks a cobalt dress and come-fuck-me pumps like no earthly creature has a right to.

Oh, yeah. And rage. She's rocking just a bit of that too.

"You are taking the truck again?"

"Ella—"

"By yourself...*again*?"

Maybe more than just "a bit."

I pocket the keys. Brace both her shoulders in order to guide her a few feet away from Doyle and Scott. She fumes through every step, despite how I show her my deep breath in. Back out.

My devil in a blue dress shuns the nonverbal cues. Matches my determined stance by parking her own feet at shoulder width, fists jammed at her hips.

"Okay," I begin carefully. "Listen—"

"Listen?" She bursts with a bitter laugh. "Are we really right back here, Cassian? At the place where I get to scream that all I *want* to do is listen? To at least *help*?"

"I know—"

"Do you? Or do I need to remind you about the last time we did this, in Bryant Park—and how the evening ended with you in surgery at New York Presbyterian?"

"I *know*, Ella."

"Apparently, you do *not*—because here you are, walling me off again. Walling *yourself* off, after that *salpu* dragged you through some of the most horrific memories of your past."

"Which she's going to pay for." I let my gritted teeth and rigid gaze fill in what my tight tone doesn't. "Which is why I have to get ahead of it right now." My grips matches the determination of hers on its way up to the sides of her neck. "That means avoiding the media three-ring as much as I can."

"And driving off like a damn Rambo, without asking for help or understanding from anyone."

She's softer about that one. Hurt. The realization wrenches more as she lifts her hands to cover mine and the bracelet sends speckles of light across her face—fairy dust for my fae.

"I already know you understand." Reverent kiss to her forehead. "Delivered with a Rambo reference, at that. There's hope for you, woman."

She yanks back. No more magic dust. "*Is* there?"

I give in to three seconds of a grimace. She's right. This is everything I said I wouldn't do—but this is also TGN treading way over the line in the name of ratings pay dirt. We came to be nice in their sandbox, and they played rough and dirty. If bullies are given second chances, they'll hit again—and no way in hell am I risking they'll hurt Ella any more than they have.

Enough is fucking enough.

"I'm asking for help too," I defend. "You *did* hear Doyle's to-do list for the day?"

Doyle cocks a dark brow but stops tapping on his cell. "I *love* it when you give me honey-dos, baby."

Ella, usually charmed by our dry smackdowns even if she doesn't understand them, only tosses a glower at us both. *Dammit.* Chantal's bombshell clearly gutted her as much as me, and I know she needs a rehash and a long, mushy recovery session, but neither long nor mushy will take care of redrawing the boundaries for Chantal Dunne and her team.

Determined exhalation. A quick jerk, to pull Ella farther away with me. One minute. I need her alone and focused for just one minute.

Ladies Room

Perfect.

"Cassian! What—"

I kiss her hard enough to make it clear I want her to back against the wall. Next to her head is a framed publicity shot of all the female TGN "celebrities." One's an "influencer" pulled from the YouTube universe; another's a former cheerleader who published a tell-all about her affair with a quarterback. Two more are B-list pop stars, and next to them is a perkily posed Chantal. They're all dressed in shades of stomach-medicine pink, a complement to wall tiles that have likely been here since the sixties.

I lift her face by nudging my bandaged knuckles beneath her chin. "I'm not 'walling you off,' Ella. Christ..." I shake my head, echoing her acerbic laugh. "Nobody's gone farther *beyond* my walls than you." I dip in, somehow needing to penetrate *her* resistance now. The hurt and doubt across her face...*dammit*... "And believe me, there's a to-do list for *you*, too..."

I get as far as tasting her breath, containing a little mint from her toothpaste and a lot of sweetness from her natural essence, before her shove stumbles me back by a couple of stunned steps.

"A list, hmmm?" She folds her arms. "With every task involving me naked in your bed?"

"What's wrong with naked and in my bed?"

Her laugh isn't bitter anymore. It's a full rush of harsh and pissed. "When it is the only way you choose to see my usefulness in your life?" Her lips twist. "Then there is plenty *wrong* with it, Cassian." A distinct sheen forms over the stormy darkness in her eyes—as she slides the diamonds off her wrist. "A wrong that cannot be made right with orgasms and bling."

As she folds my good hand around the bracelet, I fight the urge to hurl the thing—especially with that cheesy poster as a perfect target. "Is *that* what you think you are to me?"

Her gaze narrows. "Ohhhh, désonnum. I did forget about the *Scooby Doo* Monopoly tournaments."

"Ella." I don't try to tame the brutal growl. "Dammit—"

She stops me with two splayed fingers to my lips. "You are an amazing man, Cassian Court. Driven, dynamic, loyal, regal, beautiful, bold...a force of nature, captivating me as no other..."

"*Ella—*"

"Let me finish." She lifts her other fingers, spreading them out and exploring the whole curve of my bottom lip. "Let me tell you...that I *do* love you. So much..." Her touch goes still. It feels like everything else in her body does too. "But I cannot be simply your pretty, perfect toy. I need more. I am so sorry. I need..."

I dump the bracelet back into my pocket. Race my hand back up, gripping her by the back of her head, wrenching her face up for the smash of my furious, deep kiss. Only after I've tasted every tonsil in her throat do I pull back, continuing to keep her stare locked with mine.

"I'll give you more. *I'll give you more*, I promise."

Her nod is steady—but her eyes, her mouth, and her fingertips aren't. An attempt at a smile just ends up with her lip beneath her teeth and her hand gently peeling mine away. "You...you need to get going. We can talk more later."

She's as convinced of that as a prediction for raining cats and dogs.

And I can't do a fucking thing to change it.

The realization drives my head back down. I grip the back of hers, forcing her forehead to meet mine once more, praying the desperate bellows of my mind can permeate the brick barriers so clearly erected inside hers now. "You'll be there when I get home?"

She pulls in a breath between her teeth. A smile mists the edges of her lips. "Nothing has changed. Our contract is until October."

She ends it by slipping her gaze to the floor and inching her body out the door, leaving me staring at antacid tiles and the world's lamest promo poster, completely deflated of the desire to put a scratch into either.

Nothing has changed.

Then why do I feel as if everything has?

CHAPTER TWELVE

MISHELLA

"I am the damn pot who let the kettle slack."

Doyle, sprawled on the limo's back-facing seat, stops tapping on his phone long enough to narrow a questioning glance. "The pot who called the kettle black?"

I frown but do not relent my stare out the Jag's tinted window. The New York lunch rush is early, and on this sweltering summer day, it is indeed a rush. Everyone from businessmen in full suits to tourists in sandals is scurrying through the heat so as to be free from it sooner.

"That certainly fits better," I murmur. In more ways than one. The words make sense because the situation does—and I have turned myself into a vessel holding a mess of hot, sticky heartache because of it.

"How so?"

I finally swing my sights back in, certain Doyle is about to begin a new phone conversation anyway. His "honey do" list must be a mile long, filled with much more interesting people than me—but the man's phone rests on the cushion next to him, the screen dark. His eyes are twin gray pearls, lustrous but focused on me, framed by thick torrents of his chestnut hair.

"How so...what?" I sound like an idiot. Appropriate, since I feel like one right now.

"How does the analogy fit?" he clarifies. "Pot? Black?"

Our progress through the traffic is paused at a stoplight. To our left is a florist's delivery truck, emblazoned with a larger-than-life couple surrounded by dewy red roses. The man is fastening a diamond bracelet on the woman's arm. My eyes slide shut. *Creator's damn toes.*

I open my eyes and look right instead. The throngs on the sidewalk are spilling into the crosswalk—except for a young teenage couple, smashed against a light pole, kissing as if they've been granted an early visit to Nirvana.

As if they've climbed atop a rock in the sea.

Screw the Creator's toes. I shall just take his balls.

"By the powers." I mutter it while rolling eyes toward the sky, a blinding blue swath high above the building tops, almost expecting that firmament to sprout random lightning bolts just to drive the universe's point home. *All right, all right,* my psyche manages to grumble. *I get it, I get it. Now it is* my *bloody turn to "share."*

I reset my shoulders. Banish my girl growl. Doyle deserves better attitude than a slight upgrade of disgruntled teenager.

With the pout gone, I start in. "You know what I have always demanded of Cassian, more than anything, since the day he and I first met?"

One side of Doyle's mouth twitches. "Couldn't have been witty banter and clever puns. You'd have gone for me in that case."

"Astute point," I drawl.

He angles forward, tracking us back to the subject with a forthright frown. "It's his honesty and truth. You've never accepted anything less," he states. "And for a man used to women who wanted everything *but* the truth, that was a stunner. A welcome one."

"Though *someone* still was not a fan of me at first." I arch my brows to knowing points.

"I came around." He matches the arch and raises me by half a grin.

"And eventually, so did he." My first intention is to return the smile, but I cannot, weighted anew by the magnitude of everything Cassian has entrusted me with—pieces of himself that not even Doyle has. the ugliness about being raised fatherless, Damon's drug abuse and death, and the disgusting way he and Mallory lived for so many years...nobody has all the whole of that truth except for Mallory and me. *I don't want to silo the explosives anymore. Not with you.* "It was not easy for him," I rasp. "To face all of it again...for me."

Doyle's head angles over, marking his contemplation of that. "I don't imagine it was." He braces both elbows on his knees. "He'd already processed a lot of it, I think... He just had to, in order to accomplish what he did after Lily's death. Something like that either dissolves you or defines you—but I think that Cassian knew, even before that, where he came from and who he was. Then when Lily was gone, he had to define where he was going, as well. Trouble is, he's been so single-minded about it, the plan never included anyone special to share it with."

Tea room snort. A glance—just one—out the window. "Doyle, the man has had a whole string of *someone specials.*"

"A string of *someones,*" he clarifies. "Not someone *special.* Not a real partner, worthy of seeing all that he is, accepting him for it, and then walking with him *through* it to become even better because of it."

My hands twist in my lap. Perplexity zigzags my brain.

"And you think that is what...I did for him?"

He leans back again, creaking the leather seat beneath his lanky frame again. "That's the start of the list, lady."

The line feels like a standing ovation. I accept it with a grateful smile—though cannot wait for the chance to splash back into my black pot of moroseness. "Then in fairness, we must now add another important item to your 'list.'"

One of his brows jog. "This should be interesting."

"No. Just obvious." I succumb to an oh-come-*on* glower. Instantly prompt, "The disaster of what just happened in that television studio? The mess *I* suggested we walk into?"

"Okay, hold the phone, sister." He slashes a finger toward the device I yank out. "Figure of speech. Put it away. You need to hear me here. *Clearly.*" The second I comply, his stare sharpens like a pair of throwing knives. "All that shit Chantal brought out about Lily this morning... You really think she started poking around for it just last week?"

The knives sink in. I frown from their stunning impact. "She...she did not?"

"Holy shit," he mumbles. "No. Her team started digging up shit on Cassian a year ago, when he was with that Nairobian model who landed the lead in the new *Star Wars* movie. As far as we knew at the time, it was just basic trivia like his high school girlfriends, college clubs, his tight relationship with his mom. But there's a good chance that the crap with Lily goes back that far too. We'll know that soon enough."

The promise leads him back to somber tones, as well as the enigmatic Doyle with whom I am much more familiar—and comfortable. "The *main* point here is, those scumsuckers have been digging for a chink in Cassian's armor for a while—long before we took that trip to Arcadia and he even knew you existed. Whatever they found out last year, and everything since then, has been carefully stored up until the time was right."

I nod, finally beginning to understand. "And the time got right."

"More right than Chantal ever hoped for." He uncaps one of the bottled waters stored in the ice bay. Takes a quick chug before continuing. "She already had the explosion ready to detonate, Mishella." He tips the neck of the bottle toward me. "It's just a damn good thing you were at his side when that bat shit bunny decided to push the red button."

A note gets jotted in one of my mental journals. *Cassian, Doyle, and rabbits...just weird flukes?* Outwardly, my nose crinkles. Then harder. "So...this would probably be happening, no matter what?"

Doyle spreads his hands. "No matter what."

"So I am not a pot?"

He grunts. "Nor a kettle."

It takes me more long minutes to process that—though have a viable excuse due to gaping at the throng of reporters at Temptation's front gate. Did they conduct some strange mitosis while we were gone? There are four times as many of them now. It surely has something to do with Cassian's dramatic conclusion to the interview with Chantal and that "viral" phenomenon I am still not familiar with—nor am sure I wish to be. Some aspects of living in this modern world really are better as mysteries.

As Scott slows the car in front of the frosted-glass doors to the basement's elevator lobby, I look out at the portals, which are embossed with lustrous art deco lions. Blatant but appropriate irony, anyone? My lazing lion has been poked and is now awake.

Very awake.

"Doyle?"

"Hmm?"

"Do you think Cassian expected this?"

"Maybe." His head cants to the other side. "Probably. But I suspect—I'm *sure*—there was a part of him that still hoped..." He snorts, meshing his hands back together. "Ah, hell. You know Cassian, yeah? Bad-ass billionaire on the outside"—his hands fold tighter—"mush-ball of chivalry and do-right-not-easy on the inside."

My lips lift readily. How can they not, after six weeks of seeing that code at work every day? Everything from insisting Prim source most of her grocery list from local suppliers, to standing up for safer labor conditions for workers on his overseas projects, to insisting I learn every superhero's moral code during our movie nights... The man needs to believe that, in his small and not-so-small ways, he is contributing to the cause of right in this world. Balancing the wrongs from Damon and Lily—and the child he will never know.

The halves of Doyle's jaw battle each other for a second before he reaches some kind of inner resolve. "You know, he and Chantal actually used to be really fond of each other. *Not* like that," he hurries out, as if forecasting my stiffened spine. "She was a new reporter on the 'chatty news' scene and needed to make a mark. Cas has never forgotten what it was like to be the new kid and constantly judged. He had empathy and helped her out with some quality one-on-one sit-downs. When she landed at *People and Places,* Cas was even at the celebration party."

A breath whooshes from me. "Oh, my."

"Yeah." He grunts. "Oh, my."

"No wonder he reacted this morning as if his best friend had smashed a grenade into his heart."

His turn to straighten a little. Press a weirdly dainty hand to his chest. "Uh, yeah. It does."

"And...?" I prompt when his stare lifts in a bizarre spurts.

"You Arcadian women have weird violent streaks."

"So do you American men." In a mutter, I amend, "Especially Mr. Court."

"Agreed."

"Which mean he's going to destroy Chantal in court."

"Probably."

Fitting or not, it is the thought I am left to ponder as we get out of the Jag and make our way inside—which suddenly feels like as much of a cage as the confines of my mind to these whirling thoughts. Before the elevator even rumbles to life, I have punched the button for Temptation's ground floor, instead of the top.

"I need a few minutes to myself," I explain to Doyle. "Nobody can see the herb garden. I shall be all right there."

He nods, resigned. The little space, tucked against the complex's back wall, is a secret Prim let me in on just a few weeks ago, when I complimented the fresh herbs in her lasagna. She beamed when showing me the garden, a haven not only for her organically grown herbs and flavorful plants but also containing a butterfly grotto and a reading hammock beneath a sprawling linden tree.

Today, not a leaf on that tree budges in the stifling summer heat—though I am grateful for the shade and the respite of the garden after the chaos of the morning. A sigh escapes. *Chaos.* It was barely a word I knew until two months ago. It seems to be my middle name now. But given the choice, would I return to the pace and stability of Arcadia instead of this insanity?

Because two months ago, I did not know several other words either.

Like desire.

Like longing.

Like Cassian.

Like love.

With a wistful smile, I let my hand trail along a lavender bush. It is a warm-weather lover and tells me so with the bloom of soft fragrance against my fingers. "You just enjoy blooming where you are planted, hmmm?"

Do I take a cue from the flowers? Obey the call of my heart and truly try to see what will bloom if I allow some deeper roots with Cassian? Or am I destined to be nothing but a pretty window decoration here, vibrant and lovely—but trapped in the confines of a pot, set for one purpose alone, while my roots constantly fight that pot?

"Whatever it is, the fate of nations doesn't rest on it. Not today, at least."

My head snaps up at the interruption—not because I am stunned someone has found me here but because that someone is not Doyle. Nor Scott. Nor even Cassian.

Though for a second, I *did* think it was Cassian.

What. On. Earth?

Those very words race up my throat but are frozen halfway, paralyzed as if caught by an ice ray from one of Cassian's superheroes—making me wonder if the stranger standing here, tall and muscled and full of a little too much pride in his stance, might even be one of them in the flesh. He needs a better costume, though. Those faded jeans, cuffed work shirt, and sheen of sweat make me wonder if his out-of-nowhere appearance had its origin point on a mythical planet or just in the sewer just outside the mansion.

And why am I standing here, even debating these things?

Move. Move, before he realizes that you plan to. Run. Run!

"Please." Too late. He slides in front of me, dangerously fast and graceful to the point of slick, again like a scene from one of Cassian's movies—when the bad guy wants to block the hero's girlfriend from escaping his clutches. "Just hold on, okay?"

Clutches. Pegged it. He lifts a hand to my elbow, making me skitter back, swinging the only weapon in my possession: my purse. Since the Kate Spade Mini Candace only contains my phone and a lipstick, I make sure the hit counts—and am glad I paid attention when Saynt insisted on schooling me in self-defense basics.

"Ow! Shit."

"Stand back, bonsun—or I *shall* scream."

"Christ."

A schism of shock rips through my belly once more. Radiates like bolts from a plasma ball, fractioning through my toes, my fingertips, even my hair follicles. His *voice*. Why does something in its baritone timbre catch my breath and stop my senses—

As if Cassian has just walked up instead?

And with that thought, I take in the sight of him again. *Really* look at him.

Thick, dark-blond hair that seems to be the Court family trademark—though tamed more by a nearly military cut. Eyes, arrestingly green—though lighter, like Mallory's, instead of the deep forests of Cassian's.

Dear, sweet Creator...

That is not all. He has dimples—prominent ones, even with that furrowed frown on his face. And his angular, formidable jaw...and that mouth, hinting at a hundred kinds of expression...

"Wh-What—*who* are—"

The stranger steps forward, making me counter by stepping back. "I'm sorry. I didn't mean to frighten you—or hurt you. I'm here because I need to talk you." Another attempt at an advance—halted as soon as I arch the purse back once more. "Fuck. My intel was right. You *are* feisty."

Fume. Again. I like it when Cassian calls me feisty. From this stranger, it is...too personal. "What the *hell* do you want?"

He rolls those bright-green eyes. "I *told* you. To talk."

Another jolt hits my stomach. "Fine. Talk. From *over there*. You have two minutes."

His shoulders drop by an inch. He rolls them just once while resetting his chin. No more eye rolling. He drives that bright-green gaze straight into me before stating, "This may take more than two minutes."

"Why?"

He exhales. Folds his hands at the small of his back. "I'll start at the beginning. My name...is Damon Court."

★ ★ ★

My ears and my mind are mismatched fuses. The syllables have gone in, but nothing about them latches to a single anchor of comprehension—except that somewhere deep inside, my instinct connects with his truth.

"No!" My protest screams from my soul but only scrapes

the air, a rasp disappearing against the air's humid cushion. My body is a contrast of eerie composure, motionless even as Damon—*no, not Damon; who the hell are you?*—advances by another step. "That—*this* is impossible." That must be it. This is impossible. Not happening.

"I know it sounds strange—"

"Not strange!" My voice finally comes back as a gratifying snarl. "*Impossible*. What the hell did not you not understand about impossible?"

"Mishella—"

"He is dead. *You* are dead." *Which explains how you already feel you know him? How his presence just...clicks...deep within, in that same way it does with Cassian and Mallory? How he is so much like both of them, peering at you with such familiar intensity, it makes you tremble? How he steps even closer, one side of his face lifting to produce a dimple so deep, it speaks of his genes louder than the hair and the eyes and the stance and the—*

The everything.

Oh, my.

Oh...

my.

"Well." He settles his stance again, like a lion anticipating battle—just like his little brother. *Dammit.* "Clearly, I'm not dead."

"Do *not* be flippant," I retort. "You have *not* earned the right to be flippant."

The dimple vanishes—though that gleam in his eyes, a combination of assessment and enticement, pulses brighter. "Well. The Boy Wonder picked himself quite a spitfire, didn't he?"

"Who?"

The gleam softens. Just a little. "Nothing," he says softly. "Just a nickname from long ago."

From long, long *ago, you selfish bonsun.* The fury, overriding me like bloodlust on behalf of the family he has subjected to fourteen years of grief, makes me long to give the lion the fight he deserves. And the smell of his own blood. And the scars of my scratches across his serene face.

Which would do what for you? Or for Cassian?

The logic makes my stomach churn, my mind spin. I feel thrust onto a jetty in a storm, rooted on solid rock but buffeted by waves of mind-jarring force, threatening to blast me away.

Remember your rock. What would Cassian do with the waves?

Force them back. Part the damn sea. Strip everything away, until the damn sea obeyed...

I bind the thoughts to me, drawing in more strength—until they reveal a surprising shore. *Clarity.* "Wait," I murmur, gaze narrowing at Damon—or whoever the hell he is. "Have you just been *lurking*—and how long have—and exactly *how* did—" I stop my stammering to peer around, senses doused in feedback. The din of the media mini mob. The squawks of the radios from Doyle's added security guards. The added electricity in the air because of it all, despite the ten-foot-high wall bordering the entirety of the complex. "How the *hell* did you get in here?"

He jogs his head at the back wall. I cannot acknowledge it as an answer, despite the scuffs on his hands and clothes confirming his validity. "Just up and over."

I pull in a sharp breath. "You are a liar."

Well, not technically. Cassian pulled off the same move

yesterday—but that was before Doyle's new-hires started patrolling the back wall along with the automated security cameras. Cassian also owns the place—not a claim this lunatic can remotely make. The only thing he has proven accurate is his sneakiness.

"A valid point," he finally responds, all too coolly, to my allegation. "And true—about a variety of subjects. But not this one."

"So...you scrambled up and over?" I let anger cover for my incredulity. "Sweet-talked the cameras with your humility and good looks?"

"Well, there *were* those," Damon counters. "But mostly it was my training."

"Of course." I spread my hands, shrugging. *Sorry-not-sorry.* "Your 'training.' As...part of the circus you ran away with? The rogue aliens who forced you to pilot their flying saucer for fourteen years? The mob cartel who kidnapped you?"

That one makes him chuckle. "The mob. Good one. That comes the closest."

"To what?"

"To the CIA."

My jaw wants to fall. Begs me to let it simply plummet to the ground—since once more, every shred of my intuition bellows about how ridiculously, incredibly right he is. "The..."

"CIA." He repeats it as if just relaying he belongs to a book club or is allergic to chocolate. "It stands for the Central Intelligence Agency. We're an organization dedicated to protecting our country's security interests throughout the world—"

"Creator's toes." I drop my head, pinching the bridge of my nose. "I *know* what the CIA is."

"Then you also know what I'm about to tell you could get me killed."

"Good. Then your mother and brother will not have wasted the last fourteen years grieving for your sorry backside..." *Ass nozzle.* How I *yearn* to borrow the "endearment" from Vy to finish off the slam, for nothing in Arcadian comes close to fitting. But I choose the higher road, dammit, falling into fuming silence.

"All right. What I'm about to tell you could get *you* killed."

Long growl—before a prickled retort. "Then do not tell me." I could not mean anything more. Prove it by spinning on my heel, with the full intention of calling security the moment I get back inside—and then locking myself in a room to weigh out what in Creator's name I plan on doing with this landslide of revelation. How I will be able to look Cassian in the eye, or ever hear another reference to Damon again, without telling him what I now know about the man...

"Fine. Then it might get Cassian killed."

So much for that dilemma. Or for any of the tiny prickles in my nerves. All of my skin freezes—and then bears witness to it in the lengths of my limbs, which stop me totally in place. The only warm thing in my body is the core of my heart—and the beats my spirit has reserved for Cassian there. Thankfully they funnel the heat inward, giving me fortitude to turn. To brace myself for that arrogance on his face once more—and the craving to wipe it away with my open palm.

Thank the Creator, he has stowed it away himself. Now he looks sincerely grateful for my consideration—no matter how large the dose of anger with which it has come.

"Fine," I finally mutter. "*Five* minutes—which may or may not include the two you have already wasted."

Damon jerks out a nod. Repositions his stance again—which does not seem as strange, given his fresh revelation about training for an organization that specializes in secret, often nonconventional, tactics. Not that I have even *approached* an admission that his CIA fantasy is real. The man supposedly "died" at sixteen. Are there not laws in this country about recruiting a person that young?

"All right." He lets a long breath fill his chest—and a longer scrutiny of me take up his gaze. "Your rules. Ticking time clock. That means I'm going right to the ropes."

I let my head tilt, while taking out the mental journal again. *Right to the ropes.* I have no bloody idea what it means, though the sound is rather pleasant. *The ropes.* Seems like some kind of medieval torture process. If he wants to subject himself to it, he has my full support.

"Perfect," I declare. "Proceed."

That earns me a double take—though it is not a reaction I experience from most Americans. *Most* Americans—except, to this point, Cassian, and now Damon—treat the formal phrases I have learned since girlhood either as high insult or cute amusement. Cassian's enchantment with them has been just another match beneath the flames that have melted my heart. But dammit, why does his brother have to share the same wiring?

I am *not* going to be melted by Damon Court. Not by one damn degree.

His wince, filled with equal parts discomfort and resolve, is much easier to accept. *Yes. On the ropes with you, ass nozzle.* That will do. Definitely.

"Clearly, you know a little about me already," he starts in.

"Clearly." I fold my arms, giving my watch a pointed

glance along the way. I said five minutes and meant it. "And as long as we are being clear, more than a little."

He nods again. It is choppier than before, like a man accepting a lifetime jail sentence while knowing he is guilty of every crime on the indictment. "And as long as clarity is the theme, everything you've heard is probably true."

His humility makes my chest tighten. Then my arms. *I will not soften. I will* not *soften.* "All right. Enlighten me. What have I heard?"

His arms plummet next to his sides—though the fists that punctuate the move remain. "I was...a screw-up. No other way of saying it, except that whatever Mom and Cas remember likely doesn't touch the truth."

I cock both brows. "They remember a great deal."

His face twists again. I gloat inwardly. *Yes. You hurt them. Now it is time for you to know it—and to feel it too.*

"Yeah," he finally grates. "I had a lot of shit going on. Anger I didn't know what to do with. Mom did her best, but she was a single parent without a lot of time on her hands to deal with me being pissed at a father who left when I was seven and a mother who let him—at least in my eyes." He sits in the chair opposite me but stays perched on the edge, still a vigilant lion, swinging occasional, watchful glances over his shoulders. "But in truth, Dad was gone long before that. I just didn't know the difference."

"And your mother was the most convenient person to blame it on." Empathy, coming to me like second instinct, leads me to the statement—and I instantly, deeply hate myself for it. Damon's stare of celadon gratitude only makes it worse. *We owe nothing to each other, you and I. Just spit out your story and get the hell out of here, Damon Court.*

"I feel like shit for how I treated her—and Damon too."

Turn the empathy off. Do not hear the croak in his voice, or look at the sheen behind his eyes, or notice how pulses tick in place of his dimples when his heart is washed in agony...

"But you *did* treat them like shit." My spine pulls up. Better. The accusation may be as rough as the gravel under our feet but is as firm as the concrete slab beneath *that*. Perhaps I can be a messenger of the true heartache his deception has inflicted on Cassian and Mallory. "The worst kind of it. You lied to them...in the most devastating way poss—"

"I was at rock *fucking* bottom!"

The explosion of his body is obliterated by the blast of his emotions—a collision like hydrogen and uranium, wasting my senses with the searing force. I glare up at him from where I have been blown back, gripping the curves of the chair's arms, lungs detonated by fury and fear.

"Do you *think*, for a *second*, that I haven't spent every day since then regretting the choice I made?" His lips shake. His stare burns. "Goddammit. The choice *they* made for me..."

His face contorts harder, turning him into a creature of self-loathing and hate—something I no longer can liken to Cassian, which does not bring the relief I expected. Instead, I am...sad. An unfair word for a big, awful emotion...

"Then why...did you make it?" I finally manage to whisper.

"Because I was sixteen, Mishella." He stumbles away, steps heavy and clumsy, as if the words have been his daily mantra for fourteen years and he is weary from the weight of them. "I was *sixteen,* dammit, and I didn't know any better— only that what was supposed to be a 'one-time thing' to get away from my pain had turned into a drug dealer's wet dream. I needed meth or coke every morning just to get up and get through school, and sleep was only possible with a shit ton of booze or, better yet, sedatives—reds, yellows; fuck, I'd lick the goddamn rainbow if it helped me pass out—to the point that I was skipping class to run shipments for my dealers in order to pay for my next high." He lowers back into the chair, skittering gravel with the violence of his movements. Harsh exhalation. Labored inhalation. "Well, one day, one of those runs went sideways."

Dammit. Empathy crushes me again. Even with the physical similarities diminished, he is so much like Cassian. His powerful, plunging movements. His restless energy. The way I am pulled toward understanding him...needing him to know he is not alone. "Your buyers were actually...CIA?"

He braces elbows on his knees and steeples his fingers—*again, so much like Cassian*—and turns his face up with what I expect to be an implied yes. And yes, his gaze conveys conviction—but not that one. A story about to take a different twist...

A darker truth.

"They were CIA...but they weren't."

"Huh?"

A vacillation across his face, reminding me of those scenes from Cassian's superhero movies in which the hero debates revealing his truth or not. As soon as he does, the poor soul to whom he has entrusted his secret inevitably has a cinematic target on their back—to ensure what Cassian calls the "ker-ching factor" for the sequel, of course.

But this is no movie.

It is confirmed by the watchful solemnity of the man in front of me. It adds a new layer to my sadness. It makes me... restless. In a heartbeat, I understand why. I have never known strange silence like this with Cassian—because his soul is always open to me, speaking on its electric arc with mine. I do not know anything more about Damon than what he chooses to show. At this moment, that window is cracked only by inches.

"They started out the bust the typical way." His explanation begins slowly, his eyes going hazy as distant memories are accessed. "Well, I *guess* it was typical... Badges were flashed and infractions were cited, including references to other deals I'd helped on for a few months. It was very clear, very fast, that they'd been watching me for a while and waiting for the right time to pick me up." Contemplative shrug. "Now that's not *un*common, especially if a task force wants to make something stick—but why all that trouble for stick factor on a sixteen-year-old bit player in the game?"

I lean forward. "You must have been confused." I add, however reluctantly, "And frightened."

He lets me off easier for the compassion this time, chuffing wryly. "Tried to tell myself the same thing, especially when they didn't formally charge me. I was never cuffed or read my rights, and they didn't call my mom. When I asked if *I* could do it, and if they could tell me what police precinct they'd be taking me to, they blinked like I'd just asked the damn question in Klingon."

"I know the feeling." All too well. Again, more common ground I did not ask for.

The tips of his fingers turn white as he pushes them harder together. "Even as an underage punk blazed on a cocktail of who-the-fuck-knows and who-the-fuck-cares, I started putting together the pieces. Those bastards were throwing their own damn party, and local law didn't know a thing about it."

I do not understand all the complexities of the statement but glean enough to respond, "So they sought you out specifically...recruited you *because* you were so young and would not register on anyone's radar?"

One end of his mouth kicks up again. "Feisty *and* smart. The boy wonder *did* grow up to pick them well."

I narrow a glare. "Save it, bonsun. Charm earns nobody extra points except Cassian."

"Duly noted."

"So what happened then?" My mind fills in the answer with a hundred possibilities, all inspired by the only exposure I have had so far to CIA agents: their portrayals in movies. The truth is likely painted with much different brushes, though... "You said...you were given no choice..."

"Should've phrased that better." The grin disappears. As in, vanishes completely—beneath a glower worthy of a Batman reel. "Depends on what you call a choice."

I relent, giving him a moment of silence to assemble his composure. Finally prod, "Well, what did *they* call it?"

I am not surprised when he chooses to gain his feet again—nor by the fact that it is a careful, resigned flow instead of a defensive explosion. "Well...they definitely had the royal flush over my pair of eights," he mutters. "That means their mountain of evidence was huge enough to keep me in a juvenile facility until I was eighteen, with a transfer to 'grown-up prison' for at least ten to fifteen after that."

"By the powers." I gasp it on Mallory's behalf. While making her accept his "death" was the ultimate crime, the situation had clearly not gotten that extreme yet. And he *was* just a kid, with a brain scrambled on drugs... "But they needed your pair of eights too?"

"Even the royals need their essential numbers sometimes, yes?"

His knowing glance betrays he knows more about me than just my name—another nonsurprise, though certainly not a comfort. "And you were that...to them?" I counter with open skepticism. "An 'essential number'?"

"Turns out...I kind of was."

"I do not understand."

"Neither did I...at first." He stops, making a couple of butterflies skitter from the nearby rosemary, and tugs a hand at his nape. The half smile tugs at his mouth again, though snark does not define the look now. He gazes at me in what looks like...bewilderment. "You...ever had a single minute that changed your whole life?"

"Yes." Rarely have I felt as confident about a comeback or the proud stance I take for it. I gain my feet once more too, lifting my gaze to meet his with all the pride and love that has spurred me. "The moment in which I met your brother."

And instantly beheld worlds of loss in his eyes—that you had helped cause.

He blinks and backs up, the conviction clearly getting to him—as I hoped it would. But he recovers instantly, as I *knew* he would. Clearly, façades have become a life specialty for Damon Court.

Still, as he speaks again, I sense his effort to strip back even that suave pretense, coming as clean as possible. "The two men who busted me that afternoon were the game changers for me," he states. "Their names were Chris Maxmillan and Pete Shotwell—though I tried getting away with the typical sixteen-year-old bullshit like Lucy and Ricky, Mulder and Scully, Ketchum and Pikachu..."

"Gesundheit," I murmur. His forehead, more prominent than Cassian's due to his tighter haircut, furrows until I prod, "So when exactly did the 'life changing' part occur?"

He takes a few steps deeper, beneath the arbor. Again, his pace seems to represent more deliberate thoughts, and I have trouble being patient about it. His five minutes are nearly up, and I am ready to walk back inside, with or without an explanation.

"They revealed...that they'd been scouting me."

"Scouting?" I echo it after a long, puzzled pause. The verb is not unfamiliar to me—though all the contexts to which it applies in American culture are far cries from the CIA. Baseball players, movie locations, fashion models, CIA superspies... *Circle the one that does not belong...*

"That's how *I* reacted." He shrugs with much less aplomb than he obviously would like. "Until Max and Shot fired up their laptop and showed me all the stats. *My* stats." His head tick-tocks on a slow, dazed shake. "There were at least a hundred categories of criteria, from my talent at running track even after sucking down a reefer, to my curiosity about people and my ability to remember shit about them. *Lots* of shit." The last is muttered nearly in a moan, as if he is a teenager once again and simply recalling hordes of homework. "Those criteria, paired with my age, made me a perfect candidate for an elite team they were putting together..."

"A team? Of *what*?" It stammers out, a reaction to the conclusion he is clearly leading to. "Teenage super spies?"

A loud laugh. The burst does not help my bewilderment because it reflects the exact same sentiment. "I know how it sounds. Even fourteen years after the fact, I still keep waiting to wake up and learn it was all a damn dream and I was just punked bad by one of those asshole dealers I used to run dust, rocks, and flakes for." His mirth fades. Despite the sun dancing along the gold spikes of his hair, a new darkness drapes his whole demeanor. The Batman comparison does not seem like such a joke. "But suddenly, the good guys wanted *my* help in putting down the scum—the biggest ring of them in all of the tristate area, as a matter of fact—so huge, their ties had origins in international cartels who were rewarding dealers for trickling the drugs down to the elementary school level."

My stomach pitches. "They rewarded dealing to *children?*"

Tight nod. "It was why the FBI gave the CIA leeway at all—but only nine months' worth, meaning it'd be impossible to integrate regular operatives at the high schools. So, the CIA did what it needed to do." He returns to the formidable stance, hands locked behind his back. "Bent a few rules."

It gives my belly no rest, and the reason is not difficult to discern. "By recruiting children for their mission."

"A mission that saved a lot of *those* children too."

Stomach, meet real pain.

My glare whips up as everything beneath my navel is wrenched in. "What does *that* mean?"

His stance broadens. I am not the only one in this confrontation with a truth to be obstinate about. "It means that I might have been coerced into that insanity, but that insanity also gave me purpose. That things were about more than my pain... That someone *else's* pain might actually be worse." His head dips. His body stills. He is like that for such a long pause, I have no choice about accepting his diligence as sincere. "In helping save those kids' lives, my own was transformed."

With uncanny coincidence—or is it?—the two butterflies return to the bush behind him. They rest, silent but strong, amazing products of an extreme metamorphosis—just like his. But I can open up a science book and figure out the rest of their story. There is still a huge piece of his missing. An epic tale with blank pages of its most awful twist. When the bard of the story remains eerily silent, I grow angry again.

"All right. Your life was 'transformed.'" I step forward, unwavering in my own intent. "But why did that mean giving it up—*completely*?"

His stance stiffens, but his face does not. Clearly, the query is not a slap from nowhere—though it is still the lash he has been avoiding.

And continues to avoid.

"Damon?" I finally prompt again.

Finally, he grits out, "It was necessary, dammit." He ducks his head, leading the way into a violent spin. "It was... necessary."

"Necessary." If not for the anger practically sparking off of him, I would step over and jerk the stubborn lout back around. I battle to do it with my voice instead. "Why? How? Was *that* part of your buddies' package deal too? 'Here, kid. Purpose, direction, and getting to wear the white hat. Just ignore the fine print about having to *die* for us on the way to the good guys' party."

At least it gets him to turn around. "It wasn't Max's or Shot's fault," he retorts. "It was mine. Nobody's. But. Mine."

For one moment, I regret my sardonicism—but only for only one. While I believe his story, I am still not sympathetic to it. Inside the soul of the man I love, there will always be a boy on the cusp of manhood, mourning for the big brother he loved and worshiped...

"We were running tight with the Noriega cartel," he finally

ANGEL PAYNE

rasps. "I got sloppy one night...left my phone lying behind me, without the password lock on it. One of Noriega's men found it—along with the string of texts from Max on it. My buddy, Louis, covered for the bungle, but the entire team was nearly made—and Noriega started suspecting hinky play." The words might as well be vomit, and I have no doubt they taste the same to him. He might have been an addict as a kid but has grown into a man who prioritizes his duty to others—along with the regrets of having compromised it too. "So I went to Max and Shot and offered to do the right thing."

Suddenly, the acid burns up *my* throat. "Creator's teeth." Comprehension turns it into a croak. "The *right* thing, as in..."

"Yeah. I was prepared to die. Had letters written to Mom and Cas and even binged on every sixteen-year-old's favorite last meal—triple cheeseburger, large chili fries, and six glazed donuts, washed down with an extra-thick chocolate frosty."

Groan. "And *that* did not slay you first?"

He snorts. "As opposed to the typical daily junkie diet?"

I concede the point with half a nod. "So why was it not your last meal, after all?"

"Because of Pete Shotwell's brilliance." His features warm before he dips his head, all but bowing in honor to the reference of his mentor. "In addition to being a Krav Maga master and an awesome mechanic, the man was into all that weird apothecary crap. He borrowed a page right out of fucking Shakespeare..."

"And made you drink something that made you *appear* dead..."

"For twelve hours only." His face hardens with a new chill. "Revivable only with an antidote."

My eyes cannot widen enough to fulfill my shock. "Long

241

enough that everyone, including your family, would assume you were dead."

"Which was necessary so the most important person thought I was dead." His jaw jogs up as he supplies, firm and resolved, "Santiago Noriega."

A shiver courses through me despite the summer's muggy blanket. *Noriega.* His name alone carries haunting meaning—as anyone on staff at the Palais Arcadia has learned over the last year. Our island's re-entry into the modern world has exposed us to all of its modern wonders—and all of its leading monsters. Noriega, a despot who rules from his hole somewhere in a South American jungle, is a fitting pig for the second category.

Still...pigs can be duped...

"There was *no* way for you to get even a message to Cassian and your mother?" I persist. "Have your miracle-working friend arrange for a secret meeting, even years after?"

The edges of Damon's mouth twitch again—but his gaze remains ominous as a sky of green thunder. "The day I drank that nasty shit in Shot's vial was the day I gave up being Damon Court. It had to remain that way, if I wanted to be sure Mom and Cas stayed alive." The storm relents, but only for a second. "From then on, I could only participate in their lives from afar," he grits. "I saw how they struggled and what they went through...*fuck.* I couldn't send them a damn dime or even leave a bag of groceries on their front stoop. To this day, I have no fucking idea if Noriega hasn't learned the truth and isn't watching every move I make."

The words, in any other circumstance, would sound like melodrama. Horrifically, I know they are not. Santiago Noriega and his organization tiptoe the line between organized crime and radical religious terrorism in the almighty church of wealth.

But that means they lead to another glaring issue. "So why are you here now?" If Noriega could still be tracking his every step...

Unbelievably, the air around Damon Court buzzes with more tension. His posture tautens with it; his face ages at least five years from it. "Because Cassian is in danger from a bigger monster than Noriega—and I'm going to stop him from that mistake."

"What?" The gravel flying from my stumbling feet feels more like ice chips. This bonsun has brought the filthy name of Santiago Noriega into Temptation with him and now blithely drops the word *danger* into the same sentence as Cassian's name? "Who?" I demand. "And why? And what the *hell* are you going to do about it?"

"Okay—*calm down.*"

"Shut. Up." I wrench back, wiping where he tries gripping my shoulders. "You have not earned the right to tell me that, either. Just stick to the damn facts. Why is Cassian in danger, and what are you going to do about it?"

Damon backs off. *Not* a reassurance, since he returns to the smug-as-smoke expression with each defined step. "You mean...what are *we* going to do about it?"

Leaden gulp.

Torn gut.

Protesting senses.

"Wh-What—do you—"

"I'm going to get my little brother out of this, Mishella—but not without *your* help."

CASSIAN

"Hi, honey. I'm home."

Ella hops up from the chaise nestled in the curve of Turret One, arms wide for me, face even more open. There are many awesome facets about falling in love with a girl from a society nearly sealed off from the world—one of them definitely being her ignorance of every inane modern cliché.

"Hi, honey." After giggling when using the word in return, she pops on tiptoes to kiss me. "So you are."

"And so *you* are. Wow." I sweep her with a head-to-toe stare while the tips of our fingers remain clasped. "Heels... makeup...hair? Does that dress have...that tutu shit underneath it?"

She laughs again, suffusing my senses with the music I've craved all day. After the disaster of a morning at the TV set with Chantal and then meetings with the legal and PR teams on next steps for handling it all, I took advantage of being at the office to actually *work* at the office. Lunch was eaten in, followed by ordering Rob to hold calls from everyone except Ella—who was the only person who *didn't* call. Nearly seven hours later, she's the only perfect medicine for my soul...the beauty for my beast.

"The 'tutu shit' is called a crinoline." She grins pertly, swaying like a bell to make the flowered frock move. "It makes the dress pretty."

"It makes the dress fluffy." I wrap an arm around her waist, pulling her in for a more meaningful kiss. "*You* make the dress pretty."

"Why, thank you, Mr. Court."

"Most welcome, sorceress."

Her tickled smile turns my chest to six kinds of mush. Dear fuck, if the woman ever completely comprehends what she does to me...

Especially in moments like this, when her fingers tug at the ends of my hair, coaxing me down to her for more kisses...

Gladly, my beauty.

There's tongue involved this time, and I groan from the sizzling satisfaction of it. God*damn*, she tastes amazing...fruity tea, tangy toothpaste, desire-filled woman... How have I gone seven fucking hours without this? The answer doesn't matter because I waste no time making up for the loss, pulling on her, sucking on her, feasting on her, until we have to breathe through our noses and she clings to me harder just to stay standing. Yeah. *Just the way I like it...*

Only with a growled effort do I finally force myself to stop—but not before I try to poke through the tutu shit with the fresh bulge in my crotch. "Shit," I finally grumble. "We'd better stop before I can't or won't."

Her eyes drag open, entrancing me with their aqua lust. "And the problem with that would be...?"

I chuckle. "That clearly, you want to go out?"

Her head tilts. "Why would I want to do that? Prim made shrimp scampi." She smiles, seductive and coy, as I follow the twirls of a curl newly tumbled into her cleavage. "And...I might have helped your maimanne make some lemon bars too."

I moan all over again. "That's almost as delicious a thought...as *this*..." Let my finger trail lower, sliding under the edge of her bra...

"Mmmm. I thought so."

She moves in closer, pushing herself beneath my hand. I fight my way back to rational thought, despite the perfect pucker of her areola and the erotic heat of her nipple. "But you're all dressed up..." Something doesn't make sense. As gorgeous as she is in designer finery, her preferred look behind closed doors is the way in which I most prefer her: messy bun, loose tank top, leggings or shorts requiring no underwear to get in my way... "Why isn't it Batgirl PJs time?"

I bought her the lounging set two weekends ago at a flea market. She's been nearly inseparable with it since—only now, the mention of it makes little creases across her forehead. "Just not in a Gotham heroes mood tonight."

There's something off about that assertion, too—something I should dig deeper into—but dammit if the woman doesn't peel every coherent thought from my mind with the flick of her tongue, sliding over my Adam's apple, as she loosens my tie. Before I can stop her, the silk strip is gone and tossed to the floor, replaced by bolts of raw heat emanating from the spot where she nips, bites, and teases at my skin...

"Ohhhh kay..." I conclude it with a hiss as she dips fingers beneath my shirt...and rubs a thumb across my nipple. "What *are* you in...the mood...for?"

"My own hero." She lets the breath of it curl up the column of my neck—as she pinches harder at my flesh. I look down to watch the light gleam off her bracelet, raining across the V of my bared torso, as she does. The sight is so damn sublime. She is mine, just as much as I am hers. Only one element would make the snapshot complete.

My ring on her finger.

Christ.

Am I out of my damn mind?

And if I am, do I even want that mind back?

Ella plucks back by an inch, far enough to yank up her

head, her timing making me wonder if my spirit has betrayed me to her yet again. But that's not it. There's more in her eyes, across her face...a searching question of her own...a lunging of her soul for mine. A needy roll of her body against mine...

A connection of her heart to mine, rendering us both mute in its inexplicable force. Caught, Immobilized. Breathless. Overwhelmed.

"Dear God." It finally chokes out of me.

"By the Creator," she practically gurgles in return.

"What the hell are you doing to me?"

I don't expect the hard contortion of her face...the thick tears that brim in her eyes. But I don't question them, either. I just...let them be. Kiss at them, reverent and grateful for them, as she finally husks out, "Just loving you, Cassian." She presses back in, twining her arms around my neck. Tighter. Then even tighter. "Just let me do that, okay?"

I nod, letting my nose bump hers in the doing. Letting my mouth find hers and seal back over hers. Letting my tongue sink back against hers, plunging and wet and passionate. "You're on, lady."

She smiles, sucking the breath from my body and injecting the blood into my dick, in the two seconds I allow before claiming her again. Our tongues swirl and dance as our mouths open and taste. Our hands explore and delve, enticing what arousal they can despite the maddening state of our clothes—*too damn much*—and the insane state of our lust—*too damn hot*—until I've pushed her against the chaise and suddenly flip her around, facing the thing.

"Get on," I instruct in a pair of terse growls. "Grab the headrest with both arms and then kneel with your ass facing me."

She is breathless and flushed, nodding before she obeys. As soon as she does, I center myself on the cushion behind her and start to flip up those ridiculous tutu layers between my body and her heat. With every swipe of motion, I get a waft of her exotic perfume and her needy pussy, giving me hope that—

"Yessss." I snarl it in approval, beholding the creamy sight of her bare ass—and glistening sex. "You really *did* just want to stay in tonight, didn't you?"

An adorable giggle tumbles out of her—until my touch interrupts her seduction. "Well," she rasps, "I told you...there *is* shrimp scampi."

"Which we could get during a night on the town too."

Her pout bleeds into her voice. "Oh, but then you would have underwear to deal with..."

"Oh?" I don't hold back on the sexual prowl of it, relishing how it leaves my lips, enters her ear, and resonates through her body in wave after wave of enticed shivers. "Who says I'd have underwear to deal with, armeau? You?" I run my touch from the backs of her knees to the crack of her ass and then back again. "If we went out and I told you to leave the panties at home, you'd fucking leave them at home." With dual grips on her hips, I hitch her backward and then up, rubbing her sex against my fly...spreading her intimate lips with my erection. "What do you say to that, Miss Santelle?"

She shivers again. I've just hit a hundred of her erotic buttons at once, and we both rejoice in what it does to her sweet, wet pussy.

"I—I say—" She stops, gasping hard, as I unbutton my pants...letting her feel every motion of it. "Yes," she finally blurts. "Yes, Cassian...if—if you wanted me to leave the panties at home, I would."

"Good girl," I grate into her ear. "And...if I told you that the sight of your tits in this dress made my cock drip with wanting you...what would you do?"

I watch her lush profile, tawny lashes closing against her dark pink cheeks. The wisp of a smile teases her lips. "I would... spill ice water down on my breasts," she murmurs. "Not a whole glass; just enough to get down onto my nipples and make them harder for you."

"Because they'd already be hard, from lusting after me too?"

"Yes." Her chest pumps, faster and faster, against the hand I work beneath her bodice, pinching hard at her stiff peaks. "Yes!"

I pull my hand back. Yank it at my fly and then pull my cock free with it. "You know what that would make me say to you, don't you?"

"Tell me." She pleads it as I shuttle my throbbing length past the cleft of her buttocks, notching the crown at her intimate slit.

"I'd say you were my perfect little toy, begging me to play with you—at once. I'd pull your fingers to my lips across the table and order you to go to the ladies' room and prepare yourself to be played with hard." I tease my tip at her soaked pussy, having to clench my ass to keep from ramming all the way in. "Would you know what I meant by that, Ella?"

Her whole body shakes beneath mine. *Fucking...goddess. Sweet...toy.* "Y-Yes, Cassian. I would know what that meant."

"Then tell me."

"You would play with me...by fucking me."

I thrust deeper. But not all the way. "Like this? Or... deeper?"

"Deeper. Oh...Cassian!" She rocks her hips back, fighting to get more of me. "Please!"

"Harder?"

"Yes! *Harder...*"

"But you don't have the say." I feed her more of my length, but just for a second. Withdraw until I'm circling just the head in again, taunting her tunnel with my cock and the ridge of her clit with one finger. "You're the toy. You're played with. You're fucked...as *I* please."

Another tremor hits her all at once. I feel it overtake her, as she fights—and loses—the climax from rocking her into mindless, nearly babbling, bliss. "Yes!" she screams before the streams of rambling Arcadian take over, mixed with tears that rock her more violently than the orgasm. *"Yes,* Cassian. *Admak-tana,* Cassian. *Adsek-tana,* Cassian. Désonnum. *Rahmié,* Cassian. Désonnum...désonnum..."

Within minutes, I am coming as she does again, pumping her full of the completion I've needed all day and blasting my psyche through the turret's roof in the doing.

But not all the way to the stratosphere.

Even though she has just rocked my fucking world *again*, I cannot separate the celebration my body has just had from the unnerving translation my mind has made of her words... messengered on the notes of her tears, ripping into parts of me I cannot explain away to the simple flood of her post-orgasm emotion.

I adore you, Cassian.

I love you, Cassian.

Have mercy on me, Cassian.

I'm sorry. I'm sorry.

The words taunt me, even throughout our pleasant dinner

with Mom, Prim, and Hodge. Stab at me even while Ella and I have wine on the terrace afterward and her stare fixes on points miles across the city, taking her attention along with it. Become full-blown concern as her answers to my questions start to consist of one and two words—again, some even in Arcadian and not even making sense after translation.

Lost in translation.

After the sex was done, it's described the whole damn evening...

And prompts the question that whispers from my lips, as I tenderly twirl a strand of her hair, watching her sleep through the deepest hours of the night.

"What the hell happened to you today?"

I pray—yeah, really pray—that tomorrow, an answer will come from her that makes sense. That the only thing remaining between us *tomorrow* night will once again be simple shafts of moonlight.

But prayers haven't exactly gotten me very far before.

A recognition that prompts the final oath off my lips tonight.

"Shit. Shit. Shit."

CHAPTER THIRTEEN

MISHELLA

"Shit."

At first, I am answered only with a loud *thwop* from the vicinity of the bar in the main living room of the huge suite near the top of the Marriott Marquis. As I expect, Damon closes the refrigerator and turns, bearing a large can with what looks like green neon claw marks down its front.

"Aha." He flashes a fast version of his smug smirk. "So the lady *does* like a little swearing."

I fling back a glower. "The lady hates swearing. But she hates lying to the man she loves even more, especially for ten days straight."

And yes, I am counting every single hour, minute, and second of them. But if even half the evidence displayed in this room is right, my choice to help Damon with this happy-happy-joy-joy ruse will have been worth it. More than worth it.

I will have helped him save Cassian's life.

Even staring at all of this—the bank transactions, financial records, travel documents, and grainy photos, connected by string on six huge billboards—makes it easier to deal with the terse text he has just sent. It is his tenth one today, and I am certain a healthy handful more shall follow before we see each other—when I will regale him with a review of the play I did *not* see this afternoon, added to the mountain of *other* lies from the last week and a half.

Damon's gaze falls to my phone as he takes a long swig from the can. "Can't you just tell him you've taken up yoga lessons or something?"

"In the heart of the theater district?" I motion toward the bustle of Broadway and 45th, far below. "And how is that any different than lying to him about a theater outing?"

He drops the smirk into a contemplative shrug. "Easier, I guess. Fewer variables."

"Says the guy with fourteen years of experience at the art." My skin feels like thumbtacks as soon as the words are out. Though Damon hides it better, I have a feeling his does too. "Désonnum," I instantly mutter. "That was cruel."

He spurts out a harsh laugh. "Beg your pardon, Mistress Santelle, but *gros de grawl.*"

Double take. Literally. "Excuse me?"

He sips again on his green claw drink. "You know what it means."

"Of course I know what it means." It is only that the Arcadian version of *bullshit* is the last thing I expected from his insolent lips. "How do *you*—and *why*, with *me*—"

"Because you don't have a cruel bone in your body." He means it as fact; his gaze conveys as much—but I feel a blush suffusing my face exactly like the late-afternoon sun washing over the digital billboards outside. "My boy wonder of a little bro certainly found himself a female of quality."

"Well...merderim," I finally mutter.

"You're welcome," he answers.

Curious glance. "Just learning Arcadian in your spare time, hmmm?"

"As a matter of fact, yes." His face sobers as he gazes over the boards. "If getting to Cas through you didn't work, I had to be prepared to go to the island to stop this disaster he's walking into." He lifts his head a little, presenting a profile that halts me—not for the first time—with its similarities to his brother. There is no mistaking the proud Court forehead, the stubborn jawline, and the long, noble line of that nose. "But with the intel you've been able to sneak out of the office at Temptation and some of the things you've overheard and reported back, we're gathering such a mountain of evidence, there'll be nobody willing to let these 'contractors' act on their behalf overseas."

"Even Cassian."

"*Especially* Cassian." He inhales through his nose. "We just have to make sure we bury the real evidence—*deep*. Make it look like these guys simply have shoddy workmanship and late completion dates, instead of ties to an international terrorist like Rune Kavill."

I yank in a breath too—shakier than his. "Rune Kavill." My rasp is just as rickety, still weighted by the force of my disbelief. I never expected to be uttering that filthy bonsun's name again, after he messed with my land by backing Arcadian antigovernment radicals and then kidnapping my friend, Princess Brooke Cimarron.

For that, they had killed him.

And we had celebrated.

Apparently, prematurely.

Prince Samsyn and his special military team had thwarted Kavill in a covert raid on the house where they were holding Brooke, finishing the night by making certain Kavill was killed—several times over. But like a wraith charmed by an evil spell, the monster survived his wounds and then escaped

Arcadia—only to show up here and now, as the "blind investor" of a contracting firm Cassian has signed for new projects on Arcadia.

"The asshole's good." Damon concedes it from tight lips, pacing to the next bulletin board. "We've had to follow back the trail from here to Istanbul and back again. Covering it quietly won't be easy, but we're almost there."

Another shiver conquers me. From the dark daggers in his eyes and the fresh clench of his jaw, I can already interpret the extent of his meaning. *Covering it quietly* means the use of silencers, pillows, and shadow accounts of their own, not simply pushing mute buttons and freezing bank accounts. It will be messy....but lives will be saved.

Especially Cassian's.

And Brooke's.

I just have to keep telling myself that.

A lot.

And moments like this, in which I feel like I will never breathe normally again, will eventually pass. I battle to find extra room in my chest while turning to pace in front of the huge picture windows again. Far below, tourists in flip-flops and baseball caps stream along the sidewalks, gaping at the building-size ads for cologne, watches, diamonds, and plays about witches, wizards, sorcerers, and lions. Fantasy images for them...the realities of my world now. Yes, even the noble lions. A wildcat I am desperately trying to save now...even if it means having to lie to him.

Only for a little while longer...

The juxtaposition strikes me hard. The fantasy outside... the reality in here. The contradiction gives rise to a question.

"Damon?"

"Hmmm?"

"How do you do it?"

He continues peering at the boards, though he is far from distracted. The crackle of his attention fills the ten steps between us. "Do what?"

"Make sneaking around sound heroic."

More crackles, though they are indulged within a long silence. Just as quietly, he murmurs, "How do you think I've kept sane for the last fourteen years?"

"A dozen of which were *after* you answered your debt to the government," I point out. "So why did you stay on? Make the CIA your life?"

He tilts his head. For a moment, almost appears like I have asked if he has a pulse. "Because it *is* my life." The jut of his lower lip is synched to his simple shrug. "Yeah, it was shitty to have to 'die'—but in a lot of ways, it was a gift. I received a chance most people only dream of."

The answer in that blank space is clear. "A completely clean slate."

"Damn straight," he confirms. "But more than that. A clean slate—with the custom-built opportunity to make it count for good. To turn Damon Court into Bourne Jackson— the person I always wanted to be."

"A hero."

His lips spread. His stare glitters brightly. With just two words, I have given his spirit bars of solid gold. "Yeah. A hero."

Praying he does not throttle me for ruining the moment, my mouth twitches. "All right, but..."

"But what?"

"Bourne....Jackson?" I challenge.

Fortunately, he chuckles. "Hey, it's a kick-ass name!"

Snort. "For super spies who can accomplish miracles with the help of a great computer animation department." Says the woman who has taken the art of "super girlfriend" into a new cosmos this week, including viewing *way* too many super spy movies.

"And your point would be?"

"That we do not have the luxury of special effects."

It is a little harsher than I first intended—perhaps because I realize the words are for me as much as him. I act on them too, turning from the windows and leaving behind the world of fantasy for the reality of the task still before us...

And, *dear Creator please*, the finish line he has promised is in sight.

Damon, seeming to see the symbolism of my move, nods as I rejoin him—though his next drag on the energy drink appears more like a fortifying gulp from a cocktail. The impression is heightened when he sets the thing down on a nearby table with a decisive *thwong*.

"Mishella." He approaches. Plants his stance in front of me with equal verdict. "You need to know...when we're done with all this, I promise to disappear as fast as I came. It's not my intent to fuck with Cas's life or the good thing he's found with you. I'll be gone—for good."

For many seconds, I just shift from foot to foot. Fall back on the safety of some Vylet-style snark, in hopes of masking my discomfort. "Are you looking for a medal, James Bond? Because I do not have one."

He backs away. Huffs awkwardly. "Of course not. And I know that asking you to carry my secret is suckage to the *nth*."

"It is...all right, Damon." I wave a dismissive hand, flashing flecks from my bracelet across the room and raining similar sparks across my heart. Yes, the thing is flashy—and yes, completely inappropriate for any time of the day before cocktail hour—but I refuse to remove it outside the shower or bedroom. Especially now, when I need the reminder of Cassian's love too damn much. The reminder of everything he means to me...of why I am deliberately deceiving him, and will continue to do so, until his life is safe. "What other choice do we have?" I need to say it aloud too. "To tell Cassian about all this? Then...what...we would have to kill him, right?"

My deepest hope is that Damon laughs that off. My darkest dread is that he confirms it.

Nowhere in those visceral fears have I accounted for his actual reaction.

"*We* won't kill him, Mishella." He grates it out from a jaw turned to stone—shadowed by a gaze turned dark and ruthless as a dragon's. "The bad guys will. Without mercy. And without hesitation."

CASSIAN

"I'm not the goddamn bad guy here."

Doyle lifts a brow at me. Keeps it hiked while glancing back down at my phone—and the text screen it's open to. "Did I say that?"

I rock back in my big home office chair, drumming both thumbs against the screen—battling to be casual about it. "You're very good about not *saying* anything."

D angles back in his own chair. Hikes his legs up, crossing them at the ankles atop the small conference table. "You're also very good about not needing lip gloss to get through your day, honey."

"What the hell is that supposed to—"

He smirks as my phone dings. Stabs a finger down at the thing. "Lip gloss."

"Shut up." I bite it with extra vehemence after reading Ella's newest reply to me.

Thanks for checking in! Intermission right now. Show is very good. Be home soon. I love you. Toodles.

"Toodles?" I glare at the screen, feeling like goddamn Mr. Magoo, too blind and stupid to see the Mack truck about to flatten me. Blind because I can't see straight from loving her. Stupid because it's turned me into a paranoid sonofabitch merely existing between texts from the woman who is doing exactly what I exhorted her to do since the second she got to New York: getting out and enjoying the city. And how have I reacted about it? Tethered her to me with these nonstop, needy texts—even though every night, she has been a lover like none I've ever known, open and generous, nearly desperate in her desire...

And there it is.

The one cog that won't fit in the machine.

The fissure in the castle walls.

The smear of the goddamn lip gloss.

Her desperate, constant need to keep pleasing me.

Lip gloss—across the demeanor of a woman who has never wanted or needed that kind of pretense before. Suddenly, everything about Ella is slicked in this weird version of the stuff—from the princess-perky way she greets each day, to the toe-curling passion with which she ends my nights, to all the strange, Stepford wife moments in between. Constant back and foot rubs. Agreeing to a week's worth of spy movies without a concession from me to a musical. My favorite sandwiches at lunch, joined by plates of nonstop lemon bars...

Followed by all the afternoons *away* from the house.

In damn near the same part of town.

Always, *always,* somewhere near or in the theater district.

Most times, she just wants to see a matinee or get some shopping done. Two days ago, it was a nail appointment. Four days ago, a hair trim.

Only who goes to the theater district for shit like that?

Doyle snorts—hard enough to ensure he has read those thoughts just by looking at me. "You know you're beyond pussy-whipped, don't you?"

I push up from the chair. "You know I told you to shut up, don't you?" I jam a hand through my hair. I'm in home office attire, tailored but casual pants and a V-neck tee, but everything still feels too tight and hot. "And get your feet off the fucking furniture."

He answers by recrossing his ankles. "Scott's already texted too, hasn't he? Assured you she texted him too and he's already waiting outside the theater? Ahhhh"—he finger-guns me with both forefingers—"I'm *right!*"

"Big fucking deal." I descend back into my chair. "So am I."

"Says what fucking judge and jury?"

"Says this one."

The declaration is menacing as a grizzly—fitting, since Hodge resembles a new breed of the animal from where he hulks in the doorway, hair semiwild and eyes black with vengeance.

And making every hair on my neck seize as if I were sitting here with a packed picnic basket.

While every instinct in my body screams from the truth

stamped across his face.

The contents on the data stick in his hand won't divulge a goddamn picnic.

I push back to my feet. Suddenly, my legs are blocks of ice, fed by the glacier already dominating my chest, sluicing ice water through my veins. Not even my hard swallow redistributes the heat from the only thing on fire inside: the pain burning in my eye sockets, already dreading the images that stick will ignite to life on my desk monitor.

Hodge lumbers across to the desk but balks once he's standing in front of me. The edges of his gaze tighten, making my gut do the same thing. He's only ten years older than me, but at times like this, the paternal vibes are undeniable...

And never more appreciated.

Despite what I spit the next second.

"Shit."

"What?" Doyle charges. "What the *hell* is—"

"How bad, Hodge?" I grate.

His mouth twists. "She hasn't been going to the theater, Cas. Or to the salon."

"*What?*" It snarls from Doyle as I stab the stick into the port on my laptop. I add nothing to it—verbally. The cloud of my fury on the air is likely enough to blow the building, even without a match.

"Fuuuuck." Again, Doyle supplies the soundtrack for our shock. He repeats the word in several forms as image after image blares to life on the screen.

Ella, getting out of the Jag in front of the Majestic theater. The iconic phantom mask posters beneath the wooden balconies.

Ella, *leaving* the theater's back entrance.

Ella, crossing 45th Street...

And running into the Marriott Marquis.

On a different day, Hodge has caught a full video of her...

Entering the same hotel, through the front entrance.

Still images return—with shots of her inside one of the hotel's clear glass elevators. Then a video of the same thing, on a clearly different day.

I tear the stick out of the drive. Clench fingers around it so hard, the plastic casing cracks beneath my thumb. Hodge and Doyle are still and silent—poised as if ready for anything. But I have no fucking idea what that "anything" is. I spin away from them, elbow propped on the arm of my chair, thumb digging at the two inches' worth of data that have imploded my soul, wondering how the hell I'm going to take my next breath let alone move my body or form coherent words.

"Christ." Doyle finally slices it into the silence like a dagger on silk. "Jesus *Christ*, I thought she was"—he clears his throat—"different."

"Me too, lad," Hodge murmurs. "Me too."

I yearn to wheel back around and punch them both. Strain the astonishment from their statements, and there's one thing left. Their pity.

Goddammit, not for me. Not now.

My lips finally part. And shockingly, a word stammers out. "Name."

When neither of them answer, I bark it.

"*Name*, Hodge." I spin back around. Slam the drive to the desk. "She's going to the same goddamn room, isn't she?"

"Y-Yeah," he stammers.

"So *what* is the fucker's name?"

Hodge straightens. Jerks up his chin, grimly accepting

exactly where I'm going with the interrogation. "He's in a suite on the high floor."

"Of course he is," Doyle spits.

"His name is Bourne Jackson."

At once, the wrath drops out Doyle's composure.

As the bottom drops out of my damn soul.

No.

Shit. Fuck.

No.

The room lurches, even as it's filled with a fresh sound: Doyle's howl of a disbelieving laugh. "Bourne...*what?*"

"Jackson." Hodge glances from D to me, confused. But his perplexity comes nowhere close to mine, still hanging on for its fucking life as the room keeps cavorting like a seaside funhouse—

The kind Damon and I used to spend hours in...

"That is *not* the asshole's name." Doyle's protest pings through my conscious, disembodied and fuzzy, like someone trying to communicate over the funhouse's PA.

"That's the name on the room." Hodge's voice isn't much clearer, still replete with bewilderment.

"Dude," Doyle asserts. "I'm telling you—"

"He's right." I bite it out while yanking open the top drawer of my desk. "Hodge," I clarify, while sliding out a piece of paper that's folded into fourths, "Hodge...is right, D..."

"What the fuck?"

I don't answer him. I can't, propelled backward by over fifteen years as I stare at the paper, printed on one side with algebra equations. The answers, all in pencil, have faded with time. On the other side of the paper, in pen, is a page full of adolescent scribbles, topped by a headline in careful block lettering.

THE ARTICLES OF THE SUPER SECRET BROTHERHOOD

Bourne Jackson, President and CEO and Secretary (better at cursive)

Bond Connery, Vice-President and COO and Treasurer (better at math)

My psyche is a windstorm. A turbulent, flailing mess, whirling rage and confusion and anguish through the glass of my soul and the boundaries of my heart, until I am decimated past all else but one certain plan of action—which I begin by jolting to my feet and impaling Hodge and Doyle with a pair of take-no-prisoners stares.

"Call Scott," I charge to Hodge. "And tell him if Ella 'gets out of her show' before I arrive, he is to tell her to walk her ass back into the Marquis and wait for me there."

I flip my attention to Doyle—but he is already on his feet, truck keys in hand. "I'll drive. You're not seeing anything straight at all right now."

I nod and follow him out the door.

I don't argue with the man when he's right.

CHAPTER FOURTEEN

MISHELLA

"Please tell me we are done."

I punctuate it with a long groan, a longer stretch, and a tired glance over at Damon. We have been, in his words, "hitting it hard" for the last two and a half hours, attempting to connect the final name on Cassian's Arcadian contractor list to any known entities associated with Rune Kavill. So far, it looks like we have a connection: a steel company who will make custom girders for several bridges to be rebuilt within the next five to ten years.

Damon rises too. Rolls his head, making his neck crack several times, while making another pass in front of the billboards. "For today, we are," he answers to my question. "Overall, I'd say we're damn close." He scrubs both hands down his face. "At least I fucking hope we are."

A breeze of concern blows nettles through my belly. "Because...?"

"Because I was only given clearance to chase this shit for two weeks." He lets his arms fall, stretching his hands and wiggling his fingers. Everything we have mapped out on the boards, he has also carefully recorded on his smart pad—meaning all ten of his digits have had no rest for the last week and a half. "We don't have it all buttoned down, but it's enough to make the higher-ups listen and hopefully start on some action against all these fuckers."

"When?"

"End of the week, likely," he responds. "If not, first thing next week."

It is not the answer I'd expected—but so much better. Relief hits me in a rush, making me drop back down to the couch. "Thank the Creator," I blurt, also in a rush—but hurry to fix the fallout as the man's shoulders visibly slump. "Damon... hey..." *Ugh.* Why am I actually stumped here? He is a grown man. A *spy*, for the love of the powers. "It has...been real," I stammer, going for one of Vy's favorite trite-isms. "And it has been fun. Just cannot say it has been real fun, okay?"

He groans. Chuckles. Shakes his head. "Where the hell did you scrape that one up, Sancti girl?"

I grin. "Somewhere in Sancti, I think."

"Right."

He rocks back on his heels. A long moment stretches by, thick with us both scuffing toes into the carpet, awkward as a pair of tortoises on a dance floor.

Finally, I query softly, "There is no spy movie precedent for this, is there?"

"Not a damn one," Damon mutters.

"Or any obscure CIA handbook thing?"

"Only if one of us was getting ready to diffuse a bomb first."

Tick...

Tock...

The pounds at the door, three demanding blows in a row, lurch me to my feet, heartbeat surging to my throat. Though Damon's reaction is not so skittish, his face creases and his body tenses. In seconds, his Court lion takes over. He prowls across the room, silencing me with a finger at his lips—stunning me by brandishing a revolver that seems to appear from nowhere.

Three seconds. Three knocks. And everything has changed. Less than a minute ago, we were sitting here laughing about spy movies. Rune Kavill was just a black and white name up on a board. Now, there is a gun in Damon's hand and Kavill could be the fiend on the other side of that door, blasting through because he really *is* unkillable...

This is dangerous.

The awareness stabs deep and hard, gushing raw terror to my throat as Damon motions for me to duck behind the couch.

This is real.

I cower, trembling and cold, as he creeps coolly to the door. I am almost angry at him. Spy or not, how can he be so calm?

This is truly insane.

Every cell in my body freezes as he yells out, "Who is it?"

I could truly die.

And am now certain that I *will*, as the intruding assholes do not wait to knock again.

They break down. Crash in. Invade, whooshing in like a clash of Titan-class superheroes—only a thousand times more loud, terrifying, and floor-shaking.

"Room service, motherfucker."

Doyle?

"Drop the heat. *Now.*"

Hodge?

"Against the wall. Do it!"

Oh, dear Creator. No.

I forget about cowering now. My shock propels down my arms and pulls me up on knees still made of mush and feet still formed of lead. Compels my gaping eyes to comprehend the surreal truth of the scene in front of me.

"*Cassian?*"

I am answered only with a look full of so much fire and agony and pain, it forces me to drop again. I kneel on the couch, every nerve clenching, my stomach turning inside out, as I realize exactly why his face is contorted like that and why his eyes pierce me with such glimmering green allegation. He has leapt to the same conclusion *I* would in his place. A lover gone every afternoon. Vague texts during those hours. Every night, giving him a pretty, perfect toy to make up for it.

How much of a fool have I taken him to be?

The pain of that same question is hard as jade in his eyes, coarse as granite across his lips...

Violent as a pissed-off Titan in the blow he drives into Damon's face.

"Cassian!" I scream. "Dear Creator! *Stop!*"

"Stop?" It rips from somewhere deep within him, sounding like an erupting volcano—in the middle of the Antarctic. Fire and ice, fury and pain, laughter and tears all roll from him, sloppy as the steps he traces in a wide circle before wheeling around, honing in again on Damon. "Fuck, I'm just getting started."

Hodge and Doyle grab Damon by the elbows. Hoist him back up for Cassian's second punch.

"*Cassian! Calmay olmak!* Plait! Plait!"

Damon groans. "Christ, Cas. Just—"

"Don't 'Christ, Cas' me. Don't *speak* to me until I get to twenty-four on this count, you motherfucker." He rains two more blows. "One for every year you were gone. Another one for every day you fucked my woman. The last of it's going right up your ass, you selfish excuse for a human being."

"By the Creator." I scramble off the couch. Stumble over and twist a fist into Cassian's shirt, though the effort feels like trying to use a dinner napkin to stop the *Titanic*. I throw a beseeching stare to Doyle and Hodge, but it is just as useless. "Cassian, *please!*"

"Get away, Ella. I'm warning you. *Now.*"

"For the love of your God, we did not—*he* did not—"

"I never touched her," Damon snarls.

Cassian flinches. Just a little. I accept it as a toehold—and after a hard gulp, use *his* shoulder to swing myself around, directly in the path of his fist.

"He was saving your life, dammit!"

His teeth lock. Seethe. His chest pumps. Heaves. His gaze glitters. Shatters. Turns to heavy, agonized liquid, sliding down over his beautiful, broken face...

As his fist spreads apart. Tremors.

And falls, cupping my face instead.

"*We* were saving your life." I lift my arms. Delve my hands into his hair, pulling him down for a shaking, sweaty kiss. "Just let him explain. Let him tell you everything. He—he saved your life fourteen years ago, and he is doing it again now."

His fingers tighten against my skin, betraying the terrible conflict of his decision...the incriminating toll it already racks from his spirit. Hating Damon has become the default of his heart, a setting achieved through years of such pain and sorrow that changing it now is unfathomable to him...a darkness I am begging him to plunge right back into...

I pull him closer as he plummets to his knees, rocking into me and pushing his forehead against mine. "I know what I am asking." I whisper it, hovering our lips close, swiping the salty drops from his face with my thumbs. "I know how deeply this hurts, how terrifying this is...that I am asking you to trust our future over your past. But think about what I am saying. *Our* future, Cassian. This is for me as much as you. Please...listen!"

Breaths blow in and out of him, rough and desperate and shaking. A low keen echoes up his throat, like a wounded animal begging to simply be killed. "Goddammit, Ella..."

"You *must* listen to him, Cassian. For the sake of your *life*."

He jerks back. Impales me all over again with the fury of his glare. "Why the hell do you keep saying that? My life? What the hell?"

"The people you're about to sign contracts with for Arcadia... They want to ruin my country from the inside out, and they will not think twice about cutting you down to do it."

He jolts again. "What the *fuck*?"

"It's true." The croak comes from Damon, released from Doyle's and Hodge's grips and now leaning against the wall, nursing his swollen face. "I know my word means shit to you right now, but I've got a wall of proof to back it up."

Cassian follows the trajectory of his jabbing thumb. "Holy mother of..." He stops, eyeing Damon with new realization. "*Mother*. Shit. *Mom*. When she finds out that you're—"

"She won't," Damon cuts in. "I'm sorry, boy wonder. She *can't*. It's a fluke that *you* did, and now—"

"You're going to have to kill me for it?"

I mock-smack him in the jaw. "Can we *please* stop jesting about your death like it is dryer lint?"

Damon chuckles in agreement, though winces as a finish. I weather another wave of remorse, viewing what damage Cassian managed to inflict on him, before remembering the man has actually survived death already. "Maybe the best way to rectify that is to start at the beginning," he suggests.

"After we get some ice on your face," I counter.

"Not *too* much ice," Cassian quips. "I sort of like being the prettier one for once."

Damon snorts. "Oh, you were *always* the prettier one, honey."

"Shut it, douche bag."

"Just help me up, sweet pea."

And I am unable to hold back the fresh sting behind my eyes as I watch Cassian reach out to his brother...

and hold on tight.

CASSIAN

Okay, so this isn't the craziest day of my life.

Who the hell am I kidding?

It's the craziest fucking day of my life.

I shake my head while finally letting myself sit again. Ella remains pressed to my side, where she's been every second since I decided to hear Damon out instead of killing him, and I gratefully tug her close. Right now, she's the only thing resonating as real in all this. Maybe I really *am* going to wake up next to her any second, watching the sunlight play through her curls before I rouse her with a soft kiss, a hard fuck, and then the insane details of this dream...

So get this, armeau. *I dreamed Damon was alive and told me he faked his own death to protect Mom and me from a drug cartel before taking a new name to work for the CIA. He came out of hiding because he discovered a new threat—to Arcadia. Terrorists were posing as contractors for the new infrastructure projects for Court Enterprises, and he needed to warn me, so...*

"So what happens next?" She asks it with her head against a pillow—just not the right one. Doesn't stop the sight of her from sucking the breath from my lungs as her hair fans over the tapestry pattern of the hotel's decorative bolster. With one hand wrapped around my knee and the other assisting in her question of Damon, it's almost as if we're sitting in the den at Temptation and Damon's just relaying the plot of a good spy movie.

The only thing missing now...is Mom.

And a completely different set of circumstances.

Not so goddamn dangerous ones.

Damon plants his stance on both long legs. I'm struck anew by how little he's changed but how *everything* has changed. He's just a couple of inches taller than he was at sixteen, though now buffed-out as hell. His skin glows with health instead of the pasty paleness that once broadcasted his drug addiction. And he's still an arrogant son of a bitch, despite the bruises from the blows I inflicted.

I'm not sorry for them either.

I'm also not sorry that I didn't kill him.

I was prepared to, though. I couldn't see past the rage or through fourteen years of accumulated loneliness and heartbreak. Seeing him in the flesh had triggered shock, betrayal, and insult topped only by the moment Lily committed suicide before my eyes. I'd wanted Damon to pay. Parts of me still do, even after hearing his story about what happened at the hands of Santiago Noriega, who remains a key nemesis in the global drug wars even now. Doing business across the globe means having to be aware of that kind of filth too.

Which leads back to the present issue.

The projects on Arcadia.

ANGEL PAYNE

And the fact that two-thirds of my vendor list has to be tossed out.

"What *does* happen now?" I echo Ella's question, unnerved that I don't have even the beginnings of an answer myself. "I've already got materials ordered...project managers working with locals on the island..." How many of them can be trusted now? *Who* among them is really a puppet for Rune Kavill, and what kind of violence might he be planning as we speak, not only for Arcadia but the whole Mediterranean region?

Damon slants a determined stare. "Crazy as this sounds, you remain at business-as-usual, brother."

"*What?*" Ella pushes up, gaze glittering. "That monster's minions might be running around on Arcadia as we speak—"

"In disguise," Damon prompts, spreading both hands. "They have to lie low too. They're not going to just storm the palais—"

"Like they did less than six months ago?" she retorts. "Breaking in on Queen Camellia in her private chambers—before they took Brooke Cimarron hostage? *That* kind of lying low?"

"Which means they won't get so bold again. Not right away."

"Damon's right." I endure her—*and* Damon's—stunned stares while leaning forward, squaring my posture into the all-business he's asking for. "I'm sorry, armeau." I reach for her hand, encouraged when she lets me hang on. "But he is. If I start pulling contracts right and left, that'll throw up red flags. They'll know we're on to their game."

Her nose crunches. "And puts you right into their path."

I stroke across her knuckles before lifting them to my lips. For a respite of a moment, I let myself swim in the azure seas of her eyes. "Now I'm *really* glad I asked you to blow up that contract and stay longer."

Doyle yanks me out of the water with his I'm-not-really-coughing cough. Too late. Damon is already shooting a look of strange curiosity.

"Contract?" he demands. "What the—"

"Yes, well." Ella scoops up her phone and flits to her feet, distracting everyone by whirling her hair and dress with the ease of a model in a shampoo ad. "I still owe my parents *that* particular update. Excuse me for a moment?" Before Damon can get in another word, she's disappeared into the suite's second bedroom.

Before she can fully unlock her phone once she's there, I've joined her.

And shut the door. And locked it.

And pulled her to the bed. And down into a long, wet, I-need-you-more-than-air kiss. In response, she moans into my mouth, tangles her fingers in my hair, and fits her body to mine in all the best, curviest places. I accept every scintilla of her passion, letting her magic drench me, devour me, control me. Though my jewels are on her wrist, *she* is the one who holds *me* captive—and I never want to be set free.

Many minutes later, I finally let her pull away a little. With hooded eyes and a sultry smile, she traces the edges of my mouth with the oval of one fingernail. "Hmmm. I like what sibling rivalry does to you, Mr. Court."

I let her emphasize that with a brush of her lips, answering with a long, rough purr. "Thank fuck you stepped in when you did. The punches for touching you would've been twice as hard."

"*Cassian.*" She jabs a soft knee into my ribs. "He was a

gentleman. Always."

"I know," I console. "I know. But if he *had*—"

"*Aggghh.*" The knee thrusts harder. I laugh softly.

"Didn't you come in here for a reason?" Time to change the subject before I switch it up by myself—like conjuring an excuse to lift her skirt, shove aside her panties, and get inside her while my brother, my valet, and my houseman listen enviously from the next room. "Something about a text to your mom and dad...?"

She huffs. Rolls her eyes. But finally mutters, "Yes. Regrettably. I updated them briefly once we decided to appear on Chantal's show but was vague about how."

I scowl. "And they didn't blow up your phone *after* we went on?" More importantly, they didn't blast her about how the whole damn thing ended?

"Surprisingly, no—but that was likely because the media sentiment swayed with *you*." She punctuates with a soft snarl. "As it should have. Chantal pulled a smarmy move, and everyone knows it."

"I'm also a little protective, and everyone knows it."

"And everyone *loves* you for it." She wriggles closer, turning up her face with that corner lip bite that makes me a little crazier for her with every new incarnation. "My passionate, neurotic warrior."

I dip in. Am unable to resist tasting her again. "Neurotic warrior. Hmmm. *That* ought to go over well with Maimanne and Paipanne."

She giggles. "Definitely."

I brush some curls off her face...and let a rush of instinct rise within me. Higher. Stronger. Guiding words out of me that I've not expected...but feel so damn right.

"You know what might go over better?"

"What?"

"'Neurotic fiancé.'"

Heavy blink. Complete stillness. I'm not even sure she's breathing, until a deep gulp moves down her throat. "Wh-What?"

I let a smile rise up, originating from the depths of my heart. Gather a handful of her soft, golden curls in my hand, making sure her gaze is subject to the full intent of mine...all the love inside me...all the completion my soul will know with no one else...

"Mishella DaLysse Santelle, I want you become Mishella DaLysse Court. To be with me forever. To keep saving my ridiculous life...so I can keep owing you every inch of my heart...my body...my spirit."

"Cassian. I—"

"I already know your heart belongs to me." I lift my fingertips to her jaw, running them over that proud angle... the outline of the face I now know I cannot live without. "And I already know your soul won't be so easy because part of it belongs to Arcadia. Well, now part of mine does too." I answer her questioning gape with a resolved nod. "This craziness Damon has presented, making me reevaluate and rethink all the projects we have there, has made me realize they aren't just 'projects' anymore. I care about making things right in Arcadia...for you. *With* you."

She answers that with a high gasp. A joyous sigh. An excited little nod—before the fervent, passionate press of her lips and the sweet, salty flow of her tears, melding her heat and her life and her love into me...

Until the door to the living room is nearly unhinged from

the beats of an urgent knock.

We break apart. Sit up on the bed.

"*What?*" I bark.

"Put your clothes on." Doyle's bellow is no-nonsense. "And get your ass out here."

Something in the timbre of his voice sparks me to move faster than usual. Ella clearly detects the same urgency. She has herself righted and out the door before me...

Making me regret instantly that I let her win the race.

Just steps into the living room, she halts on a horrified cry. It's layered by the most stunned version of the F-word that's ever left my lips. Hodge and Doyle are on my train, gritting the word as well. The only silent person in the room is my brother. The grim line of his mouth and the terse set of his shoulders surpasses the boundary of words—perhaps the most fitting reaction to what we witness on the huge TV monitor on the wall.

The Grand Sancti Bridge, connecting the two halves of Arcadia's capital city over the wide Mousselayan River, is one of the architectural icons Arcadia got right the *first* time, an engineering triumph as well as an artistic jaw-dropper. Its soaring towers were designed to resemble a pair of flying dragons, named Pan and Faunus after the Greek and Roman versions of the god who lived in the mythological version of Arcadia. They were constructed with massive sheet metal "wings" that would balance on the wind to emulate flight...

Right now, only one of those dragons flies over the river.

The other is slowly sinking into it.

Along with half the bridge.

TGN's live feed is dominated by shades of yellow, red, and black—the flames engulfing one end of the bridge. In a corner of the screen is the slow-motion explanation for the disaster: a detonation in the center of the expanse that cannot be interpreted as anything but a purposeful act of violence.

In TGN's give-us-the-ratings style, the replay of the explosion isn't edited. At least a dozen men, all in Arcadian security forces uniforms, are thrown high into the air—and then into the river's churning waters. Several more fall directly in, already hopelessly incinerated.

"Oh...*Creator*!" Ella sags against me, grief claiming her like an earthquake, buckling her body as her spirit falls apart. I hang on tight, knowing the worst hasn't even hit her. But as soon as it does...

"*Saynt*."

Yeah. There it is.

She grips my shirt with strength only possible from pure fear, her eyes wide and white, her lips dripping with tears.

"Saynt! No! Oh, Saynt!"

"Her brother," I explain to Damon.

"He serves?" he inquires.

I get out half a nod before her phone blares from the bed where we were just kissing in joy. I pray, with everything in me that still believes in that shit, that the karma from *that* moment continues.

Doyle brings her the device, still rocking with Patrick Stump's voice. With a shriek I can't define as happy or crushed, she punches it to speaker mode.

"S-Saynt? *Saynt?* Dear Creator, p-please—oh please tell me—"

"Ssshh. Mishella. I am here. It is me, *fembla*."

"Praise to the saints!" She crumbles to the couch. I sit with her, mentally overriding my body's instinct to pace, to respond, to *act*. Right now, the top of my action list—the *only* thing on my action list—is being here for her. Holding her. Supporting her.

Cassian...you are my rock...

Damn straight. And this time, I intend to prove it.

"Are—are you all right?" she demands at her brother. "Are you injured? What the *hell* happened?"

"I am fine." Now that the initial rush of relief is behind us, more sounds are discernible over the line. Sirens. Shouts. Barking dogs, likely on the hunt for more explosives. "The night watch on the bridge found the bomb. Samsyn ordered it be closed, but a group of teenagers wanted to get closer and watch the 'action.' A team had to chase them..."

When he interrupts himself with a choke, Ella's face twists, also in pain. The woman's middle name should be Empathy, but the connection with her brother is especially tight. Even from thousands of miles away, she hears—and feels—the anguish in his voice.

"And then what?" she insists. "Saynt—*tell me*."

"Alak Navarre was on the team that chased the kids."

Her body quivers. Caves in, shoulders hunching, as she stabs a hand through her hair, whispering, "Wh-What? *Vylet's* Alak?"

"Mishella. He—he did n-not make it."

"Ella." I reach for her hand. She latches on like I'm driftwood in a storm, twisting her arms around me from wrist to elbow. I wrap my bandaged hand around her shoulders, hugging her trembling form more tightly.

"Where—where is Vylet?" she asks into the phone.

"At his parents' home. As Alak's *betranli*, she will assist them in the mourning process."

"I have been away for two months, brother, not two years. I will call—"

"She is not accepting any calls."

"She will accept mine."

"Respectfully, sister, I do not think so."

"It does not matter. I will be there in person anyway."

"Ella—"

"I am on my way, Saynt."

"*No.*" The protest belongs to Damon. I warn him off with a glare, but he persists, "If Kavill has sniffed that we're on to him, this move could've been made in retaliation. In that case—"

"Kavill?" Saynt interjects on a snarl. "What the *hell*? Is that *kimfuk* not rotting in his own half-dead carcass somewhere?"

"Regrettably not," Damon growls.

"So how the hell is *he* mixed up in all this? And who the fuck was *that*?"

"Saynt." I lean forward, speaking to him as I always have: as equals. "It's Cassian. We'll explain more once we're there. My plane can be ready to go in a couple of hours, and then—"

"*No.*" Saynt's rebuttal is swift and certain. "Even twelve hours ago, *I* would have been sending *you* forty million for that promise, Court, but the situation is different now." A tired sigh churns out of him. "Arcadia is different now."

"Which is why I need to be there." Aftershocks still rule Ella's every movement, but she stands, rising to a regal stance that crashes me with brand-new admiration and adoration for her. *Dear God, what a woman you have brought to me.*

"Ella," Saynt intones. "It is not safe—"

"I do not give a *shit* about safe!" Her arms twist at her sides, ending in stubborn fists. Her nose is a bellow of incensed breaths. Her face is a collection of fury and fire and take-no-shit resolve.

And goddammit if she isn't more beautiful now than the day I met her.

Which is why, without hesitation, I reach for her once more. Link my spirit with hers as I mold my body against hers, silently pledging all my tomorrows to her, no matter what the risks or dangers. I pour that vow into a tender kiss, pressed into her crumpled forehead, as she turns once more into me. Grips me so hard she trembles. Clings to me like her rock in the sea. And with the action, though she is lost to so much grief and pain, *she* is *my* rock too.

"Cassian?" Her scent, floral and tropical and all her, wraps around me. Her warmth surrounds me.

"Armeau." I breathe it into her hair, sensing she needs to know it...to feel it. *You are my gift, Mishella. Always.*

"I—I am scared."

I grip her closer. "It's all right to be scared."

"You make it better, though."

"You make *everything* better, Ella."

"Promise me...no matter what happens when we get back...you will not let me go."

I slide both hands beneath her face. Tilt it up until I'm lost once more in her crystalline eyes, her brave face, the joyous connection of her heart and soul to mine. "As long as you promise the same thing."

Her lips edge up. "I promise."

I capture her lips in a soft kiss. "You know I love you."

"I love you too."

"We're going to get through this mess, okay?"

Her smile turns into a little tease. "Probably the first of

many in our lifetime."

I kiss her again—with all the feeling flooding my heart, pouring through my soul, solidifying my existence.

It doesn't get more perfect than this.

Continue the Temptation Court Series with Book Three

Bold Beautiful Love

Keep reading for an excerpt!

EXCERPT FROM *BOLD BEAUTIFUL LOVE*

BOOK THREE IN THE TEMPTATION COURT SERIES

CASSIAN

A sky of stars. A cushion of clouds.

Heaven is nearly close enough to touch, and it doesn't matter.

The woman I love, attempting to sleep as we fly through the night to the middle of the Mediterranean Sea, is going through hell.

The recall of what sent her there still burns hard in my mind. We'd clutched each other in the middle of a suite at the Marriott Marquis, oblivious to the bustling heart of Manhattan below, as a news report dominated the monitor on the wall in front of us. The images, fed live from the only home she'd ever known before coming to New York with me two months ago, depicted Arcadia island's main bridge as it exploded apart. The river below it had instantly been turned into a mire of floating wreckage...

And carnage.

The bodies of people she'd known. The friends she'd loved.

Soldiers...protecting the country she was equally devoted to.

Including the man who'd been preparing to marry her best friend.

That had been four hours ago.

Fifteen minutes after I'd proposed to *her.*

Fifteen minutes before I'd picked up my phone and ordered this jet be prepared to take off so we could immediately fly back to that island.

It wasn't a decision that made my CIA super spy of a brother—or *her* Arcadian super soldier of a brother—anything close to thrilled. Not that their stress could be blamed. There was a damn good chance the explosion had been orchestrated by a terrorist not even bearing a holy cause for his evil. Rune Kavill's simply a sick fuck who jacks off to the idea of global domination and is hell-bent on acquiring Arcadia as his forward operating base from the Mediterranean. Add the masochistic ax he has to grind against the Arcadian royal family, and the recipe's been right for the bastard to form a dozen shell companies, all disguised as contractors for the infrastructure projects I've been getting ready to start on the island.

Because God forbid Mishella Santelle and I have a *moment* of smooth waters during this wild ride we're calling a relationship.

Or that the world will ever let us think otherwise.

Ella mumbles and sighs. Turns to her side and burrows against me.

Her tawny lashes flutter open—with new tears sparkling on their russet crescents.

I settle to the pillow next to her, brushing red-gold coils off her lush face...the features I've fallen hopelessly in love with. Hers is a face so unlike any other, as if clinging to the past just like the ways of her island home. Until recently, Arcadia was a kingdom stoically committed to old-fashioned ways and a more pastoral lifestyle. In the same way, Ella's face belongs more in a Victorian cameo instead of paparazzi glare—to which she's been ruthlessly exposed since I dragged her back to New York with me two months ago.

Dragged.

It's the word that says too much and not enough at the same time—referring to one of the most brilliant business moves I've ever made, yet the one inducing my harshest cringe of shame. There was likely another way to free Ella from her parents' stifling grip, but at the time, it sure as hell wasn't making itself known, so I resorted to the drastic. Put a number on it. Purchased six months of her life for forty million dollars.

Worth.

Every.

Penny.

No. Not even that. Not anymore. Beyond that.

Far beyond.

The thought sears me as her beauty overwhelms me...as her tears gut me. I'd cut off my balls to prevent even one more of them from leaving her in sorrow—but as more trickle down her creamy cheeks, I must accept that for now, this is all I *can* do. Gather her closer, silently willing the plane to go faster, to get her to the land she loves so deeply...

Ripped apart by a tragedy we still can't fathom.

"Cassian."

Her whisper, a broken breath against my chest, heightens my senses. I smell her, flowers and sleep and the wine I made her sip after we boarded. I feel her, full of nerves despite the Cabernet. I crave her, just as strongly—*stronger*—as the last time she was on this plane and we were headed for the six months in New York I'd planned on using to flush her from my system. I'd been determined to take her virginity, pay her back for the gift with self-confidence to last a lifetime, and then send her into that life without a backward thought for New York or me. My own sanity would be free for the same focus, back to running Court Enterprises with the same single-minded aim on my three-pronged formula for success: taking care of my mother, taking care of my employees, and taking care of my dick.

Three prongs. Simple, right? First rule of engineering: *keep it simple, shithead.*

Well, I got the "shithead" part right.

Forming even three *syllables* seems impossible at the moment, but I manage. "Hey, sweet girl."

Ella rolls a little, peering into the darkness beyond the window. "Where are we?"

"Still over the Atlantic. We will be for a while yet."

Wistful sigh. "All right. I just wish—"

"If I could speed up time I would, *armeau.*"

My favorite endearment from her language causes her to turn back, one hand raising to my chest. "Perhaps I am better off wishing for something else."

I scoot a finger beneath her chin. Tug up. "Like what?"

"Maybe for time to stand still instead."

I rub my thumb over the gentle curve of her chin. "Why?"

She captures the corner of her lip beneath her teeth. Exhales shakily. "What if...things are different when we return?" More tears glisten in her bright-blue gaze. "Not just the bridge and Sancti itself, but"—she drops her stare to the bottom of my throat—"everyone."

"Everyone...like Vylet?"

As I invoke her best friend's name, her features contort. "Oh, dear Creator!" More of those damn tears fall. "She and

Alak...they were everyone's hope..."

"Hope of what?" It's a quiet utterance—probably too much so—but what she needs more than anything right now isn't more tears. She needs fortitude. A wide shoulder. And dammit, I plan on being that shoulder...for the rest of her life.

"That—that it all worked," she rasps. "That two people could be 'arranged' but still find it all. Devotion, connection... love."

I hear her final word but don't comprehend it. Not really. I'm still stuck on the other word in the statement that should negate it. "Wait. *Whoa.* Vylet and Alak are—*were*—" Shit. I hate changing the tense, but the sooner I get used to it, the sooner I'll start getting *her* used to it. "Your best friend, and the fiancé she was bat-shit in love with, were—"

"Arranged." She supplies it with a stunning jolt of pragmatism. Blinks at me, almost angrily. "Yes. By their parents, at the age of thirteen." A shrug hitches at the shoulder she isn't lying on. "It was a little early, but it was also clear to everyone that Vy and Alak were meant to be—"

"A little *early*?" I cut in.

A scowl, edged in more peevishness. "You do know most highborn unions, with the exception of the Cimarron royals, are contracted between the ages of sixteen and nineteen?"

"No." I don't hesitate to match her expression. "I didn't know." But in a strange way, understand her irritation that I didn't. Arcadia is a land in a bizarre state of flux, caught between the security of their old ways and the light speed of a modern new world. Logically, ways of forging marriages and families will be one of the last social components to stick—exhibited by the very situation she was in when we met and the reason I had to act fast with my contracting creativity.

My confession buffs the edge on her ire. She cups my face with a gentled expression. "The only reason *I* was not betrothed years ago is because my parents enjoy diving their heads in the sand." She pouts when my lips quirk up. "Oh, my. How badly did I mess *that* one up?"

I laugh and shake my head. My woman and her talent for butchering idioms is close to legend across Manhattan, though this time I get to say, "Close enough for a backboard shot, armeau. Why did your parents bury their heads in the sand about your betrothal? Better yet, let me guess. They kept holding back for something better?"

She takes a whirl at the twitching lips. For good measure, adds an adorable little roll of her eyes. "Something like that... yes."

I work my head a little closer to hers. Get so close, I damn near bump our noses. "Well. They were smart, then."

"Oh?" Her features flare, a sardonic little move. "Please share, Mr. Court...how is *that* so?"

"They *did* get something better."

"Really, now?" Her eyes flare in mock astonishment.

"Uh-huh." I slant a soft but decidedly sultry kiss across her lips. As we move apart, add in a growling husk, "Really."

"Hmmm." She issues it with more deliberation, knowing exactly how that specific utterance affects me...and my cock. "And I suppose that 'something'...is you."

I let another rough rumble curl up my throat while sliding tighter to her from the waist down. Groan deeper as I slide a thigh between hers, pressing my crotch against her lower belly. Dear Christ, she feels good. The softness to my hardness. The relief for my ache. The kindness and light and passion my life has needed for so damn long...

"Well...I'd never just presume I had the position." A smirk curls up one side of my mouth, betraying how I don't mean a word of it. Thank fuck for the answering heat in her eyes, confirming my cockiness is well-justified—though if I had to fight anyone to earn her, including the pair of social schemers who call themselves her parents, I would summon a whole goddamn army to do it.

But I'd much rather focus on what I was destined to do from the first moment our eyes met.

Love her.

I'm a goner to the cause already—especially as she slants a little glance, blue eyes sparkling, and rasps, "Presuming is never the wisest option, you know."

I tilt my head. "Wise advice from a brilliant woman."

Her gaze narrows. "Now you are just trying to flatter me."

"Now I'm just trying to *compliment* you." I swallow hard, struggling to maintain the charming banter—*not* easy with her silken body shifting against me, tempting me even through my pants and her skirt. "Flattery is for empty words. No words I speak to you are empty, *favori.*"

Her fingers, still against my face, spread wide. Her expression shifts, firming into solemnity. "Nothing about you is empty, Cassian."

The grate to her words is my undoing...and my invitation. I heed both, giving in and moving in, taking her mouth with a deeper sweep of passion, a growing swell of desire.

With a gorgeous sigh of surrender, she lets me in.

Her tongue, wet and warm, dances with mine. Her body, sweet and soft, trembles for me. Soon, a mewl undulates up the length of her throat. I answer with a long, dark moan, not certain if it's in warning or capitulation. Maybe a little of both.

Dear fuck, she makes it so hard to think sometimes. When she gives me her desire like this...exposes her need like this...craves me so earnestly like this...

...all I want to do is give her every damn thing she wants...

...all I want to feel is the completion of her soul...

...all I want to hear is the fulfillment of her need...

"*Cassian.*"

Exactly like that.

"I know, armeau." I rasp it while pressing over, rolling her fully to her back. She sprawls against the cushions, where the moonlight bounces off the clouds and glows across the bed. After a few deft slides of fabric, it also illuminates the perfect curves of her bare hips...and the triangle of white lace at the juncture of her thighs. *White.* Never before have I found the color an appealing one for lingerie—if the occasion ever called for it—but for my little Arcadian, no other color seems worthy. She is the purest part of my spirit. The unfiltered path to my light. The perfect start of a joy I never thought I'd know again.

"Oh *my.*" Her whisper matches the slip of the lace as I peel the panties down. Every muscle in my body craves to twist and tear the things free, but right now she needs release and rapture, not a grunting caveman. So I clench everything back as I bare her and then spread her, soothing her back against the pillows the moment she rises up, almost seeming embarrassed.

"*Yaslan riére, armeau. Je yorum conne-toi.*"

She stills. Her eyes widen. I'm usually the one benefiting from the arousal her native language induces. With the tables turned, she's a quivering deer in the headlights...my sexy-as-fuck little Bambi.

"Wh-What?" she finally blurts.

I kiss her again. Take my time, slow and sensual, to part

the seam of her lips. Coax my tongue inside the heated recesses beyond, ravishing and taunting and seducing. At the same time, I swirl fingers along the inside of her thigh. Higher...higher...

"Hmmm. What part didn't you understand, beautiful? Isn't *'lie back, little gift...I want to taste you'* pretty clear?"

She swallows. "Y-Yes...but..."

"But what?" I slide her forward, parting her legs wider in the doing. "I've got at least another four hours to prove I was well worth your wait, Miss Santelle...and I plan on putting them to damn good use."

***This story continues in Bold Beautiful Love
Temptation Court Book Three!***

ALSO BY ANGEL PAYNE

Temptation Court:
Naughty Little Gift
Pretty Perfect Toy
Bold Beautiful Love

Cimarron Series:
Into His Dark
Into His Command
Into Her Fantasies

Suited for Sin:
Sing
Sigh
Submit

The Bolt Saga:
Bolt
Ignite
Pulse
Fuse
Surge
Light

Honor Bound:
Saved
Cuffed
Seduced
Wild
Wet
Hot
Masked
Mastered
Conquered
Ruled

Secrets of Stone Series:
No Prince Charming
No More Masquerade
No Perfect Princess
No Magic Moment
No Lucky Number
No Simple Sacrifice
No Broken Bond
No White Knight
No Longer Lost
No Curtian Call

Lords of Sin:
A Fire In Heaven
Promise of Your Touch
Redemption
Surrender of the Dawn
Tradewinds

**For a full list of Angel's other titles,
visit her at AngelPayne.com**

ABOUT ANGEL PAYNE

USA Today bestselling romance author Angel Payne loves to focus on high-heat romance starring memorable alpha men and the women who love them. She has numerous book series to her credit, including the action-packed Bolt Saga and Honor Bound series, Secrets of Stone series (with Victoria Blue), the intertwined Cimarron and Temptation Court series, the Suited for Sin series, and the Lords of Sin historicals, as well as several standalone titles.

Angel is a native Southern Californian, leading to her love of being in the outdoors, where she often reads and writes. She still lives in Southern California with her soul-mate husband and beautiful daughter, to whom she is a proud cosplay/culture con mom. Her passions also include whisky tasting, shoe shopping, and travel.

Visit her at AngelPayne.com